D0861390

A RUSSIAN GENTLEMAN

By SERGHEI AKSAKOFF

Fredonia Books
Amsterdam, The Netherlands

A Russian Gentleman

by
Serghei Aksakoff

ISBN: 1-58963-951-0

Fredonia Books
Amsterdam, The Netherlands
http://www.fredoniabooks.com

SERGHEI AKSAKOFF

Born, Ufa .   .   .   .   .   20 September 1791
Died, Moscow   .   .   .   .   30 April 1859

'*A Russian Gentleman*' (*called by its author '*Family History*') was first published serially in 1846 and in book form in 1856.*

INTRODUCTION

SERGHÉI AKSÁKOFF, older by eight years than Púshkin, and by nearly twenty years than Gógol, was born at Ufá in the district of Orenburg on 20 September 1791. His father, Timothy, was then in the public service, as an official in the law-courts at Ufá ; and his grandfather lived in the country as the owner of large estates, to which Aksákoff himself ultimately succeeded. At that time the Russians were only settlers in the country, and the population consisted mainly of Tartars and a number of Finnish tribes—Bashkirs, Mord-vinians, and Choovashes, who spoke their own language and professed the religion of Islam.

When the grandfather died in 1796, Aksákoff's parents removed to their estate of Aksákovo, and here the boy lived till the winter of 1799. He was then sent at eight years old to a boarding-school at Kazán, but suffered so terribly from home-sickness that his mother came to the rescue and carried her darling back to the home which to him seemed like heaven. After a year's respite a second experiment was made with better success : he was still at Kazán when his school was converted into a university by imperial edict in 1805, and he remained there till 1807, when he entered the

civil service. His first post was that of translator
to the Legislative Committee at Petersburg. It
cannot be said that he was well qualified for the
post : he knew something of French, but nothing
of any other foreign language, and he had never
even studied Latin.

From 1811 to 1826 he held no public office. He
lived in Moscow or near it and was much taken up
with various literary and theatrical enterprises.
He had also abundant opportunities of gratifying
his lifelong passion for field-sports of all kinds. He
married in 1816 the daughter of General Zaplátin ;
and his two sons, Constantín (1817–60) and Iván
(1823–86), early became leaders of the Slavophile
party, which sought to preserve from European
contamination the language, religion, and institu-
tions of Russia. Aksákoff was by his nature
inclined to sympathize with these objects, and the
tendency was confirmed by the influence of his
elder son. Constantín Aksákoff never married :
he always lived with his father and did not long
survive him : he never recovered from the stroke
of his father's death. In 1827 Aksákoff was
appointed censor of the press at Moscow and held
this office till 1834 ; he retired finally from the
public service in 1839.

Aksákoff lived for twenty years after his retire-
ment, and all his best work as a writer was done
during those twenty years. All his life his interest
in literature was keen, but he was surprisingly

long in finding out where his real strength lay. From 1812 to 1826 he was closely connected with the theatre at Moscow ; and much of his time was spent in the green-room, or in the society of a group of second-rate authors who produced ephemeral work for the stage. He was thus led aside to the French drama, no congenial food for his real genius : he translated some plays of Molière into Russian alexandrines, and even the Satires of Boileau. He produced some original work ; but there was not much of it, and none of it was the real thing. The change came about between 1830 and 1840. During those years he saw much of Gógol and conceived an intense admiration for him. Gógol's influence and example were decisive. Aksákoff cast off the French shackles which bound him, and made himself immortal by descriptions of what he knew and loved, Russian landscape and Russian character.

He began his Memoirs by publishing in a Moscow magazine (*Moskóvsky Sbórnik,* i. e. *Moscow Miscellany*) his *Family History*, called in this translation *A Russian Gentleman* ; this appeared in successive instalments during 1846. Two books, one on fish and fishing, the other on birds and shooting, followed in 1847 and 1855. In 1856 *Family History* was published as a whole, and with it *Recollections*, called in this translation *A Russian Schoolboy.* His last book, *Years of Childhood*, was published in 1858. The three books of Memoirs form the

first two volumes in the collected edition of his
works. After a long and painful illness, borne
with singular courage and cheerfulness, he died
at Moscow on 30 April 1859.

Aksákoff is a classic in his own country. Every
educated Russian knows these books. ' At the
present time,' wrote a Russian man of letters in
1912, ' the normal education of a child in Russia
is inconceivable unless Aksákoff's *Family History*
and Tolstóy's *Childhood* form part of it.' His
vocabulary is purely Russian, without any admix-
ture of foreign words ; his style is charming in
its purity and simplicity. He had astonishing
powers of observation and memory : he seems to
have noticed everything and forgotten nothing.
His vivid and minute account of Russian family
life in the reign of the Empress Catherine is an
important contribution to history. And even
these are not his highest merits. His books are
fragrant with the flavour of a marked and most
attractive personality. ' One is spellbound by
the charm, the dignity, the good-nature, the
gentle easy accent of the speaker, in whom one
feels convinced, not only that there was nothing
common or mean, but to whom nothing was
common or mean, who was a gentleman by
character as well as by lineage, one of God's as
well as of Russia's nobility.' [1] And lastly, Aksákoff, for all his air of simplicity, is a great literary

[1] Baring's *Russian Literature*, p. 157.

artist. If any reader is inclined to doubt this, let him consider the way in which each chapter of this narrative is brought to a conclusion; and he will not remain in doubt for long.

A Russian Gentleman is a suitable title for this book, because the whole stage, on which a large number of actors play their parts, is dominated by the tremendous personality of Aksákoff's grandfather, Stepán Miháilovitch. Plain and rough in his appearance and habits, but proud of his long descent; capable of furious anger and extreme violence in his anger, but also capable of steadfast and even chivalrous affection; a born leader of men and the very incarnation of truth and honesty —Stepán Miháilovitch is more like a Homeric hero than a man of modern times. This portrait of his grandfather is the masterpiece in Aksákoff's gallery; and his descriptions of his parents' courtship and marriage are just as vivid and minute as his pictures of his own early childhood.

The reader, when he reflects that this narrative ends with the day of the narrator's own birth, will be inclined to think that Aksákoff must have had a lively imagination. But Skabitchévsky, a critic of reputation, begins his review of Aksákoff's work by saying:

' Aksákoff's books are remarkable, first of all on this account, that one finds in them no trace of creative or inventive power.'

I venture, however, to differ from the Russian critic on this point. Aksákoff's mother may have told him much, and he may have remembered all she told him, but I am convinced that most of the detail in which these books abound can have been derived from no other source than his own imagination.

This translation was made from the Moscow edition of 1900. I may say here (1) that I have omitted from the topographical detail some lists of obscure place-names which could mean nothing to English readers (or indeed to most Russian), and (2) that I have incorporated in the text a certain amount of matter which Aksákoff, when reprinting, was only able to add in the form of notes.

These Memoirs in their original tongue were given to me in 1908 by my dear friend Aleksándra Grigóryevna Páshkova, who has loved Aksákoff from her childhood and spent much of her life in the country which Aksákoff described. The translation was first published in 1915; it has long been out of print, and I have taken advantage of this reprint to correct some errors.

J. D. DUFF.

November 1, 1922.

CONTENTS

A RUSSIAN GENTLEMAN

FRAGMENT I

STEPAN MIHAILOVITCH BAGROFF

1. THE MIGRATION

WHEN my grandfather lived in the Government of Simbirsk, on the ancestral estate granted to his forefathers by the Tsars of Muscovy, he felt cramped and confined. Not that there was really want of room ; for he had arable land and pasture, timber, and other necessaries in abundance ; but the trouble was, that the estate which his great-grandfather had held in absolute possession, had ceased to belong to one owner. This happened quite simply : for three successive generations the family consisted of one son and several daughters ; and, when some of these daughters were married, their portions took the shape of a certain number of serfs and a certain amount of land. Though their shares were not large, yet, as the land had never been properly surveyed, at this time four intruders asserted their right to share in the management of it. To my grandfather, life under these conditions was intolerable : there was no patience in his passionate temperament ; he loved plain dealing and hated complications and wrangles with his kith and kin.

For some time past, he had heard frequent reports about the district of Ufá—how there was

land there without limit for the plough and for
stock, with an indescribable abundance of game
and fish and all the fruits of the earth ; and how
easy it was to acquire whole tracts of land for a very
trifling sum of money. If tales were true, you had
only to invite a dozen of the native Bashkir chiefs
in certain districts to partake of your hospitality :
you provided two or three fat sheep, for them to
kill and dress in their own fashion ; you produced
a bucket of whisky, with several buckets of strong
fermented Bashkir mead and a barrel of home-
made country beer—which proves, by the way,
that even in old days the Bashkirs were not strict
Mohammedans—and the rest was as simple as A B C.
It was said, indeed, that an entertainment of this
kind might last a week or even a fortnight : it was
impossible for Bashkirs to do business in a hurry,
and every day it was necessary to ask the question,
' Well, good friend, is it time now to discuss my
business ? ' The guests had been eating and drinking, without exaggeration, all day and all night ;
but, if they were not completely satisfied with the
entertainment, if they had not had enough of their
monotonous singing and playing on the pipe, and
their singular dances in which they stood up or
crouched down on the same spot of ground, then
the greatest of the chiefs, clicking his tongue and
wagging his head, would answer with much dignity
and without looking his questioner in the face :
' The time has not come ; bring us another sheep ! '
The sheep was forthcoming, as a matter of course,
with fresh supplies of beer and spirits ; and the
tipsy Bashkirs began again to sing and dance,
dropping off to sleep wherever they felt inclined.
But everything in the world has an end ; and a

day came at last when the chief would look his
host straight in the face and say : ' We are obliged
to you, *bátyushka*,[1] ever so much obliged ! And
now, what is it that you want ? ' The rest of the
transaction followed a regular fashion. The
customer began with the shrewdness native to
your true Russian : he assured the Bashkir that
he did not want anything at all ; but, having heard
that the Bashkirs were exceedingly kind people,
he had come to Ufa on purpose to form a friendship
with them, and so on. Then the conversation
would somehow come round to the vast extent of
the Bashkir territory and the unsatisfactory ways
of the present tenants, who might pay their rent
for a year or two and then pay no more and yet
continue to live on the land, as if they were its
rightful owners ; it was rash to evict them, and
a lawsuit became unavoidable. These remarks,
which were true enough to the facts, were followed
up by an obliging offer to relieve the kind Bashkirs
of some part of the land which was such a burden
to them ; and in the end whole districts were
bought and sold for a mere song. The bargain was
clinched by a legal document, but the amount of
land was never stated in it, and could not be, as it
had never been surveyed. As a rule, the boundaries
were settled by landmarks of this kind : ' from
the mouth of such and such a stream as far as the
dead beech-tree on the wolf-track, and from the
dead beech-tree in a bee-line to the watershed,
and from the watershed to the fox-earths, and from
the fox-earths to the hollow tree at Soltamratka,'
and so on. So precise and permanent were the
boundaries enclosing ten or twenty or thirty

[1] ' Father,' a title of respect or affection.

thousand desyatinas [1] of land !   And the price of
all this might be about one hundred roubles [2] and
presents worth another hundred, not including
the cost of the entertainments.

Stories of this kind had a great attraction for
my grandfather. As a man of strict integrity he
disapproved of the deception practised on the
simple Bashkirs ; but he considered that the harm
lay, not in the business itself, but in the method
of transacting it, and believed that it was possible
to deal fairly and yet to buy a great stretch of
land at a low price. In that case he could migrate
with his family and transfer half of his serfs to the
new estate ; and thus he would secure the main
object of this design. For the fact was, that for
some time past he had been so much worried by
unending disputes over the management of the
land—disputes between himself and the relations
who owned a small part of it—that his desire to
leave the place where his ancestors had lived and
he himself was born, had become a fixed idea.
There was no other means of securing a quiet life ;
and to him, now that his youth was past, a quiet
life seemed more desirable than anything else.

So he scraped together several thousand roubles,
and said good-bye to his wife, whom he called
Arisha when he was in a good humour and Arína
when he was not ; he kissed his children and gave
them his blessing—his four young daughters and
the infant son who was the single scion and sole
hope of an ancient and noble family. The daughters
he thought of no importance : ' What 's the good
of *them* ? They look out of the house, not in ; if

[1] 100 desyatinas = 270 acres.
[2] A rouble was worth about 2*s*.

their name is Bagróff [1] to-day, it may be anything on earth to-morrow ; my hopes rest entirely on my boy, Alexyéi '—such were my grandfather's parting words, when he started to cross the Volga on his way to the district of Ufa.

But perhaps I had better begin by telling you what sort of a man my grandfather was.

Stepán Miháilovitch Bagróff—this was his name —was under the middle height ; but his prominent chest, uncommonly broad shoulders, sinewy arms, and wiry muscular frame, gave proof of his extraordinary strength. When it happened, in the rough-and-tumble amusements of young men, that a number of his brother-officers fastened on him at once, he would hurl them from him, as a sturdy oak hurls off the rain-drops, when its branches rock in the breeze after a shower. He had fair hair and regular features ; his eyes were large and dark blue, quick to light up with anger but friendly and kind in his hours of composure ; his eyebrows were thick and the lines of his mouth pleasant to look at. The general expression of his features was singularly frank and open : no one could help trusting him ; his word or his promise was better than any bond, and more sacred than any document guaranteed by Church or State. His natural intelligence was clear and strong. All landowners of that time were ignorant men, and he had received no sort of education ; indeed he could hardly read and write his native language. But, while serving in the Army, and before he was promoted from the ranks, he had mastered the elementary rules of arithmetic and the use of the reckoning-board— acquirements of which he liked to speak even when

[1] Bagróff is a pseudonym for Aksákoff.

he was an old man. It is probable that his period
of service was not long ; for he was only quarter-
master of the regiment when he retired. But in
those days even nobles served for long in the ranks
or as non-commissioned officers, unless indeed they
passed through this stage in their cradles, first
enrolled as sergeants in the Guards and then making
a sudden appearance as captains in line regiments.
Of the career of Stepan Mihailovitch in the Army
I know little ; but I have been told that he was
often employed in the capture of the highway-
men who infested the Volga, and always showed
good sense in the formation of his plans and reckless
courage in their execution ; that the outlaws knew
him well by sight and feared him like fire. On
retiring from the Army, he lived for some years on
his hereditary estate of Bagróvo [1] and became very
skilful in the management of land. It was not his
way to be present from morning to night where his
labourers were at work, nor did he stand like a
sentry over the grain, when it was coming in and
going out ; but, when he was on the spot, he looked
to some purpose, and, if he noticed anything amiss,
especially any attempt to deceive him, he never
failed to visit the offender with a summary form
of punishment which may rouse the displeasure of
my readers. But my grandfather, while acting in
accordance with the spirit of his age, reasoned in
a fashion of his own. In his view, to punish a
peasant by fines or by forced labour on the estate
made the man less substantial and therefore less
useful to his owner ; and to separate him from his
family and banish him to a distant estate was even
worse, for a man deprived of his family ties was

[1] Bagróvo is a pseudonym for Aksákovo.

sure to go down hill. But to have recourse to the
police was simply out of the question ; that would
have been considered the depth of disgrace and
shame ; every voice in the village would have been
raised to mourn for the offender as if he were dead,
and he would have considered himself as disgraced
and ruined beyond redemption. And it must be
said for my grandfather, that he was never severe
except when his anger was hot ; when the fit had
passed away, the offence was forgotten. Advantage
was often taken of this : sometimes the offender
had time to hide and the storm passed by without
hurting any one. Before long, his people became
so satisfactory that none of them gave him any
cause to lose his temper.

After getting his estate into good order, my
grandfather married ; his bride was Arína Vassíl-
yevna Nyeklyoodoff, a young lady of little fortune,
but, like himself, of ancient descent. This gives
me an opportunity to explain that his pedigree was
my grandfather's foible : he was moderately well-
to-do, owning only 180 serfs ; but his descent,
which he traced back, by means of Heaven knows
what documents, for six hundred years all the way
to a Varyag [1] prince called Shimon, he valued far
more than any riches or office in the State. At one
time he was much attracted by a rich and beautiful
girl, but he would not marry her, merely because
her great-grandfather was not a noble.

After this account of Stepan Mihailovitch, let
us go back to the course of the narrative.

[1] The earliest Russian chronicles report that the Russian
empire was founded in the ninth century by certain foreign
princes called *Varyags*. The nationality of these princes
has been a subject of endless controversy, some historians
maintaining that they were Norsemen, others denying it.

My grandfather first crossed the Volga by the ferry near Simbirsk, and then struck across the steppe on the farther side, and travelled on till he came to Sergievsk, which stands on a hill at the meeting of two rivers and gives a name to the sulphur springs twelve *versts* [1] from the town. The deeper he plunged into the district of Ufa, the more he was impressed by the spaciousness and fertility of that country. The first place where he found trees growing was the district of Boogoorooslan ; and in the town of that name, perched on a high hill above the river, he made a halt, wishing to make inquiries and learn more particulars of the lands that were for sale. Of land belonging to the Bashkirs there was little left in this district : some of the occupiers were tenants of the Crown, whom the Government had settled on lands confiscated for rebellion, though later they granted a general pardon and restored their territory to the Bashkir owners ; part of the land had been let to tenants by the Bashkirs themselves ; and part had been bought up by migrating landowners. Using Boogoorooslan as a centre, my grandfather made expeditions to the surrounding districts and spent some time in the beautiful country watered by the Ik and the Dyoma. [2] It is an enchanting region ; and even in his old age Stepan Mihailovitch often spoke with enthusiasm of the first impression produced on him by the astonishing richness of that soil. But he did not allow himself to be carried away. Ascertaining on the spot that any purchaser of Bashkir land was quite sure to be involved in endless disputes and

[1] A *verst* is two-thirds of a mile.
[2] Pronounce Dyáw-ma.

lawsuits—for it was impossible for the acquirer to make sure either of his own title or of the number of the former owners—my grandfather, who feared and hated like poison the very name of a lawsuit, resolved to buy no land direct from the Bashkirs or without formal legal documents to confirm his ownership. Thus he hoped to exclude the possibility of disputes, and surely he had reason for such a hope ; but things turned out very differently, and the last claim was only settled by his youngest grandson when he was forty years old.

My grandfather returned reluctantly from the banks of the Ik and the Dyoma to Boogoorooslan, where he bought land from a Russian lady near the river of that name and distant twenty-five *versts* from the town. The river is rapid and deep and never runs dry. For forty *versts*, from the town of Boogoorooslan to the Crown settlement of Fair Bank, the country on both sides of the river was uninhabited, so that there was ample room ; and the amenities of the spot were wonderful. The river was so transparent that, if you threw in a copper coin, you could see it resting on the bottom even in pools fifteen feet deep. In some places there was a thick border of trees and bushes—birches, poplars, service-trees, guelder-roses, and bird-cherries, where the hop-bines trailed their green festoons and hung their straw-coloured clusters from tree to tree ; in other places, the grass grew tall and strong, with an infinite profusion of flowers, including tall meadowsweet, lords' pride (the scarlet lychnis), kings' curls (the martagon lily), and cat-grass or valerian. The river flows along a valley varying in breadth and bordered on both sides by sloping hills with

a steep cliff here and there ; the slopes were thickly
covered with hard-wood trees of all sorts. As you
got out of the valley, the level steppe spread out
before you, a black virgin soil over two feet in
depth. Along the river and in the neighbouring
marshes, wild ducks of all kinds, and geese, wood-
cocks, and snipe made their nests and filled the air
with their different notes and calls ; while on the
table-land above, where the grass grew thick and
strong, the music in the air was as rich and quite
distinct. Every kind of bird that lives in the
steppe bred there in multitudes—bustards, cranes,
and hawks ; and on the wooded slopes there were
quantities of black-game. The river swarmed with
every variety of fish that could endure its ice-cold
water—pike, perch, chub, dace, and even salmon.
Both steppe and forest were filled beyond belief
with wild creatures. In a word, the place was, and
still is, a paradise for the sportsman.

My grandfather bought about 12,000 acres for
2,500 roubles. That was a large sum in those days,
and the price was much higher than was generally
paid. When he had assured his title by legal
documents, he went back with a light heart to his
expectant family in the Government of Simbirsk.
There he set to work with fierce energy and made
all preparations for transferring at once a portion
of his serfs to the new estate. It was an anxious
and troublesome job, because the distance was
considerable—about 400 *versts*. That same autumn
twenty families of serfs started for the district
of Boogoorooslan, taking with them ploughs
and harrows with rye for sowing. They chose
their ground and set to work on the virgin soil.
Two thousand acres were lightly ploughed, then

harrowed, and sown with winter rye ; two thousand more were ploughed in preparation for the spring sowing ; and some cottages were built. When this was done, the men travelled back to spend the winter at home. When winter was over, twenty more labourers again went forth ; and, as the spring advanced, they sowed the two thousand acres with spring wheat, erected fences round the cottages and byres, and made stoves for the cottages out of clay. The second party then returned home. These were distinct from the actual settlers, who remained at home, preparing for their move and selling off what they did not need—their houses and kailyards, stock and corn, and all sorts of odds and ends.

The date fixed was the middle of June, that the colonists might reach their destination before St. Peter's Day,[1] when hay-cutting begins. The carts were packed with the women and children and old people, and awnings of bast bent over them to protect them from the sun and rain ; the indispensable pots and pans were piled up inside, the cocks and hens perched on the top, and the cows tied on behind ; and off they started. The poor settlers shed bitter tears as they parted for ever with their past life, with the church in which they had been christened and married, and with the graves of their fathers and grandfathers. Nobody likes moving, and a Russian peasant least of all ; but to move in those days to an unknown land inhabited by unbelievers, where the churches were so distant that a man might die without confession and infants remain long unchristened, a land of which rumour reported evil as well as good—this

[1] June 29.

seemed a terrible ordeal. When the peasants had gone, my grandfather started after them. He had taken a vow that, when circumstances allowed, he would build a church dedicated to the Presentation of Our Lady—it was actually built by his son—and he named the new settlement after the festival. But the peasants, whose example was followed by their neighbours, called it New Bagrovo, after their master and in memory of Old Bagrovo, from which they had come ; and to this day the formal name is only used in legal documents. No one knows the village, with its fine stone church and high manor-house, by any other name than Bagrovo. With unremitting care and attention my grandfather watched the labour of the people on their own land and on his ; the hay was mown, the winter rye and spring corn were cut down and carried, and the right moment was chosen for each operation. The yield of the crops was fabulous. The peasants thought things were not so bad after all. By November, cottages were built for them all, and the beginning of a house for the owner was run up. All this was not done without help from neighbours. In spite of the long distances, they came willingly to lend a hand to the new land-owner, who proved to be sensible and friendly ; they ate and drank and turned to with a will, and sang as they worked. In that winter my grand-father went to Simbirsk and brought back his wife and children with him.

Next year forty more serfs were transferred and set up in their new abodes ; and this proved an easier job. My grandfather's first operation in this year was to build a mill ; without it, it had been necessary to drive forty *versts* to get his corn

ground. A spot was chosen where the river was
not deep, the bottom sound, and the banks high
and solid. Then a dam of earth and brushwood
was started from each bank, like a pair of hands
ready to clasp ; next, the dam was wattled with
osiers, to make it more substantial ; and all that
remained was to stop the swift strong current and
force it to fill the basin intended for it. The mill
itself, with two pairs of millstones, was built beforehand on the lower bank. All the machinery was
ready and even greased. It was the business of
the river, when checked in its natural course, to
fill the broad dam and pour through wooden pipes
down upon the great wheel. When all was ready
and four long oaken piles had been firmly driven
into the clay bottom of the river, my grandfather
invited his neighbours to lend him their assistance
for two days ; and they came, bringing horses and
carts, spades, forks, and axes. On the first day,
great piles of brushwood, straw, manure, and
fresh-cut sods were heaped up on both banks of
the Boogoorooslan, while the river continued to
pour down its waters at its own sweet will. Hardly
any one slept that night, and next morning at
sunrise about a hundred men set to work to dam
the stream ; they all looked solemn and serious, as
if they had important business before them. They
began on both sides at the same moment. With
loud cries they hurled with sturdy arms faggots of
brushwood into the water ; part was carried down
by the stream, but part stuck against the piles and
sank across the channel. Next came bundles of
straw weighted with stones, then soil and manure,
then more brushwood, followed by more straw and
manure, and, on the top of all, a thick layer of sods.

All this accumulation was swallowed up till it rose at last above the surface of the water. At once, a dozen strong and active men sprang on to the barrier and began to tread it and stamp it down. The operation was performed with the utmost speed ; and the general excitement was so great and the noise so vociferous, that a passer-by, if he had not known the reason of it, might have been frightened. But there was no one there to be frightened by it : only the uninhabited steppes and dark forests and all the region round re-echoed the shouts of the labourers. The voices of women and children swelled the chorus ; for such an important affair aroused interest in every breast, and the noise and excitement were universal. The resistance of the river was not overcome at once. For long it tore away and carried down brushwood and straw, manure and turf ; but man at last conquered. The baffled water stopped, as if reflecting ; then it turned back, and rose till it poured over its banks and inundated the fields. By evening the mill-pond had taken shape ; or one might call it a floating lake, where the banks and all the green grass and bushes had disappeared ; only the tops of submerged trees, doomed to die, stuck up here and there. Next day the mill began to work, and goes on woiking and grinding to this day.

2. The Government of Orenburg

How wonderful in those days was that region, in its wild and virginal richness ! It is different now ; it is not even what it was when I first knew it, when it was still fresh and blooming and unde-flowered by hordes of settlers from every quarter.

It is changed ; but it is still beautiful and spacious,
fertile and infinitely various, the Government of
Orenburg. The name sounds strange, and the
termination ' burg ' is inappropriate enough. But
when I first knew that earthly paradise, it was still
called the ' Province of Ufa.'

Thirty years ago, one who was born within it [1]
expressed in verse his fears for the future of the
land ; and these have been realized in part, and
the process still goes on. But still hast thou power
to charm, wondrous land ! Bright and clear, like
great deep cups, are thy lakes—Kandry and
Karatabyn. Full of water and full of all manner
of fish are thy rivers, whether they race down the
valleys and rocky gorges of the Ural Mountains, or
steal softly, glittering like a string of jewels, through
the prairie-grass of the steppes.   Wondrous are
those rivers of the steppe, formed by the union of
countless little streams flowing from deep water-
holes—streams so tiny that you can hardly see the
trickle of water in them. And thy rivers that flow
swift from fountain-heads and run under the shade
of trees and bushes are transparent and cold as ice
even in the heat of summer ; and all kinds of trout,
good to eat and beautiful to see, live there ; but
they soon die out, when man begins to defile with
unclean hands the virgin streams of their clear
cool retreats. Fertile is the black soil of thy corn-
land, and rich thy pastures ; and thy fields are
covered in spring with the milk-white blossom of
the cherrytree and wild peach, while in summer
the fragrant strawberries spread over them like
a scarlet cloth, and the small cherries that turn
purple later when they ripen in autumn. Rich is

[1] Aksákoff himself.

the harvest that rewards the peasant, however idle
and ignorant, when he scratches with his rude
ploughshare the surface of thy soil. Fresh and
green and mighty stand thy forests of all manner
of trees ; and buzzing swarms of wild bees fill their
self-chosen nests among the leaves with the fragrant
honey of the lime blossom. The Ufa marten, with
its priceless fur, is still to be found in the wooded
head-waters of the great rivers.

The original inhabitants of the land are men of
peace, the wandering tribes of Bashkirs. Their
herds of horses and cattle and flocks of sheep,
though far smaller than they were once, are still
numerous. When the fierce storms of winter are
over, the Bashkirs crawl forth, thin and wasted
like flies in winter. With the first warmth and the
first sprouting of the grass they drive out into
the open their half-starved herds and flocks, and
drag themselves after them, with their wives and
children. A few weeks change them beyond recog-
nition, both men and animals. What were mere
skeletons have become spirited and tireless horses ;
and the stallion proudly guards his mares as they
graze, and keeps both man and beast at a distance.
The meagre cattle have grown fat, and their udders
swell with milk. But for cow's milk the Bashkir
cares nothing. For the *koumiss* [1] is now in season
and already fermenting in the bags of horse-hide ;
and every creature that can drink, from the infant
in arms to the tottering old man, swallows the
health-giving beverage, a drink for heroes. And
the result is marvellous : all the traces of winter
and starvation soon disappear, and even the
troubles of old age ; their faces fill out, and pale

[1] Mare's milk, fermented.

sunken cheeks take on the hue of health. But
their deserted villages are a sad and even alarming
sight. A traveller unfamiliar with the country
might well start, appalled by the emptiness and
deadness of the place. There stand the deserted
huts with their white chimneys, and the empty
window-frames look mournfully at him like human
faces with no eyes in the sockets. He may hear
the bark of a half-starved watch-dog, whom his
master visits and feeds at long intervals, or the
mewing of a cat that has run wild and finds food
for herself; but that is all : not one human being
remains.

How varied and picturesque, each in its own
way, are the different regions of the land—the
forests, the steppes, and, more than all, the hills,
where all metals, even gold, are found along the
slopes of the Ural ridge ! How vast the expanse,
from the borders of Vyatka and Perm, where the
mercury often freezes in winter, to the little town
of Guryeff on the edge of Astrakhan, where small
grapes ripen in the open air—grapes whose wine
the Cossack trades in and drinks himself for coolness
in summer and warmth in winter. How noble is
the fishing in the Urals, unlike any other both
in the fish that are caught and in the manner of
catching them ! It only needs a faithful and lively
description to attract general attention.

But I must ask pardon. I have gone too far in
the description of the beautiful country where I
was born. Now let us go back and observe the life
and unwearied activity of my grandfather.

3. Fresh Scenes

Stepan Mihailovitch had peace at last. Many
a time he thanked God from the bottom of his
heart, when the move was completed and he found
elbow-room on the banks of the Boogoorooslan.
His spirits rose, and even his health was better.
No petitions, no complaints, no disputes, no disturbance !   No tiresome relations, no divided
ownership !   No thieves to fell his trees, no tres-
passers to trample down his corn and meadows !
He was undisputed master at last in his own house,
and beyond it : he might feed sheep, or mow grass,
or cut firewood where he pleased without a word
from any one.

The peasants too soon became accustomed to
the new habitation and soon grew to love it. And
that was but natural. Old Bagrovo had wood, but
little water ; meadow-land was so scarce that it
was hard for them to find grazing for one horse and
one cow apiece ; and, though the natural soil was
good, it had been cropped over and over from time
immemorial till its fertility was exhausted. The
new site gave them wide and fertile fields and
meadows, never touched till now by ploughshare or
scythe ; it gave them a rapid river with good fresh
water, and springs in abundance ; it gave them
a broad pond with fish in it and the river running
through it ; and it gave them a mill at their very
doors, whereas before they had to travel twenty-
five *versts* to have a load of corn ground, and
perhaps to wait after all a couple of days till their
turn came.

It surprises you perhaps that I called Old
Bagrovo waterless ; and you may blame my

ancestors for choosing such a spot to settle in.
But they were not to blame, and things were
different in old days. Once on a time Old Bagrovo
stood on a pretty stream, the Maina, which took
its rise from the Mossy Lakes three *versts* distant ;
and also along the whole settlement there stretched
a lake, not broad but long and clear, and deep in
the middle, with a bottom of white sand ; and
another streamlet, called The White Spring, issued
from this lake. So it was in former times, but
it is quite another story now. Tradition tells
that the Mossy Lakes were once deep round pools
surrounded by trees, with ice-cold water and
treacherous banks, and no one ventured near them
except in winter, because the banks were said to
give way under foot and engulf the bold disturber
of the water-spirit's solitary reign. But man is
the sworn foe of Nature, and she can never with-
stand his treacherous warfare against her beauty.
Ancient tradition, unsupported by modern in-
stances, ceased to be believed. The people steeped
their flax on the banks and drove their herds
there to water ; and the Mossy Lakes were polluted
by degrees, and grew shallow at the edges, and
even dried up in places where the wood all round
was cut. Then a thick scurf formed on the top ;
moss grew over it, and the vein-like roots of water-
plants bound it together, till it was covered with
tussocks and bushes and even firtrees of some size.
One of the pools is now entirely covered ; of the
other are left two deep water-holes, which even
now are formidable for a stranger to approach,
because the soil, with all its covering of plants and
bushes and trees, rises and falls beneath the foot
like a wave at sea. Owing to the dwindling of

these lakes, the Maina now issues from the ground some distance below the settlement, and its upper waters have dried up. The lake by the village has become a filthy stinking canal; the sandy bottom is covered to a depth of over seven feet by mud and refuse of all kinds from the peasants' houses; of the White Spring not a trace is left, and the memory of it will soon be forgotten.

When my grandfather had settled down at New Bagrovo, he set to work, with all his natural activity and energy, to grow corn and breed stock. The peasants caught the contagion of his enthusiasm and worked so hard and steadily that they were soon as well set up and provided for as if they had been old inhabitants. After a few years, their stackyards took up thrice as much room as the village-street; and their drove of stout horses, their herds and flocks and pigs, would have done honour to a large and prosperous settlement.

After the success of Stepan Mihailovitch, migration to Ufa or Orenburg became more fashionable every year. Native tribes came streaming from every quarter—Mordvinians, Choovashes, Tatars, and Meshchers, and plenty of Russian settlers too—Crown-tenants from different districts, and landowners, large and small. My grandfather began to have neighbours. His brother-in-law, Ivan Nyeklyoodoff, bought land within twelve *versts* of Bagrovo, transferred his serfs there, built a wooden church, named his estate Nyeklyoodovo, and came to live there with his family. This afforded no gratification to my grandfather, who had a strong dislike to all his wife's relations—all ' Nyeklyoodovdom,' as he used to call them. Then a landowner called Bakmétyeff bought land still closer, about ten *versts* from Bagrovo, on the upper waters of the Sovrusha, which runs to the south-west like the Boogoorooslan. On the other side, twelve *versts* along the river Nasyagai, another settlement was planted, Polibino, which now belongs to the Karamzin family. The Nasyagai is a larger and finer river than the Boogoorooslan, with more water and more fish in it, and birds still breed there much more freely. On the road to Polibino, and eight *versts* from Bagrovo, a number of Mordvinians settled in a large village called Noikino, and built a mill on the streamlet of Bokla. Close to the mill, the Bokla runs into the Nasyagai, which rolls its swift strong current straight to the south-west, and is reinforced by the Boogoorooslan not far from the town of that name. Then the Nasyagai unites with the Great Kinel, and loses thenceforth its sounding and significant [1] name.

The latest arrivals were some Mordvinian colonists, a detachment from the larger settlement at Mordovsky Boogoorooslan, nine *versts* from Bagrovo. This smaller settlement, called Kivatsky, was within two *versts* of my grandfather, down the river ; and he made a wry face at first ; for it reminded him of old times in Simbirsk. But the result was quite different. They were good-tempered quiet people, who respected my grandfather as much as the official in charge of them.

Before many years had passed, Stepan Mihailovitch had gained the deep respect and love too of the whole district. He was a real benefactor to his neighbours, near or far, old or new, and especially to the latter, owing to their ignorance of the place and lack of supplies, and the various difficulties

---

[1] Na-sya-gái = ' Pursuer.'

which always befall settlers. Too often people
start off on this difficult job without due preparation, without even providing themselves with bread
and corn or the means to buy them. My grandfather's full granaries were always open to such
people. ' Take what you want, and pay me back
next harvest, if you can ; and if you can't—well,
never mind ! '—with such words as these he used
to distribute with a generous hand seed-corn and
flour. And more than this : he was so sensible, so
considerate towards petitioners, and so inflexibly
strict in the keeping of his word, that he soon
became quite an oracle in that newly settled corner
of the spacious district of Orenburg. Not only did
he help his neighbours by his generosity, but he
taught them how to behave. To speak the truth
was the only key to his favour : a man who had
once lied to him and deceived him was ill advised
if he came again to Bagrovo : he would be certain
to depart with empty hands, and might think
himself lucky if he came off with a whole skin. My
grandfather settled many family disputes and
smothered many lawsuits at their first birth. People
travelled from every quarter to seek his advice
and hear his decision ; and both were punctiliously
followed. I have known grandsons and great-
grandsons of that generation and heard them speak
of Stepan Mihailovitch ; and the figure of the strict
master but kind benefactor is still unforgotten. I
have often heard striking facts told about him by
simple people, who shed tears and crossed themselves
as they ejaculated a prayer for his soul's rest. It is
not surprising that his peasants loved so excellent
a master ; but he was loved also by his personal
servants who had often to endure the terrible

storms of his furious rage. Many of his younger servants spent their last days under my roof ; and in their old age they liked to talk of their late master—of his strict discipline and passionate temper, and also of his goodness and justice ; and they never spoke of him with dry eyes.

Yet this kind, helpful, and even considerate man was subject at times to fearful explosions of anger which utterly defaced the image of humanity in him and made him capable, for the time, of repulsive and ferocious actions. I once saw him in this state when I was a child—it was many years after the time I am writing about—and the fear that I felt has left a lively impression on my mind to this day. I seem to see him before me now. He was angry with one of his daughters ; I believe she had told him a lie and persisted in it. It was impossible to recognize his former self. He was trembling all over and supported on each side by a servant ; his face was convulsed, and a fierce fire shot from his eyes which were clouded and darkened with fury. ' Let me get at her ! '—he called out in a strangled voice. (So far, my recollection is clear ; and the rest I have often heard others tell.) My grandmother tried to throw herself at his feet, to intercede for the culprit ; but in an instant her kerchief and cap flew to a distance, and Stepan Mihailovitch was dragging his wife, though she was now old and stout, over the floor by her hair. Meantime, not only the offender, but all her sisters, and even their brother with his young wife and little son,[1] had fled out of doors and sought concealment in the

---

[1] i.e. the author, who in childhood was called Seryózha (short for Serghéi).

wood that grew round the house. The rest of them
spent the whole night there ; but the daughter-in-
law, fearing that her child would catch cold, went
back and passed the night in a servant's cottage.
For a long time my grandfather raged at large
through the deserted house. At last, when he was
weary of dragging his wife about by the hair, and
weary of striking his servants, Mazan and Tanaichonok, he dropped upon his bed utterly exhausted
and soon fell into a deep sleep which lasted till the
following morning.

At dawn Stepan Mihailovitch woke up. His
face was bright and clear, and his voice cheerful
as he hailed his wife. She hurried in at once from
the next room, looking as if nothing had happened
the day before. ' I want my tea ! Where are the
children, and Aleyxéi and his wife ? I want to
see Seryozha '—thus spoke the madman on his
waking, and all the family appeared, composed and
cheerful, in his presence. But there was one
exception. His daughter-in-law was a woman of
strong character herself, and no entreaties could
induce her to smile so soon upon the wild beast of
the day before ; and her little son kept constantly
saying, ' I won't go to grandfather ! I'm frightened ! '
She really did not feel well and excused herself on
that ground ; and she kept her child in her room.
The family were horrified and expected a renewal
of the storm. But the wild beast of yesterday had
wakened up as a human being. He talked play-
fully over his tea and then went himself to visit the
invalid. She was really unwell and was lying in
bed thin and altered. The old man sat down beside
her, kissed her, said kind things to her, and caressed
his grandson ; then he left the room saying that

he would find that day long 'without his dear daughter-in-law.' Half an hour later she entered his room, wearing a pretty dress which he used to say especially became her, and holding her son by the hand. My grandfather welcomed her almost in tears : ' Just see ! ' he said fondly ; ' though she was not well, she got up and dressed, regardless of herself, and came to cheer up an old man.' His wife and daughters bit their lips and looked down ; for they all disliked his favourite ; but she answered his affectionate greeting with cheerful respect, and looked proudly and triumphantly at her ill-wishers.

But I will say no more of the dark side of my grandfather's character. I would rather dwell on his bright side and describe one of his good days, which I have often and often heard spoken of.

4. My Grandfather on one of his Good Days

It was the end of June, and the weather was very hot. After a stifling night, a fresh breeze set in from the East at dawn, a breeze which always flags when the sun grows hot. Just then my grandfather awoke. It was hot in his bedroom ; for the room was not large, and, though the window with its narrow old-fashioned sash was raised as high as it would go, he had curtains of home-made muslin round his bed. This precaution was indispensable : without it, the wicked mosquitoes would have kept him awake and devoured him. Those winged musicians swarmed round the bed, each driving its long proboscis into the fine fabric which protected him, and kept up their monotonous serenade all through the night. It

sounds absurd, but I cannot conceal the fact that
I like the shrill high note and even the bite of the
mosquito ; for it reminds me of sleepless nights in
high summer on the banks of the Boogorooslan,
where the bushes grew thick and green and all
round the nightingales called ; and I remember
the beating heart of youth and that vague feeling,
half pleasure and half pain, for which I would now
give up all that remains of the sinking fire of life.

My grandfather woke up, rubbed the sweat off
his high forehead with a hot hand, put his head out
between the curtains, and burst out laughing.
His two servants, Mazan and Tanaichonok, lay
stretched on the floor ; their attitudes might have
made any one laugh, and they snored lustily.
' Confound the rascals ! How they snore ! ' said
my grandfather, and smiled again. You could
never be sure about Stepan Mihailovitch. It might
have been expected that such forcible language
would have been followed up by a blow in the ribs
from the blackthorn staff which always stood by
his bed, or a kick, or even a salutation in the form
of a stool. But no : my grandfather had laughed
on opening his eyes, and he kept up that mood
throughout the day. He rose quickly, crossed
himself once or twice, and thrust his bare feet into
a pair of old rusty leather slippers ; then, wearing
only his shirt of coarse home-made linen—my
grandmother would not give him any better—he
went out upon the stoop,[1] to enjoy the freshness
and moisture of the morning all around him.

I said just now that Arina Vassilyevna would
not give her husband finer linen ; and the reader

---

[1] This word from S. Africa seems best for an unroofed
veranda. such as this was.

will remark with justice that this is inconsistent
with the relations between the two. I am sorry,
but I cannot help it. It is really true that female
persistence triumphed, as it always does, over
male violence. My grandmother got more than
one beating over the coarse linen, but she continued to supply him with it till at last her husband
got used to it. He resorted once to extreme
measures : he took an axe and chopped up all
his objectionable shirts on the threshold of his
room, while my grandmother howled at the sight
and implored him to beat *her* rather than spoil his
good clothes. But even this device failed : the
coarse shirts appeared once more, and the victim
submitted. I must apologize for interrupting my
narrative, in order to meet an imaginary objection
on the part of the reader.

Without troubling any one, he went himself
to the store-room, fetched a woollen mat, and
spread it out on the top step of the stoop ; then
he sat down upon it, meaning to follow his regular
custom of watching the sun rise. To see sunrise
gives every man a kind of half-conscious pleasure ;
and my grandfather felt an added satisfaction
when he looked down over his court-yard, by this
time sufficiently equipped with all the buildings
necessary for his farming operations. The court
was not, indeed, fenced ; and the animals, when
turned out of the peasants' yards, used to pay it
passing visits, before they were all gathered
together and driven to the common pasture. So
it was on this morning ; and the same thing was
repeated every evening. Some pigs, fresh from the
mire, rubbed and scratched themselves against the
very stoop on which my grandfather was sitting,

while they feasted with grunts of satisfaction on
shells of crayfish and other refuse from the table,
which that unsophisticated household deposited
close to the steps. Cows and sheep also looked in,
and it was inevitable that these visitors should
leave unsightly tokens behind them. But to this
my grandfather did not object in the least. On
the contrary, he looked with pleasure at the fine
beasts, taking them as a certain indication that his
peasants were doing well. The loud cracking of
the herdsman's long whip soon evicted the tres-
passers. Now the servants began to stir. The
stout groom, Spiridon—known even in advanced
old age as 'little Spirka'—led out, one after
another, three colts, two bays and one brown. He
tied them to a post, rubbed them down, and
exercised them at the end of a long halter, while
my grandfather admired their paces and also
admired in fancy the stock he hoped to raise from
them—a dream which he realized with entire
success. Then the old housekeeper came forth
from the cellar in which she slept, and went down
to the river to wash. First she sighed and groaned,
according to her invariable custom ; then she
turned towards the sunrise and said a prayer, before
she set to work at washing and scrubbing plates
and dishes. Swallows and martins twittered cheerfully as they cut circles in the air, quails called
loudly in the fields, the song of the larks rained
down from the sky, the hoarse note of the sitting
landrails came from the bushes, and the bleat of
the snipe from the neighbouring marsh, the mock-
ing-birds imitated the nightingales with all their
might ; and forth from behind the hill issued the
bright sun ! Blue smoke rose in columns from the

peasants' houses and then swayed in the breeze
like the fluttering flags of a line of ships ; and soon
the labourers were plodding towards the fields.

My grandfather began to feel a desire for cold
water to wash in and then for his tea. He roused
his two servants from their ungainly attitudes ;
and they jumped up in a great fright at first, but
were soon reassured by his good-humoured voice :
' Mazan, my washing things ! Tanaichonok, wake
Aksyutka and your mistress, and then tea ! '
There was no need to repeat these orders : clumsy
Mazan was already flying at top speed to the spring
for water, carrying a glittering copper basin, while
handy Tanaichonok woke up Aksyutka, a young
but ugly maid ; and she, while she put straight the
kerchief on her head, called her mistress, Arina
Vassilyevna, now grown old and stout. In a few
minutes all the household were on their legs, and
all knew by this time that the old master had got
out of bed on the right side ! A quarter of an hour
later, a table was standing by the stoop—the white
tablecloth was home-made and adorned with a
pattern—a samovár [1] in the shape of a large
copper teapot, was hissing on the table, and
Aksyutka was busy about the tea. Meanwhile
Arina Vassilyevna was greeting her husband. On
some mornings it was the etiquette to sigh and look
sorrowful ; but to-day she asked after his health
in a loud cheerful voice : ' How had he slept ?
What dreams had he had ? ' Stepan Mihailovitch
greeted his wife affectionately and called her
' Arisha ' ; he never kissed her hand, but sometimes

[1] An urn, with a central receptacle for hot charcoal. In
this case, the receptacle is inserted where the teapot lid
should be.

gave her his to kiss as a sign of favour. Arina Vassil-yevna, in her pleasure, looked quite young and pretty; one forgot her stout awkward figure. She brought a stool at once and sat down on the stoop beside my grandfather, which she never ventured to do unless he was in a very good humour. 'Come, Arisha, let us have a cup of tea together before it gets hot,' said Stepan Mihailo-vitch; 'it was a stifling night, but I slept so sound that I have forgotten all my dreams. How did you sleep?' This question was a signal mark of favour, and my grandmother replied at once that, when Stepan Mihailovitch had a good night, she of course had one too, but that Tanyusha [1] was restless all night. Tanyusha was the youngest daughter and, as often happens, her father's favourite. He was vexed to hear this account of her, and ordered that she was not to be called but to sleep on till she woke. She had been called at the same time as her sisters Alexandra and Eliza-beth, and was dressed already; but no one ventured to mention this fact. She made haste to undress, got back into bed, and had the shutters drawn. She could not get to sleep, but she lay in the dark for two hours; and her father was pleased that Tanyusha had had her sleep out. The only son, [2] who was now nine, was never wakened early. But the two elder daughters appeared immediately; and Stepan Mihailovitch gave them his hand to kiss and called them by their pet names, Lexanya and Lizanka. They were both clever girls, and

[1] A diminutive form of Tatyána.
[2] The author's father, called throughout Alexyéi; his real name was Timoféi (Timothy). So his mother, whose name was Márya (Mary) is called Sófya (Sophia).

Alexandra had also inherited her father's active mind and violent temper but none of his good qualities. My grandmother, a very simple woman, was entirely under the thumb of her daughters ; and whenever she ventured to play tricks upon Stepan Mihailovitch, it was because they had put her up to it ; but she was so clumsy that she seldom succeeded, and her husband knew very well who was at the bottom of it. He knew also that his daughters were prepared to deceive him whenever they got the chance—though, for the sake of a quiet life, he let them suppose that he was blind to their goings on. But this only lasted while he was in a good temper : as soon as he got angry, he stated his view of their conduct in the most unsparing and uncomplimentary terms, and sometimes even chastised them. But, like true daughters of Eve, they were not discouraged. When the fit of anger passed and the cloud lifted from their father's brow, they started again upon their underhand schemes, and pretty often they were successful in carrying them out.

When he had drunk his tea and talked about things in general with his womankind, my grandfather got ready to drive out. Some time before, he had said to Mazan, ' My horse ! '—and an old brown gelding was already standing by the steps, harnessed to a long car, a very comfortable conveyance, with an outer frame-work of netting and a plank, covered with felt, to sit on. Spiridon, the driver, wore a simple livery : he had bare feet and nothing on but his shirt, with a red woollen belt, from which hung a key and a copper comb. On a similar occasion on the previous day, he had worn no hat ; but this had been disapproved of, and he

now wore some head-gear which he had woven out
of broad strips of bast.[1]   My grandfather made
merry over this ' sun-bonnet.'   Then he put on his
own cap and long coat of unbleached home-made
cloth, placed his heavy cloak beneath him in case
of rain, and took his seat on the car.   Spiridon also
folded his coat and sat upon it; it was made of
unbleached cloth but dyed bright red with madder.
Madder grew freely in the fields round Bagrovo,
and was so much used that the servants about the
house were called by the neighbours ' redbreasts ';
I have heard the nickname myself fifteen years
after my grandfather's death.

In the fields, Stepan Mihailovitch found everything to his mind.   He examined the rye-crop;
it was now past flowering and stood up like a wall,
as high as a man; a light breeze was blowing, and
bluish-purple waves went over it, now lighter
and now darker in the sunlight; and the sight
gladdened his heart.   He visited the young oats
and millet and all the spring-sown crops, and then
went to the fallow, where he ordered his car to be
driven backwards and forwards over the field.
This was his regular way of testing the goodness of
the work : any spot of ground that had not been
properly ploughed and harrowed gave the light car
a jolt; and, when my grandfather was not in a
good humour, he stuck a twig or a stick in the
ground at the place, sent for the bailiff if he was not
present, and settled accounts with him on the
spot.   But to-day all went well : his wheels may
have encountered such obstacles, but he took no
notice of them.   His next point was the hay-fields,

---

[1] The inner bark of the limetree, used for many purposes
in Russia.

where he admired the tall thick steppe-grass which
was to fall beneath the scythe before many days
were past. He paid a visit to the peasants' fields
also, to see for himself who had a good crop and
who had not ; and he drove over their fallow to
test it. He noticed everything and forgot nothing.
Passing over an untilled strip, he saw some wild
strawberries nearly ripe ; he stopped and, with
Mazan's help, picked a large handful of splendid
big berries, which he took home as a present for his
'Arisha.' In spite of the great heat he was out till
nearly noon.

As soon as my grandfather's car was seen
descending the hill, dinner was set on the table,
and all the family stood on the steps to receive
him. 'Well, Arisha,' he called out cheerfully,
'what splendid crops God is giving us this year !
Great is His goodness ! And here are some strawberries for you ; they are nearly ripe ; the pickers
must go out to-morrow.' This attention was
almost too much for my grandmother. As he
spoke, he walked into the house, and the smell of
the hot cabbage-soup came to meet him from the
parlour. 'Ah ! I see dinner 's ready ; good ! ' said
Stepan Mihailovitch more cheerfully than before,
and walked straight into the parlour and sat down
at table, without visiting his own room. I should
mention that my grandfather had a rule : at
whatever hour, early or late, he returned from the
fields, dinner must be on the table, and Heaven
help the women, if they did not notice his coming
and failed to serve the meal in time ! There were
occasions when such neglect gave rise to sad
consequences ; but on this happy day, everything
went without a hitch. Behind my grandfather's

241   C

chair stood a stout lad, holding a birch-bough with
the leaves on to drive away the flies. The hottest
weather will not make a true Russian refuse
cabbage-soup, and my grandfather supped his
with a wooden spoon, because silver would have
burnt his lips. Soup was followed by a fish-salad,
made of kippered sturgeon as yellow as wax, and
shelled crayfish. All the courses were of this light
kind, and were washed down with *kvass* [1] and
home-made beer ; the drinks were iced and so was
the salad. There were days when dinner was eaten
in terrible stillness and silent dread of an explosion ;
but this was a cheerful meal, with much loud
talking and laughing. Every boy and girl about
the place had heard that the master was in a
cheerful temper, and they all crowded into the
parlour in hopes of a ' piece.' He gave them all
something good to eat ; for there was five times
as much food on the table as the family could
eat.

Immediately after dinner he went to lie down.
All flies were expelled from the bed-curtains, and
the curtains drawn round him with the ends
tucked under the mattress ; and soon his mighty
snoring proclaimed that the master was asleep.
All the rest went to their rooms to lie down.
Mazan and Tanaichonok, when they had had their
dinner and swallowed their share of the remnants
from the dining-room table, also lay down in the
passage, close to the door of my grandfather's
bedroom. Though they had slept before dinner,
they went to sleep again at once ; but they were
soon wakened by the heat and the burning rays of
the sun coming through the windows. They felt

[1] A drink made of malt and rye.

a strong desire to cool their parched throats with
some of their master's iced beer ; and the bold
scamps managed to get it in the following way.
My grandfather's dressing-gown and night-cap
were lying on a chair near the half-open door of
his room. Tanaichonok put them on and sat down
on the stoop, while Mazan went off to the cellar
with a jug and wakened the old housekeeper, who
like every soul in the house was fast asleep. He
said his master was awake and wanted an iced
tankard at once. She was surprised at his waking
so soon ; but Mazan then pointed to the figure in
the dressing-gown and night-cap sitting on the
stoop. The beer was drawn at once and ice added ;
and Mazan went quickly back with his prize. The
cronies shared the jug between them and then
replaced the garments. An hour later their master
awoke in excellent humour, and his first words
were, ' Iced boor !' This frightened the rascals ;
and when Tanaichonok hurried off to the cellar,
the housekeeper guessed at once where the previous
jug had gone. She produced the liquor, but followed
the messenger back herself, and found the real
Simon Pure sitting on the stoop and wearing the
dressing-gown. The truth came out at once ; and
Mazan and Tanaichonok shaking with fear fell at
their master's feet. And what do you think my
grandfather did ? He burst out laughing, sent for
his wife and daughters, and told them the story
with loud bursts of laughter. The culprits breathed
again, and one of them even ventured to grin. But
Stepan Mihailovitch noticed this and very nearly
grew angry : he frowned, but the composing effect
of his good day was so strong that his face cleared
up, and he said with a significant look, ' Well,

I forgive you this once, but if it happens again
. . .'—there was no need to end the sentence.

It is certainly strange that the servants of a man
so passionate and so violent in his moments of
passion should dare to be so impudent. But I
have often noticed in the course of my life that the
strictest masters have the most venturesome and
reckless servants. My grandfather had other
experiences of a similar kind. This same servant,
Mazan, was sweeping out his master's room one
day and preparing to make the bed, when he was
suddenly tempted by the soft down of the bedding
and pillows. He thought he would like a little
taste of luxury ; so down he lay on his master's
bed and fell asleep. My grandfather himself came
upon him sound asleep, and only laughed ! He
did, indeed, give the man one good rap with his
staff ; but that was nothing—he only did it in
order to see how frightened Mazan would be.
Worse tricks than these were played upon Stepan
Mihailovitch in his time. During his absence from
home, his cousin and ward, Praskovya Ivanovna
Bagroff, was given in marriage to a dangerous and
disreputable man whom he detested ; the girl, who
was only fourteen and a great heiress, was an
inmate of Bagrovo and very dear to its owner. It
is true that the plot was executed by the girl's
relations on her mother's side ; but Arina
Vassilyevna gave her consent, and her daughters
were actively engaged in it. But I shall return to
my narrative for the present and leave this
incident to be told later.

He woke up at five in the afternoon and drank
his iced beer. Soon afterwards he wanted his tea,
in spite of the sultry heat of the day ; for he

believed that a very hot drink makes hot weather more bearable. But first he went down to bathe in the cool waters of the river, which flowed under the windows of the house. When he came back, the whole family were waiting for him at the tea-table—the same table set in the shade, with the same hissing teapot and the same Aksyutka. When he had drunk his fill of his favourite sudorific beverage, with cream so thick that the curd on it was yellow, my grandfather proposed that the whole party should make an expedition to the mill. The plan was received with joy; and Alexandra and Tatyana, who were fond of angling, took fishing-rods with them. Two cars were brought round in a minute. Stepan Mihailovitch and his wife took their seats on one, and placed between them their one boy,[1] the precious scion of their ancient and noble line; while the other carried the three daughters, with a boy to dig for worms on the mill-dam and bait their hooks for the young ladies. When they reached the mill, a seat was brought out for Arina Vassilyevna, and she sat down in the shade of the building, not far from the mill-race where her daughters were fishing. Meanwhile Elizabeth, the eldest, partly to please her father and partly from her own interest in such matters, went with Stepan Mihailovitch to inspect the mill and the pounding machine. The little boy either watched his sisters fishing—he was not allowed to fish himself in deep places—or played beside his mother, who never took her eyes off him, in her fear that the child would somehow tumble in.

Both sets of mill-stones were at work, one making

[1] The author's father.

wheat-flour for the master's table, and the other
grinding rye for a neighbour; and there was millet
under the pounding-machine. My grandfather
was well acquainted with all farming operations:
he understood a mill thoroughly and explained all
the details to his attentive and intelligent companion. He saw in a moment any defect in the
machinery or mistake in the position of the stones.
One of them he ordered to be lowered half a notch,
and the rye-meal came out finer, to the great
satisfaction of its owner. At the other stone, his
ear detected at once that one of the cogs on the
small wheel was getting worn. He stopped the
current, and Boltunyónok,[1] the miller, jumped
down beside the wheel. He looked at it and felt it
and then said, 'You are quite right, *bátyushka*
Stepan Mihailovitch! One of the cogs is a little
worn.' 'A little you call it!'—said my grandfather, not at all vexed: 'but for my coming, the
wheel would have snapped this very night!' 'I
am sorry I did not notice it, Stepan Mihailovitch.'
'Well, never mind! Bring a new wheel, and take
the worn cog off the other; and mind the new cog
is neither thicker nor thinner than the rest; the
whole secret lies in that.' The new wheel, fitted
and tested beforehand, was fixed at once and
greased with tar; and the current was turned on
by degrees, also by my grandfather's instructions;
at once the stone began to hum and grind smoothly
and evenly, with no stumbling or knocking. The
visitors went next to the pounding-machine, where
my grandfather took a handful of millet from the
mortar. He blew the chaff away and said to the

---

[1] A nickname: 'Little Chatterer,' a diminutive of
boltún.

man who had brought the grain to the mill, a Mordvinian and an old acquaintance : ' Have a care,
friend Vaska ! If you look, every grain is pounded
already, and if you go on, you will have less of it.'
Vaska tried it himself and saw that my grandfather
was right. He said, ' Thank you,' ducked his head
by way of bowing, and ran off to stop the current.
Their last visit was to the poultry-yard, where a
large number of ducks and geese, hens and turkeys,
were looked after by an old woman and her little
grand-daughter. Everything here was in excellent
order. As a sign of special favour, my grandfather
gave both of them his hand to kiss, and ordered
that the hen-wife should get an extra allowance of
20 lb., of wheat-flour every month to make pies
with. Stepan Mihailovitch rejoined his wife in
good spirits. Everything had gone right : his
daughter had shown intelligence, the mill was
working well, and the hen-wife, Tatyana Goro-
ohnua,[1] was attending to her duties.

The heat had long been abating ; coolness came
from the water and from the approach of evening ;
a long cloud of dust drifted along the road and
came nearer the village with the bleating of sheep
and lowing of cattle ; the sun was losing light and
sinking behind the steep hill. Stepan Mihailovitch
stood on the mill-dam and surveyed the wide
mirror of the pond as it lay motionless in the frame
of its sloping banks. A fish jumped from time to
time ; but my grandfather was no fisherman.
' Time to go home, Arisha,' he said at last : ' I

[1] She had got this nickname (' the townwoman ')
because she had spent part of her youth in some town
(*Author's Note*).

expect the bailiff is waiting for me.' Seeing his
good humour, his daughters asked leave to fish on :
they said the fish would take better at sunset, and
they would walk home in half an hour. Leave
was given, and the old couple started for home on
one of the cars, while Elizabeth took her little
brother in the other. As Stepan Mihailovitch had
expected, the bailiff was waiting for him by the
stoop, and some peasants and their wives were
there with him ; they had got a hint from the
bailiff, who knew already that his master was in
the right mood, and now seized the opportunity
to state some exceptional needs or prefer some
exceptional requests. Not one of them was
disappointed. To one my grandfather gave corn,
and forgave an old debt which the man could have
paid ; another was allowed to marry his son before
the winter [1] and to a girl of their own choosing ;
he gave leave to a soldier's wife,[2] who was to be
turned out of the village for misconduct, to go on
living with her father ; and so on. Nor was that
all : strong home-made spirits were offered to each
of them, in a silver cup which held more than an
ordinary dram. Then my grandfather gave his
orders to the bailiff, shortly and clearly, and went
off to his supper which had been standing ready
some time. The evening meal did not differ much
from the midday dinner ; but the cooler air
probably gave a keener edge to appetite. It was
a custom with Stepan Mihailovitch to send his
family off to bed and sit up for half an hour or so
on the stoop, with nothing on but his shirt, for the

[1] After harvest is the normal time for peasants' marriages.
[2] A *soldatka* is a woman whose husband is away serving
in the Army.

sake of coolness. This day he stayed there longer
than usual, laughing and jesting with Mazan and
Tanaichonok; he made them wrestle and fight
with their fists, and urged them on till they began
to hit out in earnest and even clutched each other
by the hair. He had laughed his fill; and now
a word of command, and the tone it was spoken in,
brought them to their senses and parted them.

All the landscape lay before him, still and
wonderful, enfolded by the summer night. The
glow of sunset had not yet disappeared, and would
go on till it gave place to the glow of dawn.
Hour by hour, the depths of the vault of heaven
grew darker; hour by hour, the stars flashed
brighter, and the cries of the night birds grew
louder, as if they were becoming more familiar
with man; the clack of the mill sounded nearer in
the misty damp of the night air. My grandfather
rose from his stoop, and crossed himself once or
twice, looking at the starry sky. Then, though the
heat in his bedroom was stifling, he lay down on
the hot feather-bed and ordered his curtains to be
drawn round him.

FRAGMENT II

MIHAIL MAXIMOVITCH KUROLYESSOFF

I PROMISED to give a separate account of Mihail
Maximovitch Kurolyessoff and his marriage with
my grandfather's cousin, Praskóvya Ivánovna
Bagróff. This story begins about 1760, earlier
than the time described in the First Fragment of
this history, and ends much later. I shall now
fulfil my promise.

Stepan Mihailovitch was the only son of Mihail
Bagroff; Mihail had a brother Peter, whose only
daughter was Praskovya Ivanovna. As she was
his only cousin and the sole female representative
of the Bagroff family in that generation, my
grandfather was much attached to her. While
still in the cradle she lost her mother, and her
father died when she was ten. Her mother, one of
the Baktéyeff family, was very rich and left to her
daughter 900 serfs, a quantity of money, and still
more in silver and valuables, and her father's
death added 300 serfs to her property. Praskovya
Ivanovna was therefore a rich orphan, and would
bring a great fortune to her future husband. After
her father's death she lived at first with her grandmother, Mme. Baktéyeff; then she paid a long
visit to Bagrovo; and finally Stepan Mihailovitch
took her to his house as a permanent inmate. He
was quite as fond of his orphan cousin as of his
daughters and was very affectionate to her in his
own way. But she was too young, too babyish,
one might say, to appreciate her cousin's love and

tenderness, which never took the form of spoiling,
while, under her grandmother's roof, where she
had spent some time, she had grown accustomed
to indulgence. So it is not surprising that she
grew tired of Bagrovo and wished to go back
to old Mme. Baktéyeff. Praskovya Ivanovna,
though she was not beautiful, had regular features
and fine intelligent grey eyes ; her dark eyebrows,
long and rather thick, were a sign of her masculine
strength of character ; she was tall and well-made,
and looked eighteen when she was only fourteen.
But, in spite of her physical maturity, her mind
and feelings were still those of a mere child :
always lively and merry, she capered and frisked,
gambolled and sang, from morning till night.
She had a remarkable voice and was passionately
fond of joining with the maids in their singing or
dancing or swinging ; or, when nothing of that
kind was to be had, she played with her dolls all
day, invariably accompanying her occupation
with popular songs of all sorts, of which she knew
even then an immense number.

A year before Praskovya Ivanovna went to live
at Bagrovo, Mihail Kurolyessoff, an officer in the
Army, came on leave to the Government of
Simbirsk. He belonged to a noble family in the
district, and was then twenty-eight years old. He
was a fine-looking fellow, and many people called
him handsome ; but some said that, in spite of
his regular features, there was something unpleas-
ing about him ; and I remember to have heard as
a child debates on this point between my grandmother and her daughters. Entering the Army at
fifteen, he had served in a regiment of high
reputation in those days and had risen to the

rank of major. He did not often come home on leave, and he had little reason to come, because the serfs—about 150 in all—who formed his property, owned little land and were scattered about. As a matter of course, he had received no proper education, but he had a ready tongue and wrote in an easy correct style. Many of his letters have passed through my hands; and they prove clearly that he was a man of sense and tact and also firm of purpose and businesslike. I don't know his exact relationship to our immortal Suvóroff;[1] but I found in the correspondence some letters from the great captain, which always begin thus—

'Dear Sir and cousin, Mihail Maximovitch,' and end—

'With all proper respect for you and my worthy cousin, Praskovya Ivanovna,

'I have the honour to be,' &c.

Kurolyessoff was little known in the Government of Simbirsk. But 'rumour runs all over the earth,' and perhaps the young officer on leave permitted himself some 'distractions', as they are called ; or perhaps the soldier servant whom he brought with him, in spite of his master's severity, let something leak out at odd times. Whatever the reason, an opinion gradually took shape about him, which may be summed up in the following statements—' Toe the line, when you parade before the Major '—' Mind your P's and Q's, when talking to Kurolyessoff '—' When one of his men is caught out, he shows no mercy, though he may try to shield him '—' When he says a thing,

---

[1] A famous general in the reign of Catherine II, and a great popular hero.

he means it '—' He's the very devil when his temper's up.' People called him ' a dark horse ' and ' a rum customer '; but every one admitted his ability as a man of business. There were also rumours, probably proceeding from the same sources, that the Major had certain weaknesses, which, however, he gratified with due regard to time and place. But these failings were excused by the charitable proverbs—' A young man must sow his wild oats,' and ' It's no crime in a man to drink,' and ' The man who drinks and keeps his head Scores two points, it must be said.' So Kurolyessoff had not a positively bad reputation ; on the contrary many people thought highly of him. Insinuating and courteous in his address, and respectful to all persons of rank and position, he was a welcome guest in every home. As he was a near neighbour of the Baktéyeff family, and indeed a distant connexion, he soon managed to make his way into their good graces ; they took a great liking to him and sounded his praises everywhere. At first he had no special object, but was merely following his invariable rule—to make himself agreeable to persons of rank and wealth ; but later, when he met in their house Praskovya Ivanovna, lively, laughing, and rich, and looking quite old enough to be married, he formed a plan of marrying her himself and getting her wealth into his hands. With this definite object in view, he redoubled his attentions to her grandmother and aunt, till the two ladies quite lost their heads about him ; at the same time he paid court so cleverly to the girl herself, that she soon had a liking for him, as she naturally would for a man who agreed to everything she said, gave her

everything she asked, and spoiled her in every
possible way. Next he showed his hand to her
relations : he professed that he had fallen in love
with the orphan girl, and they believed that he
was suffering all a passionate lover's pangs, mad
with longing, and haunted by his darling's image
day and night. They approved of his plan and
took the poor victim of love under their protection.
The favour and connivance of her relations made
it easy for him to proceed along his path : he did
everything he could to entertain and amuse the
child—taking her out for drives behind his spirited
horses, pushing her in the swing and sitting beside
her in it himself, singing with her the popular
songs which he sang very well, giving her many
trifling presents, and ordering amusing toys for
her from Moscow.

Kurolyessoff knew, however, that the consent
of her cousin and guardian was a necessary preliminary to complete success, and therefore tried
to get into the good graces of Stepan Mihailovitch.
Under various pretexts and provided with intro-
ductory letters from Praskovya Ivanovna's
relations, he paid a visit at Bagrovo ; but the
visit proved a failure. At first sight this may
seem strange ; for some of the young officer's
qualities were likely to appeal to Stepan Mihailovitch. But my grandfather, as well as his quick
eye and sound sense, had that instinct, peculiar
to men who are perfectly honest and straightforward themselves, which is instantly conscious
of the hidden guile and crooked ways even of a
complete stranger—the instinct which detects
evil under a plausible exterior and surmises its
future development. Kurolyessoff's respectful

manner and polite speeches did not take him in
for a moment : he guessed at once that there was
some knavery underneath. There were other
objections. My grandfather's own life was very
strict, and the repoits of the Major's peccadillocs
which had casually come to his ear, though many
people treated them lightly enough, filled his
honest breast with disgust ; and, though he was
himself capable of furious anger, he hated deliberate
unkindness and cold cruelty. For all these reasons
his reception of his guest was cool and dry, though
Kurolyessoff talked in a sensible practical way on
all subjects and especially the management of
land. Praskovya Ivanovna had now come to live
with my grandfather ; and when the Major began,
on the strength of their old acquaintance, to pay
her compliments which she accepted with pleasure,
his host's head bent a little to one side, his eyebrows met, and he shot a look at his guest which
was hardly hospitable. Arina Vassilyevna, on the
contrary, and her daughters, had been charmed
straight off by the young man's seductions and
were quite inclined to say kind things to him ; but
the storm-signals on the face of Stepan Mihailovitch
quenched their ardour and made them all hold
their tongues. The guest tried to restore the
harmony of the party and to resume their agreeable conversation. But it was no use : he received
short answers from them all, and his host was not
even quite polite. Though it was getting late and
an invitation to stay the night would have been
the natural thing, there was nothing for it but
to take his leave. ' The man is a knave and
rotten all through,' said Stepan Mihailovitch to
his family ; ' but perhaps he won't come here

again.' No voice was raised to contradict him;
but, behind his back, the women went on for a
long time praising the dashing young officer; and
one who liked to listen to his merits and to tell of
them herself, was the orphan girl with the large
fortune.

With the taste of this rebuff in his mouth,
Kurolyessoff went back and told Mme. Baktéyeff
of his failure. The people there knew my grandfather well, and at once abandoned all hope that
he would give his consent. Long consideration
brought no solution of the difficulty. The bold
Major suggested that her grandmother should
invite the girl on a visit, and that the marriage
should take place without the consent of Stepan
Mihailovitch; but both Mme. Baktéyeff and her
daughter, Mme. Kurmysheff, were convinced that
Stepan Mihailovitch would not let his cousin go
alone, or, if he did, would be slow about it, and the
Major's leave was nearly at an end. Then he
proposed a desperate scheme—to induce Praskovya
Ivanovna to elope with him, and to get married in
the nearest church; but her relations would not
hear of such a scandalous expedient, and Kurolyessoff went back to his regiment. The ways of
Providence are past finding out, and we cannot
judge why it came about that this nefarious
scheme was crowned with success. Six months
later, Mme. Baktéyeff heard one day that Stepan
Mihailovitch was called away to some distance by
very important business and would not return for
some time. His destination and errand I do not
know; but it was some distant place, Astrakhan
or Moscow, and the business was certainly legal,
because he took with him his man of business. A

letter was sent at once to Stepan Mihailovitch, begging that the child, during the absence of her cousin and guardian, might stay with her grandmother. A curt answer was received—that Parasha[1] was very well where she was, and if they wished to see her they were welcome to visit Bagrovo and stay as long as they liked. Stepan Mihailovitch sent this plain answer, and gave the strictest injunctions to his always submissive wife, that she was to watch Parasha as the apple of her eye and never let her go out of the house alone ; and then he started on his journey.

Mme. Baktéyeff was constantly sending letters and messages to Praskovya Ivanovna and my grandfather's womankind ; and she sent news of his departure at once to Kurolyessoff, adding that the absence would be a long one, and asking whether the Major could not come on leave, to take a personal share in the promotion of their scheme. She herself and her daughter went at once to Bagrovo. She had always been on friendly terms with Arina Vassilyevna, and now, on discovering that she also liked Kurolyessoff, revealed the fact that the young officer was passionately in love with Parasha ; she launched out into praise of the suitor, and said, ' There is nothing I wish so much as to see the poor little orphan comfortably settled in my lifetime ; I am sure she will be happy. I feel that I have not long to live, and therefore I should like to hurry on the business.' Arina Vassilyevna, on her side, entirely approved of the plan but expressed doubts whether Stepan Mihailovitch would consent : ' Heaven knows

---

[1] A short form of Praskóvya, which itself represents the Greek name Paraskevá.

why ', she said, ' but he took a strong dislike to
that delightful Kurolyessoff.'   Arina Vassilyevna's
elder daughters were summoned to a council
presided over by Mme. Baktéyeff and her daughter,
a strong partisan of the Major's ; and it was
settled that the grandmother, as the girl's nearest
relation, should manage the affair, without
involving Arina Vassilyevna and her daughters ;
it was to appear that they knew nothing about it
and took no hand in it.   I have said already that
Arina Vassilyevna was a kindhearted and very
simple   woman ;   her   daughters   sympathized
entirely with Mme. Baktéyeff, and it is not surprising that she was persuaded by them to pro-
mote a scheme which was sure to provoke the
furious rage of Stepan Mihailovitch.

Meantime the innocent victim laughed and sang,
with no suspicion that her fate was being decided.
They often spoke of Kurolyessoff in her presence,
praised him to the skies, and assured her that he
loved her more than his own life, was constantly
studying how to please her, and would certainly
bring her a number of presents from Moscow on
his next visit.   All this she heard with pleasure,
and often said that she loved Kurolyessoff better
than anyone in the world.   While Mme. Baktéyeff
was at Bagrovo, she had a letter forwarded to her,
in which Kurolyessoff assured her that he would
come, as soon as he could get leave.   Arina
Vassilyevna promised to say nothing when writing
to her husband, and also to send Parasha to her
grandmother's house, in spite of her husband's
strict orders to the contrary, on the pretext that
her nearest relative was dangerously ill.   When
the two ladies left Bagrovo and went home,

Praskovya Ivanovna cried and asked to go with them; the Major was expected soon, and that was an additional attraction; but permission was refused, out of respect, it was said, to her guardian's strict orders. Kurolyessoff had some difficulty in getting leave, and it was two months before he arrived. Immediately afterwards a special messenger was dispatched to Bagrovo with a letter from Mme. Kurmysheff to Arina Vassilyevna; the lady wrote that her mother was desperately ill and wished to see her granddaughter and give her her blessing; she therefore asked that Parasha might be sent, with an escort. She also wrote that Stepan Mihailovitch would certainly have sent the child to see the last of her grandmother, and could not possibly resent this infraction of his commands. The letter was clearly intended to be shown by Arina Vassilyevna, in order to protect herself from her husband's displeasure. True to her promise and reassured by this letter, Arina Vassilyevna made her preparations at once and took Parasha herself to the place where the grandmother was supposed to be dying; she stayed there a week and returned home charmed by the politeness of Kurolyessoff and also by some presents which he had brought from Moscow for her, and for her daughters as well. Praskovya Ivanovna was very happy: her grandmother took a sudden turn for the better; that fairy godmother, the Major, had brought her a number of presents and toys from Moscow and stayed in the house continually. He flattered her in every possible way, and soon took her fancy so completely, that, when her grandmother told her he wished to marry her, she was charmed. She

ran up and down through the house like a perfect
child, telling every one she met that she was going
to marry the Major and would have capital fun—
driving all day with him behind his fine trotters,
swinging on a swing of immense height, singing,
or playing with dolls, not little dolls, but big ones
that were able to walk and bow. You can judge
by this, how far the poor little bride realized her
position. Fearing that reports might reach Stepan
Mihailovitch, the plotters went to work quickly :
they invited the neighbours to a formal betrothal,
at which the pair exchanged rings and kisses, sat
side by side at table, and had their healths drunk.
At first, the bride got tired of the ceremony where
she had to sit still so long and listen to so many
congratulations ; but when she was allowed to
have her new doll from Moscow beside her, she
quite cheered up, introducing the doll to every one
as her daughter, and making it curtsey when she
did, in acknowledgement of their kind wishes.
A week later, the marriage took place with all due
formality ; the bride's age was given as seventeen
instead of fifteen, but no one would have guessed
the truth, to look at her.

Though Arina Vassilyevna and her daughters
knew what the end must be, yet the news of the
marriage, which came sooner than they expected,
filled them with horror. The scales fell from their
eyes, and they now realized what they had been
about, and that neither the grandmother's sham
illness nor her letter would serve to cover them
from the just wrath of Stepan Mihailovitch.
Before she heard of the marriage, Arina Vassilyevna had written to her husband that she had
taken the child to her grandmother : ' It was quite

necessary,' she wrote, ' because the old lady was
in a dying state. I stayed there a whole week, and
mercifully the invalid took a good turn; but they insisted on keeping Parasha till her grandmother got
well. I was helpless : I could not take her by force,
so I agreed against my will and hurried back to our
own children, who were quite alone at Bagrovo.
And now I am afraid that you will be angry.' In
answering, he said she had done a foolish thing
and told her to go back and fetch Parasha home at
all costs. Arina Vassilyevna sighed and shed tears
over this letter, and was puzzled how to act. The
young couple soon came to pay her a visit. Parasha
seemed perfectly happy and cheerful, though some
of her childish gaiety had gone. Her husband
seemed happy too, and at the same time so composed and sensible that his clever arguments had
power to lull Arina Vassilyevna's fears to rest.
He proved to her convincingly that her husband's
wrath must all fall upon the grandmother : ' And
she,' said he, ' owing to that dangerous illness—
though now, thank God ! she is better—had a
perfect right not to wait for the consent of Stepan
Mihailovitch ; she knew that he would be slow in
giving it, though of course he must have given it
in time. It was impossible for her to delay, owing to
her critical condition, and it would have been hard
for her to die without seeing her orphan grand-
daughter settled in life ; her place could not be
filled even by a brother, far less by a mere cousin.'
Many soothing assurances of this kind were forthcoming, backed by some very handsome presents
which were received by the Bagrovo ladies with
great satisfaction and some sinking of heart.
Other presents were left, to be given to Stepan

Mihailovitch. Kurolyessoff advised Arina Vassilyevna not to write to her husband till he answered
the letter of intimation from the young couple ;
and he assured her that he and his wife would
write this at once. He did not really dream of
writing : his sole object was to delay the explosion
and get time to take root in his new position.
Immediately after his marriage, he applied for
leave to retire from the Army, and got it very
soon. He then began by paying a round of visits
with his bride to all the relations and friends on
both sides. At Simbirsk he began by calling on
the Governor and neglected no one of any importance who could be useful to him. All were
enthusiastic in praise of the handsome young
couple, and they were so popular everywhere,
that the marriage was soon sanctioned by public
opinion. Thus several months passed away.

Stepan Mihailovitch had had no news from
home for a long time, and his lawsuit dragged on
interminably. He was suddenly seized by a longing to see his family again, and returned one fine
day to Bagrovo. Arina Vassilyevna trembled all
over when she heard the awful words, ' The master
has come ! ' Hearing that all were alive and well,
he entered his house in high spirits, kissed his
Arisha and daughters and son, and then asked in
an easy tone, ' But where on earth is Parasha ? '
Encouraged by her husband's kind manner, Arina
Vassilyevna answered : ' I don't know for certain
where she is ; perhaps with her grandmother.
Of course you heard long ago, *batyushka*, that she
was married.' I shall not describe my grandfather's amazement and fury ; but his fury became
twice as hot, when he heard the name of the bride-

groom. He was proceeding to settle accounts with his wife on the spot, when she and all her daughters fell at his feet and showed him Mme. Baktéyeff's letter ; thus she had time to convince him that she knew nothing about it and had been deceived herself. The fury of Stepan Mihailovitch was now diverted to Mme. Baktéyeff ; he ordered fresh horses to be ready, rested two hours, and then galloped straight off to her house. The battle royal that took place between the two may be imagined. The old lady stood the first torrent of unmeasured abuse without flinching ; then she drew herself up, grew hot in her turn, and delivered her own attack upon my grandfather. ' How dare you make this furious assault on me,' she asked, ' as if I was your bond-slave ? Do you forget that my birth is quite as good as yours, and that my late husband held a much higher rank than you ? I am a nearer relation to Parasha, I am her own grandmother, and her guardian as much as you are. I arranged for her settlement without waiting for your consent, because I was dangerously ill and did not wish to leave her dependent upon you. I knew your infernal temper ; under your roof, the child would have had a taste of the stick some day. Kurolyessoff is an excellent match for her, and Parasha fell in love with him of herself. Everybody likes him and praises him. I know he did not take your fancy ; but just ask your own family, and you will soon find out that they can't say enough in his praise ! '

' You lie, you old swindler ! ' roared my grandfather ; ' you deceived my wife by pretending that you were dying ! Kurolyessoff has bewitched you and your daughter by the power of the devil, and you have sold your grand-daughter into his hands ! '

This was too much for Mme. Baktéyeff, and she let out in her rage that Arina Vassilyevna and her daughters were in league with her and had themselves accepted presents at different times from Kurolyessoff. This disclosure turned the whole force of my grandfather's rage back upon his own family. He threatened that he would dissolve the marriage on the ground that Parasha was not of age, and then started home. On the way he turned aside to visit the priest who had performed the ceremony, and called him to account. But the priest met his attack very coolly, and showed him without hesitation the certificate of affinity, the signatures of the grandmother, the bride, and the witnesses, and also the baptismal certificate which alleged that Praskovya Ivanovna was seventeen. This was a fresh blow to my grandfather, for it deprived him of all hope of breaking the hateful marriage ; and it increased enormously his anger against his wife and daughters. I shall not dwell upon his behaviour when he got home : it would be too painful and repulsive. Thirty years later, my aunts could never speak of that day without trembling. I shall only say, that the culprits made a full confession, that he sent back all the presents, including those intended for himself, to Mme. Baktéyeff, to be forwarded to the proper quarter, that the elder daughters long kept their beds, and that my grandmother lost all her hair and went about for a whole year with her head bandaged. He sent a message to the Kurolyessoffs forbidding them to dare to appear before him, and ordered that their names should never be mentioned in his house.

Time rolled on, healing wounds whether of mind or body, and calming passions. Within a year Arina Vassilyevna's head was healed, and the anger in the heart of Stepan Mihailovitch had cooled. At first he refused either to see or hear of the Kurolyessoffs, and would not even write to Praskovya Ivanovna; but when a year had passed and he heard from all quarters good accounts of her way of life, and was told that she had suddenly become sensible beyond her years, his heart softened and he became anxious to see the cousin whom he loved. He reasoned that she, as a perfect child, was less to blame than any of the rest, and gave her leave to come, without her husband, to Bagrovo; and, as a matter of course, she came at once. The reports were true: one year of marriage had wrought such a change in Praskovya Ivanovna, that Stepan Mihailovitch could hardly believe it. It was puzzling also, that she now showed towards her cousin a kind of love and gratitude which she had never felt in her girl-hood, and was still less likely, one would think, to feel after her marriage. In his eyes, which filled with tears when they met, did she read how much love was concealed under that harsh exterior and that arbitrary violence? Had she any dark fore-boding of the future, or did she dimly realize that here was her one support and stay? Or did she feel unconsciously, that the rough cousin who had opposed her happiness and still disliked her hus-band, loved her better than all the women who had indulged her by falling in with all her childish wishes? I cannot answer these questions; but all were struck by the change. In her careless childhood she had been indifferent to her cousin.

thinking little of his rights and her duties; and
now she had every reason to resent his treatment
of her grandmother; yet she felt to him now as
a devoted daughter feels to a tender father when
both have long known and loved one another.
Whatever the cause of it, this sudden feeling
ended only with her life.

But what was the remarkable change that had
come over so young a woman as Praskovya Ivanovna, after one year of married life? The foolish
child had turned into a sensible but cheerful
woman. She frankly confessed that they had all
behaved badly to Stepan Mihailovitch. For herself only she pleaded youth and ignorance, and
for her grandmother, her husband, and the rest,
their blind devotion to her. She did not ask him
to pardon the chief criminal at once; but she
hoped that in time, when he saw her happiness
and the unwearied care with which her husband
managed her property and looked after her estates,
her cousin would forgive the culprit and admit
him at Bagrovo. My grandfather, though he
made no answer at the time, was completely
conquered by this appeal. He did not keep his
' clever cousin '—as he now began to call her—long
at his house; he said that her place was now else-
where, and soon sent her back to her husband.
At parting, he said: ' If you are as well satisfied
with your husband a year hence, and if he behaves
as well to you as he does now, I shall be reconciled
to him.' A year later, as he knew that Kurolyessoff
was behaving well and paying the utmost attention
to the management of his wife's property, and
found his cousin, when he saw her, looking healthy
and happy and cheerful, Stepan Mihailovitch told

her to bring her husband with her to Bagrovo. He
received Kurolyessoff cordially, frankly confessed
his former doubts, and ended by promising to treat
him as a kinsman and friend, on condition of continued good conduct. The guest behaved very
cleverly : he was less furtive and less insinuating
than he used to be, but just as respectful, attentive,
and tactful. His bearing was clearly more confident and self-assured ; he was giving the closest
attention to agricultural problems, on which he
asked advice from my grandfather—advice which
he took in very quickly and followed with remarkable skill. He was connected in some distant way
with Stepan Mihailovitch, and addressed him as
' uncle ' and treated the rest of the family as
relations. Even before the scene of reconciliation
or forgiveness, he had rendered a service of some
kind to Stepan Mihailovitch ; my grandfather
was aware of this and thanked him for it
now ; he even gave him a similar commission to
execute. In fact, the visit passed off very well.
But, though all the circumstances seemed to speak
in favour of Kurolyessoff, my grandfather still
said : ' The lad is all right : he is clever and sensible ; but somehow I don't take to him.'

It was in the course of the next year that Stepan
Mihailovitch made his move to the district of Ufa.
For three years after his marriage, Kurolyessoff
behaved with discretion and moderation, or at
least concealed his conduct with such care that
nothing got round. Besides, he was constantly
moving about and spent little time at home. There
was only one report, which spread everywhere
with exaggeration—that the young landowner was
a very strict master. During the next two years he

did wonders in the way of improving his wife's property, and established his character for unceasing activity, bold enterprise, and steadfast perseverance in the execution of his schemes. The property had been mismanaged previously : the land had been injured by neglect, and the peasants brought in very little income, not because there was no market for their grain, but because they were spoilt and lazy, and had too little land ; and another difficulty was that some of them belonged to three different owners—Mme. Baktéyeff and her daughter as well as Praskovya Ivanovna. Kurolyessoff began by transferring some of the peasants to new ground, while he sold the old land at a good profit. He bought about 20,000 acres of steppe in the Government of Simbirsk (now Samára) and the district of Stavropolsk—excellent arable land, level and easy to plough, with over three feet of black soil. The land lay on the river Berlya, which had some coppices on its banks near the source ; and there was also ' Bear Hollow,' which was left untouched for some time and is now the only forest on the property. He settled 350 serfs here. This estate turned out highly profitable, because it was only a hundred *versts* from Samára and about fifty from a number of ports on the Volga. It is well known that the value of an estate in our country depends entirely upon the market for grain.

Next, Kurolyessoff went off to the district of Ufa and bought from the Bashkirs 60,000 acres. The soil, though good, was not as productive as that in Simbirsk, but there was a considerable quantity of wood, not only fire-wood, but timber for building. He planted two colonies there, one

of 450 serfs and the other of 50 ; and he called the
larger ' Párashino ' and the smaller ' Ivánovka.'
As the Simbirsk estate was called ' Kurolyessovo,'
each of the properties bore one of the names of
his wife. Such a romantic fancy has always seemed
to me curious, considering the sort of man that
Kurolyessoff turned out to be ; but some will
maintain that these inconsistencies are common
enough. He also made a seat for himself and his
wife in the village of Choorassovo, fifty *versts* from
Simbirsk ; this was a separate property of 350
serfs which his wife had inherited from her mother.
He built there a splendid mansion, according to
the ideas of those days, with all the usual appur-
tenances ; it was finely decorated and furnished,
and painted with frescoes inside and out ; the
chandeliers and bronzes, the silver plate and china,
were a wonder to behold. The house was situated
on the slope of a hill, from which more than twenty
excellent springs came bubbling out. The house
and the hill stood in the centre of an orchard, very
large and productive, stocked with apple-trees and
cherry-trees of every possible sort. The internal
arrangements—the service and cooking, the horses
and carriages—were luxurious and substantial.
There was a constant succession of visitors at
Choorassovo, either country neighbours, of whom
there were a good many, or people from Simbirsk ;
they ate and drank, took walks and played cards,
sang and talked, and were generally noisy and
merry. Kurolyessoff dressed his wife up like a doll,
anticipated all her wishes, and entertained her
from morning till night, that is, when he happened
to be at home. In short, after a few years, he had
attained such a position all round, that good people

admired him and bad people envied him. Nor did
he forget the claims of religion : in place of an old
tumbledown wooden erection, he built a new
church of stone and equipped it splendidly ; he
even formed an excellent choir out of the household
servants. Praskovya Ivanovna was quite con-
tented and happy. She gave birth to a daughter
in the fourth year of her marriage, and to a son
a year later, but she soon lost them, the girl in
infancy, and the boy when he was three. She had
become so attached to the boy that this loss cost her
dear. For a whole year her eyes were never dry,
her excellent constitution was seriously affected,
and she had no more children. Meanwhile her
husband's reputation and influence grew by leaps
and bounds. It is true that his behaviour to the
small landowners was arbitrary and harsh ; yet
they, if they did not like him, were exceedingly
afraid of him ; and people of importance thought
it only to his credit, that he made his inferiors
know their proper place. His absences from home
became more frequent and longer, from year to
year, especially after the sad year in which Praskovya Ivanovna lost her son and would not be
comforted. It is probable that he grew weary of
tears and sighs and solitude ; for she refused to
have any visitors for a whole year. But indeed
the most cheerful and noisy society at Choorassovo
was no attraction to Kurolyessoff.

Little by little, certain rumours began to spread
abroad and gain strength. According to these
reports, the Major was not merely strict, as was
said before, but cruel ; in the privacy of his estates
at Ufa he gave himself up to drink and debauchery ;
he had gathered round him a band, with whom he

drank and committed excesses of every kind ; and, worse still, several victims had already been killed by him in the fury of his drunken violence. The police and magistrates of the district, it was said, were all his creatures : he had bribed some with money and others with drink and terrorized them all. The small landowners and inferior officials went in terror of their lives : if any dared to act or speak against him, they were seized in broad day-light and imprisoned in cellars or corn kilns, where they were fed on bread and water and suffered the pangs of cold and hunger ; and some were unmercifully flogged with an instrument called a ' cat.' Kurolyessoff had a special fancy for this implement, which was merely a leather whip with seven tails and knots at the end of each tail. Some specimens were kept long after Kurolyessoff's death in a store-room at Parashino, for show, not for use ; and I saw them there myself ; they were burnt by my father when he inherited the property. These reports were only too well founded : the reality far surpassed the timid whisper of rumour. Kurol-yessoff's thirst for blood, inflamed to madness by strong drink, grew unchecked to its full propor-tions, till it presented one of those horrible spec-tacles at which humanity shudders and turns sick. The instinct of the tiger is terrible indeed, when combined with the reasoning power of a man.

At last the rumours were changed into certain knowledge ; and of all the people with whom Praskovya Ivanovna lived—relations, neighbours, and servants,—every one knew the real truth about Kurolyessoff. When he returned to Choorassovo from the scene of his exploits, he always showed the same respect to rank, the same friendly attention

to his equals, the same anxiety to please his
wife. She had now got over her loss and had
recovered health and spirits ; the house was as
full of visitors as it used to be, and something was
always going on. At Choorassovo, Kurolyessoff
never struck any of the servants, leaving the bailiff
and the butler in sole possession of this amusement ;
but they all knew about him and trembled at a
mere look. Even relations and intimate friends
showed some discomfort and embarrassment in
his company. But Praskovya Ivanovna noticed
nothing, or, if she did, ascribed it to a quite
different cause—the involuntary respect which
every one felt for her husband's remarkable success
as a landowner, his splendid establishment, and
his general intelligence and firmness of purpose.
Sensible people who loved Praskovya Ivanovna,
when they saw her perfectly composed and happy,
were glad of her ignorance and hoped it might last
as long as possible. There were, no doubt, some
women among her dependants and humble neighbours whose tongues itched uncommonly, and who
felt a strong desire to pay the Major out for his
contemptuous treatment of them, by disclosing the
truth ; but, apart from the fear they could not
help feeling, which would probably not have de-
terred them, there was another obstacle which
prevented the fulfilment of their kind intentions.
It was simply impossible to bring any tales against
her husband to Praskovya Ivanovna. She was
clever, keen-sighted, and determined ; and, as
soon as she detected any hidden innuendo to the
detriment of Kurolyessoff, she knitted her dark
eyebrows and said in her downright way that any
offence of the kind would be punished by perpetual

exclusion from her house. As the natural result
of such a significant warning, nobody ventured to
interfere in what was not their business. There
were two servants in the house, a favourite attendant of her late father's and her own old nurse,
whom she specially favoured, though they were not
admitted to such close intimacy as old servants
often were in those days ; but they too were powerless. To them it was a matter of life and death
that their mistress should know the real truth
about her husband ; for they had near relations
who were personal attendants of Kurolyessoff's
and were suffering beyond endurance from their
master's cruelty. At last they determined to tell
the whole story to their mistress. They chose a
time when she was alone, and went together to
her room ; but the old nurse had hardly mentioned
Kurolyessoff's name, when Praskovya Ivanovna
flew into a violent passion. She told the woman
that if she ever again ventured to open her mouth
against her master, she would banish her from her
presence for ever and send her to live at Parashino.
Thus all possible channels were blocked, and all
mouths were stopped, that might have informed
against the criminal. Praskovya Ivanovna loved
her husband and trusted him absolutely. She
knew that people like to meddle with what
does not concern them, and like to trouble the
water, that they may catch fish ; and she had
made up her mind at once and laid down an absolute rule, to listen to no tales against her husband.
It is an excellent rule, and indispensable for the
preservation of domestic peace. But there is no
rule that does not admit of exceptions ; and perhaps, in the present case, the resolute temper and

strong will of the wife, added to the fact that all the wealth belonged to her, might have checked the husband at the outset of his career. As a sensible man, he would not have cared to deprive himself of all the advantages of a luxurious life ; he would not have gone to such extremes or given such free play to his monstrous passions. It is more likely that, like many other men, he would have taken his pleasures in moderation and with precaution.

Thus several years went by, during which Kurolyessoff gave himself up without restraint to his evil tendencies. His degeneration was rapid, and at last he began to commit incredible crimes, and always with impunity. I shall not describe in detail the kind of life he led on his estates, especially at Parashino, and also in the villages of the district ; the story would be too repulsive. I shall say no more than is necessary to convey a true conception of this formidable man. During the early years when his whole attention was given to organizing his wife's estates, he deserved to be called the most far-seeing, practical, and watchful of agents. To all the infinitely various and troublesome business, involved in removing peasants and settling them down in distant holdings, he gave his personal and unremitting attention. He kept constantly in view one object only, the well-being of his dependants. He could spend money where it was needed ; he saw that it came to hand at the right time and in the right quantity ; he anticipated all the wants and requirements of the settlers. He accompanied them himself for a great part of their journey, and met them himself at the end of it, where they found everything prepared for their

reception. It is true that he was too severe and
even cruel in the punishment of culprits ; but he
was just, and could keep his eyes shut at times.
From time to time he allowed himself a little
relaxation, when he disappeared for a day or two
to amuse himself ; but he could throw off the effects
of his debauchery like water off a duck's back, and
come to work again with fresh vigour.

So long as he had the burden of his work upon
his shoulders, it took up all his powers of mind and
kept him from the fatal passion for drink, which
robbed him of his senses and removed the curb
from his monstrous inhuman passions. Work was
his salvation ; but when he had got both the new
estates, Kurolyessovo and Parashino, into order,
and built manor-houses at both, with a second
smaller house at Parashino, then came the season
of little work and much leisure. Drunkenness,
with its usual consequences, and violence, gained
complete mastery over him, and developed by
degrees into an insatiable thirst for human blood
and human suffering. Encouraged by the passive
fear of all around him, he soon ceased to set any
limit to his arbitrary violence. He chose from
among his dependants a score of ruffians, fit
instruments for his purposes, and formed them
into a band of robbers. They saw that their
master bore a charmed life, and believed in his
power ; drunken and debauched themselves, they
carried out all his insane orders willingly and
boldly. If any man offended Kurolyessoff by the
slightest independence in word or action—if, for
example, he failed to turn up when invited to one
of their drunken revels—the gang set off at once
at a sign from their master, seized the culprit

either secretly or openly wherever they found him, and brought him back to Parashino, where he was treated with insult and chained up in a cellar underground or flogged by their master's orders. Kurolyessoff was a man of taste : he liked good horses, and he liked good pictures—he thought them good at least—to adorn his walls. If anything of the kind took his fancy in a neighbour's house or in any house where he happened to be, he at once proposed an exchange ; in case of a refusal, he would sometimes, if he was in a good humour, offer money ; but if this also was refused, he gave warning that he would take it and give nothing for it. And he did actually turn up with his gang a short time after, pack up whatever he wanted, and carry it off. Complaints were made, and the preliminary steps for an inquiry were taken. But Kurolyessoff saw this must be stopped at once. He sent a message to the district magistrate, that he would flay with the ' cat ' any officer of the law who dared to present himself ; and he remained master of the situation. Meantime the man who had dared to complain was seized and beaten, on his own estate and in his own house, with his wife and children kneeling round and imploring mercy. It was Kurolyessoff's custom to make it up with his victims after a time : sometimes he offered them pecuniary compensation, but more often he restored peace by terrorizing them ; in any case, the stolen goods remained his lawful property. During his carouses he liked to boast that he had taken ' that pretty thing in the gilt frame ' from so-and-so, and that inlaid writing-table from some one else ; and often these very people were sitting at the table, pretending to be

deaf or plucking up heart to laugh at their own
losses. There were even worse acts of violence,
but these also went scot-free.

Kurolyessoff had a very powerful constitution :
though he drank a great deal, it never disabled him
but only put him on the move and roused a horrible
activity in his clouded brain and inflamed body.
One of his favourite amusements was to harness
teams of spirited horses to a miscellaneous assort-
ment of carriages, to pack the carriages with his
ragtag and bobtail of men and women, and then
scour over the fields and through the villages at
full gallop, with the jingling of bells and the singing
and shouting of his drunken rabble. He took a
stock of liquor with him on these occasions and
made every one he met, without regard to calling
or sex or age, drink till they were intoxicated ; and
anyone who dared to refuse was first flogged, and
then tied to a tree or a post, though it might be
raining or freezing at the time. Of more revolting
acts of violence I say nothing. One day he was
driving in this state of mind through a village,
and, as he passed a threshing-floor, noticed a
woman of remarkable beauty. ' Stop ! ' he called
out. ' Petrushka, what do you think of that
woman ? ' ' She 's uncommonly pretty,' said
Petrushka. ' Would you like to marry her ? '
' How can I marry another man's wife ? ' asked
Petrushka with a grin on his face. ' I'll show you
how ! Seize her, my lads, and put her in the
carriage beside me ! ' They did so ; the woman
was taken straight to the parish church, and there,
though she protested that she had a husband living
and two children, was married to Petrushka ; and
no complaints were made either in Kurolyessoff's

lifetime or in that of his widow. When the estate came into my father's hands, he restored this woman with her husband and children to her former owner ; her first husband had long been dead. My father also distributed various articles of property to their former owners when they asked for them ; but many of the things had got worn out by tossing about in lumber-rooms. It is hard to believe that such things could happen in Russia, even eighty years ago ; but the truth of the narrative it is impossible to dispute.

This life of drunken and criminal violence, horrible and disgusting enough in itself, led on to worse, till the man's natural cruelty became a ferocious thirst for blood. To inflict torture became with him a necessity as well as a pleasure. On the days when he could not gratify this passion, he was depressed and listless, uneasy and even ill ; and this was why his visits to Choorassovo grew steadily rarer and his stay there shorter. But, on his return to the solitude of Parashino, he made haste to reward himself for his abstinence. He had only to watch the labourers at their work, to secure a sufficient number of victims ; no excuses were accepted, and it is always possible to find trifling cases of neglect on the land if you are determined to hunt for them. Yet it was the personal servants and people about the house who suffered most from his ferocity. He seldom flogged a peasant, unless the man had committed a serious offence or was personally known to him ; but his bailiffs and clerks suffered as much at his hands as the household servants. He spared no one : every one of his favourites had, some time or other, been flogged within an inch of his life, and some of them

many times. It is remarkable that, when Kurolyessoff got violently angry, which seldom happened,
he did not use violence ; but, when he had got
hold of a man and intended to torture him for his
own amusement, he would say in a quiet and even
affectionate tone : ' Well, my good friend Grigori
Kuzmitch ',—Grishka [1] being his usual name—' it
can't be helped ; come, and I will settle accounts
with you.' Thus he would speak to his head-
groom, who for some unknown reason was put to
the torture more often than others. ' Scratch him
up a bit with the cat,' said the master with a smile,
and then the torture went on for hours, while the
master drank tea with brandy in it, smoked his
pipe, and from time to time passed jests on his
victim till unconsciousness supervened. Trust-
worthy witnesses have assured me that only one
expedient proved successful in saving life after
such an ordeal : the lacerated body of the victim
was wrapped up in sheepskins taken warm from
the animals' backs as soon as they were slaughtered.
Kurolyessoff would carefully examine his victim ;
then, if content, he would say, ' Well, that's
enough ; take him away '—and then he became
cheerful, jocular, and amiable for the whole day
and sometimes for several days. In order to complete the portrait of this monster, I shall quote his
own words which he repeated more than once
among his boon-companions : ' Don't talk to me
of the knout or the stick ! They kill a man before
you mean it. The " cat " is the thing for me : it
gives pain without taking life ! ' I have told here
only a tithe of what I know, but perhaps I have
said enough. It is remarkable, as an instance of

[1] A diminutive form of Grigóri (Gregory).

the inexplicable inconsistencies of corrupt human
nature, that Kurolyessoff, at a time when he had
reached the extreme limit of debauchery and
cruelty, was zealously engaged in building a stone
church at Parashino. At the time I am about to
describe, the outside of the church was finished,
and workmen had been hired for the internal
decoration :   carpenters,   carvers,   gilders,   and
ikon [1]-painters had been at work for some months
and were occupying all the smaller manor-house
of Parashino.

Prashkovya Ivanovna had now been married
fourteen years. She noticed something strange
about her husband, whom for two years she had
only seen at long intervals for a few days at a time,
but she did not even suspect anything like the
truth. She went on with her easy cheerful way
of life : in summer she gave great attention to her
orchard and the water-springs which she left in
their natural state and liked to clean out with her
own hands ; at other seasons she spent her time
with her visitors and became a great lover of cards.
Suddenly she received, by post or special messenger,
a letter from an old lady for whom she had great
respect, a distant relation of her husband's. This
letter gave a full description of Kurolyessoff's life,
and ended by saying, that it would be sinful not
to open the eyes of the mistress of a thousand
serfs, when they were suffering such monstrous
cruelty and she could protect them by cancelling
the legal authority she had given her husband to
manage her estates. ' Their blood cries to heaven,'
she wrote, ' and at this moment a servant known

---

[1] An íkon is a sacred picture, kept in a church or hung
on the wall of a room.

to you, Ivan Onufrieff, is dying in consequence of cruel maltreatment. You have nothing to fear yourself from Kurolyessoff : he will not venture to show his face at Choorassovo, and your good neighbours and the Governor himself will protect you.'

This letter fell like a thunder-bolt on Praskovya Ivanovna. I have heard her say myself that she was quite stunned for some minutes ; but she was supported by her firm faith in God and the uncommon strength of her will, and soon determined on a step from which most brave men would have shrunk. She ordered horses to be harnessed, saying that she was going to Simbirsk, and then, with one maid and a man and the coachman, drove straight to Parashino. It was a long journey of 400 *versts*, and she had plenty of leisure to think over what she was doing. She used to say herself that she had formed no plan of action whatever ; she merely wished to see with her own eyes and find out for certain what her husband was doing and how he lived. She did not entirely trust the letter from his kinswoman, who lived at a distance and might have been deceived by false reports ; and she did not choose to question her old nurse at Choorassovo. The thought of danger never entered her head : her husband had always been so gentle and respectful with her, that it seemed to her quite natural and quite possible to induce him to return in her carriage to Choorassovo. She timed herself to arrive at Parashino in the evening, left her carriage outside the village, and walked unrecognized—few of the people there knew her—accompanied by her maid and man, to the court of the mansion-house. She passed through the back entrance, made her way to a wing from which loud sounds of singing and laughter were issuing, and opened the door with a steady hand.

Fortune, as if on purpose, had brought together everything that could reveal at one flash the kind of life her husband was leading. More intoxicated than usual, he was carousing with his boon-companions. Dressed in a shirt of red silk, he held a glass of punch in one hand * * *[1] while a tipsy herd of servants, retainers, and country women danced and sang before him. Praskovya Ivanovna nearly fainted at the sight. She understood all now. Unnoticed, because the room was crowded with people, she shut the door and left the house. On the steps she came face to face with one of Kurolyessoff's servants, not a young man, and, fortunately, sober. He recognized his mistress and was just calling out, ' *Mátushka* [2] Praskovya Ivanovna, is it you ? '—when she put her hand over his mouth and led him to the centre of the courtyard. She said in an ominous voice, ' Is this the way you go on behind my back ? The days of your feasting and dancing are done.' The man fell at her feet weeping and said : ' *Matushka*, do you suppose that *we* find pleasure in his goings-on, that *we* are responsible ? God himself has brought you here.' She told him to be silent and take her to see Ivan Onufrieff ; she had heard that he was still living. She found him in a dying state, lying in a cow-byre in the backyard. He was too weak to tell her anything ; but his brother, Alexyéi, a mere lad, who had been flogged only the day before,

---

[1] The asterisks apparently imply that the author is unwilling to report some details of this orgy.

[2] i.e. mother, a term of affection and respect.

crawled somehow from his pallet, fell on his knees ,
and told her what had befallen his brother and
himself and others as well. Praskovya Ivanovna's
heart swelled with pity and horror. She felt that
she also was to blame, and she formed a firm
resolve to put an end to the crimes and atrocities
of Kurolyessoff. She thought there would be no
difficulty. She gave strict orders that her presence
should be kept secret. Then, as she heard that
the smaller house, which had been built some
years before, but, from some caprice of her husband's, never furnished, contained one habitable
room unoccupied by the workmen, she went off,
intending to pass the remainder of the night there
and to speak next morning to her husband when
he was sober. But the secret of her arrival was
not strictly kept. The report reached the ear of
one of the most desperate of Kurolyessoff's gang,
and he, moved by devotion or by fear, whispered
it to his master. Kurolyessoff was dumbfounded
by the news ; it sobered him in a moment ; he
felt uneasy and scented danger ahead. His wife's
firm and masculine temper had found few opportunities to display itself hitherto, but he guessed
that it was there. Dismissing his band of revellers, he had two or three buckets of cold water
poured over his head ; and then, braced up and
invigorated by this expedient, he changed into
ordinary clothing and went to see if his wife was
asleep. He had had time to reflect and fix on a
line of action. He guessed the truth, that Praskovya Ivanovna had received from some quarter
information as to his way of life, but that she was
incredulous and had come to Parashino to ascertain
the truth herself. He knew that her eye had rested

for a moment on his revels, but he did not know that she had seen Onufrieff and that Alexyéi had told her the whole story. He intended to play the repentant sinner, to excuse himself as best he could for his riotous debauch, to pour oil on the troubled waters by his delicate attentions, and to take his wife away as soon as possible from Parashino.

It was morning by now, and the sun had actually risen. Kurolyessoff stole on tiptoe to the room occupied by Praskovya Ivanovna and softly opened the door. A bed had been made for her on the top of a chest, but the sheets were still smooth and no one had lain down on them. He looked all round the room and saw Praskovya Ivanovna. She was kneeling in prayer ; there was no ikon in the room, and her eyes, full of tears, were fixed upon the cross on the church, which was just opposite the window and glittered in the rays of the rising sun. He remained standing a few moments, and then said in a playful voice : ' You have prayed long enough, my dear ! I am delighted to see you. What made you think of coming ? ' Praskovya Ivanovna rose from her knees with no sign of confusion ; she refused her husband's embrace ; then, concealing the flame of her just anger under a cold determined manner, she told him that she knew all and had seen Ivan Onufrieff. She expressed in plain terms her aversion to the monster whom she could no longer regard as her husband, and she passed sentence upon him : he was to return the document which gave him authority over her estates, to leave Parashino at once, never to appear before her again, and never to set foot on any of her lands ; if he refused, she

would petition the Governor of the province, and
reveal all his crimes ; and his fate would be Siberia
and penal servitude. Kurolyessoff was taken by
surprise ; he foamed at the mouth with rage and
anger. ' So that is the way you talk to me, my
beauty ! Then I shall change my tune too ! '
roared the infuriated ruffian. ' You shall not
leave Parashino till you sign a document transferring all your estates to me ; if you refuse, I shall
shut you up in a cellar and starve you to death.'
Then he caught up a stick from a corner of the
room, felled his wife to the floor with his first blows,
and went on beating her till she lost her senses.
Next he ordered some of his trusted servants to
carry their mistress to a stone cellar, which he
locked with a huge padlock and put the key in his
pocket. He was a formidable figure when he
appeared before the assembled household ; he had
summoned them all, in order to discover the culprit
who had led his mistress to the cow-byre ; but the
man had already sought safety in flight, accompanied by the coachman and manservant who had
come from Choorassovo. The fugitives were pur-
sued at once. Kurolyessoff did no injury to the
maid, who had refused to desert her mistress : he
gave her directions for exhorting the prisoner to
submission, and then locked her up with his own
hands in the same cellar. What did Kurolyessoff
do next ? He began to drink and riot more
furiously than before. But alas ! in vain did he
swallow brandy like water, in vain did his revel
rout dance and sing before him—he had turned
gloomy and sullen. Yet this did not prevent him
from working indefatigably for the attainment of
his purpose. He procured from the local town

a legal document by which Praskovya Ivanovna professed to sell Parashino and Kurolyessovo to one of his disreputable friends—Choorassovo he was kind enough to leave to her—and twice a day he went down to the cellar and pressed his wife to sign the paper ; he begged pardon for his violence in the heat of the moment, promised that if she consented she should never see him again, and took an oath that he would restore all her property to her by his will. But Praskovya Ivanovna, though bruised and half-starved and suffering from fever, refused even to listen to any compromise whatever. So things went on for five days, and God only knows how it would all have ended.

All this time my grandfather Stepan Mihailovitch was living and prospering on his estate of New Bagrovo, which was 120 *versts* distant from Parashino. As I have mentioned already, he had frankly made it up with Kurolyessoff and was satisfied with him in general, though he felt no fancy for him. Kurolyessoff, on his side, showed great deference to Stepan Mihailovitch and all his family, and was ready to perform any services for them. When he had planted his colony at Parashino and was engaged in organizing it, he came every year to Bagrovo and made himself very agreeable. He appealed to Stepan Mihailovitch, as a man of practical experience in colonizing, for his advice ; he received it gratefully, wrote it all down word for word, and really followed it. He even invited Stepan Mihailovitch twice to Parashino, to judge of his pupil's proficiency ; and each time my grandfather approved entirely of what he saw ; and on his last visit, when he had inspected the arable land and all the farming arrangements,

he said to Kurolyessoff, ' You are young, friend,
but you've got on fast ; I can teach you nothing.'
And, as a matter of fact, everything at Parashino
was in excellent order. Of course the host received
the old man as if he had been his own father, with
all possible deference and attention. As years
went on, ugly rumours about Kurolyessoff found
their way to Bagrovo. As my grandfather disliked gossip, nothing was said to him at first ; but
the rumours grew steadily. The womankind at
Bagrovo knew of them ; and Arina Vassilyevna
ventured at last to tell her husband that Kurolyessoff was leading a terribly wicked life. He
would not believe it. He said : ' Once you believe
what people say, you will soon accuse your neighbour of robbing a church ! I know what the
Baktéyeff servants were like—thieves and shirkers,
to a man ! And my cousin's serfs too got spoilt, with
no master to look after them. It 's not surprising
if they're terrified of honest work and decent order.
Friend Mihail may have gone to work too fast :
what of that ? they'll learn to bear it. As to his
drinking—if he takes a glass after his work, a man 's
none the worse for that, provided he doesn't
neglect his business. There *are* beastly things a
man shouldn't do ; but there, I fancy, they're
lying. You women are too fond of listening to
gossip.' For a long time after this, Stepan Mihailovitch heard nothing more of the rumours. At
last, some Bagroff serfs, who had been transferred
from the Government of Simbirsk to Parashino
together with the serfs of the Baktéyeff family,
came to visit their relations at New Bagrovo and
told terrible stories of their master. Arina Vassilyevna again appealed to her husband, and begged

that he would himself question one of these men
who was now at Bagrovo; he was an old man
with an established character for speaking the
truth; and Stepan Mihailovitch had known him
all his life. My grandfather consented. He sent
for the man and questioned him, and heard a story
which made his hair stand on end. He could not
think what to do, or how to mend matters.
Praskovya Ivanovna's occasional letters showed
that she was quite happy and undisturbed; and
he concluded that she knew nothing of her husband's conduct. In the old days he had warned
her himself never to listen to tales against her
husband; and he felt sure that she was following
his advice only too well. He reflected that, if she
learnt the truth, it was doubtful if she could do
anything; she would distress herself terribly, all
to no purpose. It was therefore desirable that her
eyes should never be opened. He could not now
interfere; and he thought interference useless in
the case of such a man. 'I hope he will break his
neck or be tried for a murder; he deserves it. No
hand but God's can mend a man like that. He
is not so hard upon his peasants and labourers, and
the house-servants are a pack of scoundrels; let
them suffer for their sins! I have no mind to soil
my fingers with this dirty business.' Thus Stepan
Mihailovitch reasoned in his own way. He broke
off all relations with Kurolyessoff, however, and
ceased to answer his letters. This hint was understood, and the correspondence came to an end.
But to Praskovya Ivanovna, Stepan Mihailovitch
began to write oftener and more intimately than
before.

So matters remained till the morning, when the

three fugitives from Parashino made their appearance before my grandfather as he sat on his stoop.
They had spent the first day concealed in an
inaccessible swamp which joined on to the stackyards of Parashino ; in the evening they learnt
from some one in the village exactly what had
happened, and made their way straight to Bagrovo,
considering Stepan Mihailovitch as the only
possible protector and champion of Praskovya
Ivanovna. His feelings may be imagined when he
heard what had happened at Parashino. He loved
his one cousin not less, perhaps more, than his own
daughters. The image of Parasha half-killed by
her ruffian of a husband, of Parasha confined in a
cellar for three days and perhaps dead already,
presented itself so vividly to his lively imagination that he sprang up like one demented, and
rushed down the courtyard and through the village,
summoning his retainers and labourers in accents
of frenzy. Those who were not in the cottages
came running from the fields. When all were
assembled, they were full of sympathy for their
master's passionate despair and cried with one
voice that they would go on foot, if need be, to
the rescue of Praskovya Ivanovna. In a short
time three cars, drawn by teams of spirited horses
from the stables of Bagrovo, and carrying a dozen
men chosen for strength and courage, were galloping along the road to Parashino. The party in-
cluded the fugitives from Parashino, and were
armed with guns and swords, pikes and pitchforks.
Later in the day two more cars followed to rein-
force Stepan Mihailovitch ; the men were armed
in the same way ; the horses were the best the
peasants could produce. By the evening of the

second day, the vanguard was within seven *versts*
of Parashino. They fed the jaded horses, and in
the first light of the summer dawn dashed into the
wide courtyard and drove straight up to the cellar.
It was close to the rooms occupied by Kurolyessoff.
Stepan Mihailovitch jumped out and began to beat
his fist against the wooden door of the cellar. A
voice faintly asked, ' Who is there ? ' My grandfather recognized his cousin's voice ; dropping
a tear of joy that he had found her alive, and
crossing himself, he called out in a loud voice,
' Thank God ! It is your cousin, Stepan Mihailovitch ; you are safe now ! ' He sent off the
servants from Choorassovo to get ready Praskovya
Ivanovna's carriage, and posted six armed men to
defend the gate, while he himself and the rest of
his men applied axes and crowbars to the cellar-
door. It gave way in a moment; and Stepan Mihailovitch himself carried out Praskovya Ivanovna,
placed her on a car between himself and her faithful
maid, and drove unmolested out of the courtyard
with all his retainers. The sun was rising as they
drove past the church, and his first beams lit up
the cross on the roof. It was just six days since
Praskovya Ivanovna had prayed with her eyes
fixed on that cross ; and now she prayed again
and thanked God for her deliverance. The carriage
caught them up, when they were five *versts* from
Parashino ; and Stepan Mihailovitch moved his
cousin into the carriage and drove with her back to
Bagrovo.

But I shall be asked, ' How did all this happen ?
did no one see it ? what had become of Kurolyessoff and his trusty retainers ? is it possible that
he was unaware of it or absent at the time ? ' No :

the liberation of Praskovya Ivanovna took place before many witnesses ; and Kurolyessoff was at home and knew what was going on, but did not venture to show his face.

The explanation is quite simple. His men had spent the whole evening carousing with their master, and some of them were so drunk that they could not be roused. There was one sober man, a complete abstainer and a favourite. He wakened his master with some difficulty, and, trembling with fear, told him of the raid of Stepan Mihailovitch and the guns pointing straight at the windows. ' But where are all our fellows ? ' asked Kurolyessoff. ' Some are asleep, and others are hiding,' said the man ; but this was not true ; for the drunken rabble was mustering near the outside steps. Kurolyessoff thought a moment ; then with a gesture of despair he said, ' Let her go, and the devil go with her ! Lock the door, go to the window, and watch what happens.' In a few minutes, the man cried out, ' They are carrying away the mistress !—They're off ! '—' Go to your bed,' said his master ; then he rolled himself up in his blankets and either fell asleep or made a pretence of it.

Yes, right has a moral strength before which wrong must bend, for all its boldness. Kurolyessoff knew the stout heart and fearless courage of Stepan Mihailovitch, and he knew that he himself was in the wrong ; and therefore, in spite of his furious temper and unscrupulous impudence, he let his victim go without a struggle.

Tenderly and carefully Stepan Mihailovitch conveyed the sufferer, whom he had always loved and who now roused in him deep sympathy and a still greater affection. No question passed his lips on the journey; and, when he brought her in safety to Bagrovo, he forbade his womankind to trouble her with inquiries. But in a fortnight Praskovya Ivanovna was herself again, thanks to her strong constitution and high spirits; and then Stepan Mihailovitch determined to cross-examine her. In order to act, he must know the real truth, and he never trusted second-hand information. She told him the whole truth with perfect frankness, but begged that he would keep it from his family and that she should be asked no questions by any one else. She put herself altogether in his hands; but she feared his hot temper and implored him not to take vengeance on Kurolyessoff. She said positively that, on reflection, she had decided not to bring shame on her husband, or to stain the name which she must continue to bear throughout her life. She added that she now repented of the words which had burst from her lips at her first interview with Kurolyessoff at Parashino, and that nothing would induce her to make a complaint to the Governor against him. Yet she considered it her duty to rescue her serfs from his cruelty, and therefore intended to cancel the document which gave him authority over her estates. She asked Stepan Mihailovitch to take over the management himself, and also to write to Kurolyessoff demanding the document and stating that, if he refused to give it up, she would take legal steps to cancel it. She asked Stepan Mihailovitch to express this in plain terms but without any abusive epithets: and she offered to sign the letter herself to make it more convincing. I should mention that she could hardly read and write her native language. Stepan

Mihailovitch loved his cousin so well that he
bridled his rage and assented to her wishes.
But he would not hear of taking over the management. ' No, my dear,' he said ; ' I don't want
to meddle in other people's affairs, and I don't
want your relations to be saying that I feather my
own nest while looking after your multitude of
serfs. The land will be badly managed in your
hands, I don't doubt ; but you are rich and will
have enough. I don't mind saying in the letter
that I am to take over the management ; that will
give your sweet pet a turn ! All the rest you ask
shall be done.'

Strict orders were accordingly issued to the
women folk to ask no questions of the lady. My
grandfather wrote the letter to Kurolyessoff with
his own hand, Praskovya Ivanovna added her
signature, and a special messenger was dispatched
with it to Parashino. But, while they were considering and wondering and writing at Bagrovo,
all was already over at Parashino. The messenger
returned on the fourth day and reported that, by
God's will, Kurolyessoff had died suddenly and
was already buried.

Stepan Mihailovitch heard the news first. In-
voluntarily he crossed himself and said, ' Thank
God!' And so said all his family : in spite of their
former weakness for Kurolyessoff, they had long
looked on him with horror as a criminal and a
ruffian. With Praskovya Ivanovna it was different.
Judging by their own feelings, they all supposed
she would welcome the news, and told her at once.
But to the surprise of every one she was utterly
prostrated by it, and became ill again ; and when
her strength got the better of the illness, her

depression and wretchedness were extreme : for
some weeks she wept from morning till night, and
she grew so thin that Stepan Mihailovitch was
alarmed.   No one could understand the cause of
such intense sorrow for a husband whom she could
not love and who had treated her so brutally—
' a disgrace to human nature,' as they called him.
But there was an explanation, and this is it.

Many years later, my mother, who was a great
favourite with Praskovya Ivanovna, was talking
with her of past days—a thing which Praskovya
Ivanovna generally avoided—and in the open-
hearted frankness of their conversation she asked :
' Please tell me, aunt, why you took on so after
your husband's death. In your place, I should have
said a prayer for his soul, and felt quite cheerful.'
' You are a little fool, my dear,' answered Praskovya Ivanovna : ' I had loved him for fourteen
years and could not unlearn my feeling in one
month though I had found out what he was ; and,
above all, I grieved for his soul : he had no time to
repent before he died.'

After six weeks, Praskovya Ivanovna's good
sense mastered her grief to some extent ; and she
consented, or, I should rather say, did not refuse,
to travel with all the Bagroff family to Parashino,
in order to attend a memorial service at Kurolyessoff's grave.   To the general surprise, she
dropped no tear at Parashino or during the sad
ceremony ; but one may imagine how much this
effort cost her, in her condition of sorrow and
bodily weakness.   By her wish, only a few hours
were spent at Parashino, and she did not enter that
part of the house where her husband had lived
and died.

It is not difficult to guess the cause of Kurolyessoff's sudden death. When Stepan Mihailovitch
had rescued his cousin from the cellar, the people
at Parashino all plucked up heart, believing that
the end of Kurolyessoff's rule had come. They
all supposed that the owner of Bagrovo, who was
in the position of a father to their mistress, would
turn her husband neck and crop out of a place that
did not belong to him. No one dreamed that their
young mistress, insulted and beaten and half-
starved in an underground cellar in her own house,
would fail to appeal to the law for redress. Every
day they expected an irruption from Stepan Mihailovitch with the sheriff at his back; but week
followed week, and no one came. Kurolyessoff
was as drunken and violent as ever: every one of
his retainers he flogged till they were half-dead,
for having betrayed him, not sparing even the
sober man who had awakened him on the night of
the rescue; and he boasted that Praskovya Ivanovna had given up to him the title-deeds of her
estates. It was past the power of human endurance; and the future seemed hopeless.[1] Two of
the scoundrels, who had been favourites, and,
strangely enough, two who had suffered less than
the rest from his cruelty, ventured upon a horrible
crime. They poisoned him with arsenic, putting it
into a decanter of *kvass*, which Kurolyessoff generally emptied during the night; and they put in so
much, that he was dead in two hours. As they had
taken no one into their confidence, the catastrophe
startled and terrified the whole household. The
servants suspected one another, but the real crimi-

[1] From here to the end of the paragraph was removed
by the censor from the early editions of the work.

nals remained unknown for some time. Six months later one of them became desperately ill and confessed his crime before he died ; and his accomplice, though the dying man had not betrayed him, made off and was never seen again.

The sudden death of Kurolyessoff would certainly have been followed by an inquest, but for the presence at Parashino of a young clerk called Mihail Maximitch, who had only lately come to the place. By cleverness and good management, he contrived to get the affair hushed up. He became later Praskovya Ivanovna's man of business and the chief agent on all her estates, and enjoyed her full confidence. Under the name of ' Mihailushka ' he was known to all and sundry in the Governments of Simbirsk and Orenburg. He was a man of remarkable ability ; though he made a large fortune, he lived discreetly and modestly for many years ; but when he received his freedom on the death of his mistress, and lost his wife to whom he was much attached, he took to drinking and died in poverty. One of his sons, if I remember rightly, entered the official class and was eventually ennobled.

I should not conceal the fact that forty years later, when I became the owner of Parashino, I found the recollection of Kurolyessoff's management still fresh among the peasants, and they spoke of him with gratitude, because they felt every day the advantage of many of his arrangements. His cruelty they had forgotten, and they had felt it less than his personal attendants ; but they remembered his power of distinguishing guilt and innocence, the honest workman and the shirker ; they remembered his perfect knowledge of their

needs and his constant readiness to give them help.
The old men smiled as they told me that Kurolyessoff used often to say : ' Steal and rob as you
please, if you keep it dark ; but if I catch you,
then look out ! '

When she went back to Bagrovo, Praskovya
Ivanovna, soothed by the sincere and tender love
of her cousin and by the assiduous attentions of
his womankind (whom she did not much like but
who expected great favours and benefits from her),
gradually got over the terrible blow she had
suffered. Her good health came back, and her
peace of mind ; and at the end of a year she
resolved to go back to Choorassovo. It was
painful to Stepan Mihailovitch to part with his
favourite : her whole nature appealed to him, and
he had become thoroughly accustomed to her
society. Not once in his whole life was he in a
rage with Praskovya Ivanovna. But he did not
try to keep her : on the contrary, he pressed her
to go as soon as possible. ' It 's no sort of life for
you here, my dear,' he used to say ; ' it 's a dull
place, though we have got accustomed to it. You
are young still '—she was thirty—' and rich and
used to something different. You should go back
to Choorassovo, and enjoy your fine house and
splendid garden and the springs. You have plenty
of kind neighbours there, rich people who live a gay
life. It is possible that God will send you better
fortune in a second venture ; you won't want for
offers.' Praskovya Ivanovna put off her departure
from day to day—so hard did she find it to part
from the cousin who had saved her life and been
her benefactor from her childhood. At last the day
was fixed. Early on the previous morning, she

came out to join Stepan Mihailovitch, who was
sitting on his stoop and thinking sad thoughts.
She kissed and embraced him ; the tears came to
her eyes as she said : ' I feel all your love for
me, and I love and respect you like a daughter.
God sees my gratitude ; but I want men to
see it too. Will you let me bequeath to your
family all my mother's property ? What I have
from my father will come to your son in any case.
My relations on my mother's side are rich, and you
know that they have given me no reason to reward
them with my wealth. I shall never marry. I
wish the Bagroff family to be rich. Say yes, my
dear cousin, and you will comfort me and set my
mind at rest.' She threw herself at his feet and
covered with kisses the hands with which he was
trying to raise her up. ' Listen, my dear,' said
Stepan Mihailovitch in a rather stern voice : ' You
don't know me aright. That I should covet what
does not belong to me, and cut out the rightful
heirs to your estates—no ! that shall never be,
and never shall any one be able to say that of
Stepan Bagroff ! Mind you don't ever mention it
again. If you do, we shall quarrel ; and it will be
the first time in our lives.'

Next day Praskovya Ivanovna left Bagrovo and
began her own independent life at Choorassovo.

FRAGMENT III

THE MARRIAGE OF THE YOUNG BAGROFF

MANY years passed by and much happened during that time—famine and plague, and the rebellion of Pugatchoff.[1] The landowners of the Orenburg district scattered before the bands of the usurper, and Stepan Mihailovitch also made off with his family, first to Samára, and then down the Volga to Saratoff and as far off as Astrakhan. But by degrees all disturbances passed over and calmed down and were forgotten. Children became boys, boys became men, and men came to grey hairs ; and among these last was Stepan Mihailovitch. He saw this himself, but he hardly believed it. He would sometimes allude to the ravages of time, but he did so without uneasiness, as if there were no personal reference to himself. Yet my grandfather had ceased to be his old self : his herculean strength and tireless activity had gone for ever. This sometimes surprised him ; but he went on living precisely in the old way—eating and drinking to his heart's content, and dressing with no regard to the weather, though he sometimes suffered for this neglect. Little by little, his keen clear eye became clouded and his great voice lost its power ; his fits of anger were rarer, but so were his bright and happy moods. His elder daughters had all married, and the eldest had been

[1] Pugatchoff was a Cossack, who raised a formidable rebellion in East Russia ; taken prisoner by Suvóroff, he was executed at Moscow in 1775.

dead some time, leaving a daughter of three years old. Aksinya,[1] the second, had lost one husband and married again ; Elizabeth, a clever but arrogant woman, had somehow married a General Yerlykin, who was old and poor and given to drinking ; and Alexandra had found herself a husband in Ivan Karatayeff, well-born, young, rich, but a passionate lover of the Bashkirs and their wandering life— a true Bashkir himself in mind and body.   The youngest daughter, Tanyusha, had not married. The only son [2] was now twenty-six, a handsome youth with a complexion of lilies and roses : his own father used to say of him, ' Put a petticoat on him, and he'd be a prettier girl than any of his sisters ! '   Though his wife, Arina Vassilyevna, shed bitter tears and would not be comforted, Stepan Mihailovitch sent his son into the Army as soon as he was sixteen. He served for three years, and, owing to the influence of Mihail Kurolyessoff, acted as aide-de-camp for part of the time to Suvóroff.   But Suvóroff left the district of Oren-burg and was succeeded by a German general (I think his name was Treubluth) ; and he sentenced the young man to a severe flogging, from which his entire innocence, if not his noble birth, should have protected him.   His mother nearly died of grief, when she heard it ; and even my grand-father thought this was going too far. He with-drew his son from the Army and got him a place in the law court at Ufa, where he earned promotion by long and zealous service.

I cannot pass over in silence a strange fact that

[1] The popular form of Xenia; the diminutive is Aksyutka.

[2] The author's father.

I have noticed : most of the Germans and foreigners in general who held posts in the Russian service in those days were notorious for their cruelty and love of inflicting corporal punishment. The German who punished young Bagroff so cruelly was a Lutheran himself, but at the same time a great stickler for all the rites and ceremonies of the Russian Church. This historic incident in the annals of the Bagroff family happened in the following way. The general ordered a service to be performed in the regimental chapel on the eve of some unimportant saint's day ; he was always present himself on these occasions, and all officers were expected to attend. It was summer, and the chapel windows were open. Suddenly, a voice in the street outside struck up a popular song. The general rushed to the window : three subalterns were walking along the street, and one of them was singing. He ordered them under arrest and sentenced each of them to 300 lashes. My unfortunate father, who was not singing but merely walking with his friends, pleaded his noble birth ; but the general said with a sneer, ' A noble is bound to show special respect to divine service ' ; and then the brute himself looked on till the last stripe was inflicted on the innocent youth. This took place in a room next the chapel, where the solemn singing of the choir could be distinctly heard ; and the tyrant forbade his victim to cry out, ' for fear of disturbing divine worship.' After his punishment, he was carried off unconscious to hospital, where it was found necessary to cut off his uniform, owing to the swelling of his tender young body. It was two months before his back and shoulders healed up. What it must have cost his mother to hear such news of her only son whom she simply worshipped ! My grandfather lodged a complaint in some quarter ; and his son, who had sent in his papers at once, got his discharge from the Army before he left the hospital, and entered the Civil Service as an official of the fourteenth or lowest class. Eight years had now gone by, and the incident was by this time forgotten.

Alexyéi Stepanitch was now living peacefully at Ufa and performing his duties there. Twice a year he paid a visit to his parents at Bagrovo, 240 *versts* away. His life was quite uneventful. Quiet, bashful, and unassuming, this young heir to a landed estate lived on good terms with all the world, till suddenly the modest course of his existence became disturbed.

There was a permanent military administration in the town of Ufa, and next in authority to the Lieutenant-Governor was Nikolai Zubin, who resided regularly in the town. M. Zubin was an honest and able man, but his character was weak. His wife had died, leaving three children—Sonitchka,[1] a girl of twelve, and two younger boys. He was devoted to his daughter ; and it was no wonder he should love a child so beautiful and so clever, who, in spite of her tender years, soon became her father's companion and assisted him in the management of the household. Eighteen months after the death of his first wife, whom he had loved and sincerely mourned, M. Zubin found consolation by falling in love with the daughter of M. Rychkoff, a landowner in Orenburg, well-known for his descriptions of that country. The

---

[1] A pet name for Sófya (Sophia). This is the author's mother, whose real name was Márya.

marriage soon took place ; and the young wife,
Alexandra, by her intelligence and beauty, soon
gained entire control over her submissive husband.
But she was hard and unfeeling, and conceived
a hatred for her step-daughter, her father's darling,
who bade fair to grow up into a beautiful woman.
The thing is common enough. The name of step-
mother has long been proverbial for cruelty, and
it fitted Mme. Zubin precisely. But it was by no
means easy to tear Sonitchka from her place in
her father's heart : she was not a girl who could
be put down easily, and the contest which followed
inflamed the step-mother's anger to an extraordinary pitch. She swore that this hussy of
thirteen, who was the idol of her father and all the
town, should some day live in the maids' room,
wear the coarsest clothes, and carry the slops out
of the children's nursery. She kept her oath to
the letter : after two or three years, Sonitchka was
living with the servants and clothed like a scullion,
and she scrubbed and cleaned the nursery which
was now inhabited by two half-sisters. But what
was the father doing ? He had once loved her
dearly ; but now for whole months he never saw
her ; and when he did meet her going about in rages,
he turned away with a sigh, wiped away a furtive
tear, and made off as soon as possible. It is the
way of many elderly men who have married again
and are dominated by young wives. As I do not
know exactly the ways and methods by which
Mme. Zubin attained her object, I shall not speak
of them ; nor shall I dwell upon the cruelties and
sufferings inflicted upon the bereaved girl, with
her sensitive temper and strong will ; nothing was
spared her, not even the most humiliating punish-

ments and beatings for imaginary offences. I shall merely say, that the step-daughter was not far from suicide, and was only saved from it by a miracle. It happened thus. When she had decided to put an end to an intolerable existence, the poor child wished to say her last prayer before a picture of Our Lady of Smolensk, the picture with which her mother on her death-bed had blessed her. She fell on her knees in her garret before the ikon, and, with floods of bitter tears, pressed her face on the dirt-stained floor. Suffering deprived her of consciousness for some minutes; when she recovered and got up, she saw the candle, which she had put out the night before, still burning before the ikon. At first she cried out with surprise and involuntary fear; but soon she recognized that she had seen a miracle wrought by Divine Power. She took courage; she was conscious of a strength and composure she had never felt before; and she firmly resolved to suffer and endure and live. From that day the helpless child wore armour of proof against the increasing exasperation of her step-mother: whatever she was told to do, she did; whatever was inflicted upon her, she bore. Degrading punishment no longer forced the tears from her eyes, no longer made her turn sick and faint, as it used to do. 'Mean slut' had long been her title, and 'desperate wretch' was now added to it. But the measure of God's patience now brimmed over, and His thunder pealed: Mme. Zubin, in the prime of life and in the pride of her health and beauty, died ten days after giving birth to a son. Twenty-four hours before the end, knowing that she must die, she was eager to take the load off her conscience. Sonitchka was suddenly

wakened in the night and summoned to her step-
mother's bedside. The dying woman confessed
in the presence of witnesses her guilty conduct
towards her stepdaughter, begged her forgiveness,
and conjured her in the name of God to be good to
the children. The girl forgave her and promised
to care for the orphans; and she kept that promise.
Mme Zubin confessed also to her husband that the
accusations which had been brought against his
daughter were all calumnies and falsehoods.

Her death caused a complete reversal of affairs.
M. Zubin also had a paralytic stroke, and, though
he survived for some years, never left his bed again.
The oppressed and ragged Cinderella, whom the
servants—and especially those belonging to Mme
Zubin—had been mean enough to humiliate and
insult to their heart's content, suddenly became
the absolute mistress of the household, her sick
father having put everything under her control.
The reconciliation between the guilty father and
the injured daughter was touching and even
distressing to the daughter and all who saw it.
For long, M. Zubin was wrung by remorse : his
tears flowed day and night, and he repeated the
same words over and over, ' No, Sonitchka, it is
impossible you should forgive me ! ' To each one
of his acquaintance in the town he formally confessed his misconduct towards his daughter ; and
' Sofya Nikolayevna,' as she was now called,
became the object of general respect and admiration. Made wise by years of suffering, this girl of
seventeen developed into a grown woman, a mother
to the children, and the manager of the household.
She even discharged public duties ; for, owing to
her father's illness, she received all heads of depart-

ments, officials, and private citizens ; she discussed
matters with them, wrote letters and official
documents, and at last became the real manager
of the business in her father's office.   Sofya
Nikolayevna nursed her father with anxious care
and tenderness ; she looked after her three brothers
and two sisters, and even took trouble about the
education of the elder children.   Her own brothers,
Serghéi and Alexander, were now boys of twelve
and ten ; and she contrived to find teachers for
them—a kind old Frenchman called Villemer,
whom fortune had somehow stranded at Ufa, and
a half-educated Little Russian who had been
exiled to the town for an attempted fraud.   She
availed herself of the opportunity to study with
her brothers, and worked so hard that she could
soon understand a French book or conversation
and even talk French a little herself.   Eighteen
months later she sent her brothers to Moscow for
their education.   Through a certain M. Anitchkoff
who lived at Ufa, she had become acquainted with
his cousin who lived at Moscow, and they often cor-
responded. The well-known writer, Novikoff, shared
a house at Moscow with this M. Anitchkoff ; and
both friends were so struck by the letters from this
young lady on the banks of the river Byélaya, that
they sent her regularly all new and important
books in the way of Russian literature ; and this
did much for her mental development.   This
M. Anitchkoff had a special respect for her, and
considered it an honour to carry out her request.
He undertook to receive both her brothers and
place them at a boarding-school connected with
Moscow University, and performed his undertaking
punctiliously.   The boys got on well at school, but

their studies were broken off when the summons came for them to enter the Guards, in which they had been enrolled while still in the cradle.

All clever and educated people who came to Ufa hastened to make the acquaintance of Sofya Nikolayevna, were attracted by her, and never forgot her. Many of these acquaintances became in course of time the intimate friends of her children, and the relation was severed only by death. I shall name only those of them whom I knew myself— V. Romanovsky, A. Avenarius, Peter Chichagoff, Dmitri Myortvavo, and V. Itchansky. Scholars also, and travellers attracted by the novelty and beauty of the district, invariably made the young lady's acquaintance and left written testimony of their admiration for her beauty and wit. It is true that her position in society and her home helped her, and served, one might say, as a pedestal for the statue ; but the statue itself was a noble figure. I remember especially the verses of Count Manteuffel, a traveller ;   he sent them to Sofya Nikolayevna with a most respectful letter in French ; and he also sent a copy of an immense work in five quarto volumes, by a Dr. Buchan,[1] which had just been translated from English into Russian and made a great sensation in the medical world of that day. Buchan's *Domestic Medicine* was a real treasure to Sofya Nikolayevna : she was able to make use of its directions to make up medicines for her father's benefit. In his verses Count Manteuffel compared the fair lady of Ufa to both Venus and Minerva.

In spite of his enfeebled state, M. Zubin did not

---

[1] Buchan's *Domestic Medicine* was published in 1769 ; the author died in 1805.

resign his office for several years. Twice a year he
gave a ball ; he did not appear himself in order to
welcome the ladies, but the men went to see him
where he lay in his study ; and the young hostess
had to receive the whole town. Several times a year
her father insisted on her going out to balls in the
houses of the leading people, and she yielded to his
earnest entreaties and put in a short appearance
at the ball. She wore fine dresses and was an
excellent dancer in the fashion of the time. When
she had gone through a Polish minuet and a single
country-dance or schottische, she went away at
once, after flashing through the room like a meteor.
All who had the right to be so, were in love with
Sofya Nikolayevna, but they sighed at a respectful
distance ; for this young lady gave none of them
any encouragement whatever.

And with this peerless creature the son of Stepan
Mihailovitch fell in love ! He could not understand
and appreciate her fully, but her appearance alone
and her lively cheerful temper were enough to
bewitch a man ; and bewitched he accordingly
was. He saw her first in church, and the first sight
was enough for his susceptible heart. Alexyéi
Stepanitch—henceforth we shall give him both
his names—soon discovered that the fair lady
received all officials who visited at her father's
house ; and, being himself an official in the law-
court, he began to appear regularly in her drawing-
room, to pay his respects on high days and holidays.
He saw her every time, and his passion grew
steadily. His calls were so regular and so prolonged—though he hardly opened his mouth—that
they soon attracted general notice ; and it is
probable that the first person to notice them was

the young hostess herself. Rapturous looks,
flaming cheeks, helpless confusion—these are the
symbols by which love has always spoken.   A
frank passion has been an object of ridicule from
time immemorial, and all Ufa laughed at Alexyéi
Stepanitch.   He was humble and shy and as
bashful as a country girl ; and his only reply to all
jests and allusions to the subject was to blush the
colour of a peony. But Sofya Nikolayevna, so
cold and even snubbing in her manner to her
fashionable admirers, was surprisingly indulgent
to this speechless worshipper. Perhaps she was
sorry for this young man who had no armour
against all the ridicule he suffered on her behalf ;
perhaps she understood that his was no idle or
passing fancy and that his whole life was at stake ;
anyhow, the severe young beauty not only bowed
graciously and looked kindly at him, but tried
also to start conversation ; and his timid incoherent
replies and agitated voice did not seem to her
ridiculous or repulsive. I should say, however,
that Sofya Nikolayevna, though she stood on her
dignity with self-assertive people, was always kind
and condescending to humility and modesty.

Things went on thus for some time. Suddenly,
a bold thought flashed on the brain of Alexyéi
Stepanitch—the thought of getting Sofya Nikolayevna for his wife. At first he was frightened by
his own ambition, so bold and so unlikely to be
realized. How could he raise his eyes to Sofya
Nikolayevna, the chief personage in Ufa, and in his
opinion the cleverest and most beautiful woman
in the world ?   He abandoned his intention
entirely for a time. But by degrees the lady's
constant goodwill and attention, her friendly

glances which seemed to him to hold out some
encouragement, and, above all, the passion which
mastered his whole being, recalled the abandoned
ideal ; and it soon grew familiar and became part
of his life. There was an old lady called Mme
Alakayeff, then living at Ufa to look after a lawsuit,
who used to visit at the Zubins' house ; she was
distantly related to Alexyéi Stepanitch and had
always taken a great interest in him. He now
began to visit her oftener, and did his best to please
her ; and at last he confessed his love for a certain
person, and his intention to seek her hand. His
love was the talk of the town and therefore no
news to Mme Alakayeff ; but his intention of
marrying her was a surprise. 'She won't have
you,' said the old lady, shaking her head ; ' she 's
too clever, too proud, too highly educated. Plenty
of people have been in love with her, but not one
has ever dared ask the question. You're a handsome lad, certainly, well-born and fairly well off,
and you will be rich in course of time—everybody
knows that ; but then you're a plain country
fellow, no scholar or man of the world, and you're
terribly bashful in society.' Alexyéi Stepanitch
was aware of all this himself ; but love had entirely
confused his brain, and a voice whispered in his ear
day and night that Sofya Nikolayevna would
accept him. Though the young man's hopes
seemed to her unfounded, Mme Alakayeff consented to go to Sofya Nikolayevna's house, where,
without making any allusion to his wishes, she
would turn the conversation on to him and take
note of all that was said. She started at once, and
Alexyéi Stepanitch remained in the house till she
should come back. She was absent for some time.

and the lover became so distressed and despondent
that he began to cry, and then fell asleep, tired out,
with his head leaning against the window. When
the old lady came back, she wakened him and said
with a cheerful air : ' Well, Alexyéi Stepanitch,
there is really something in it ! When I began to
speak about you, and was rather hard upon you,
Sofya Nikolayevna took up the cudgels in earnest
on your behalf, and ended by saying that she was
sure you were very kind and modest and gentle,
and respectful to your parents ; and she said that
God sent His blessing on such people, and they
were much better than your pert and forward
talkers.' Alexyéi Stepanitch was so enraptured
by this report that he hardly knew where he was.
Mme Alakayeff gave him time to recover, and
then said with decision : ' If your mind is quite
made up about this, I will tell you what you had
better do. Go home at once, tell the whole story
to your parents, and ask for their consent and
blessing, before kind people put their oar in. If
they give you one and the other, I don't refuse to
work in your cause. Only don't be in a hurry :
begin by getting on the soft side of your sisters ;
your mother won't go against your wishes. Of
course, your father's consent matters most of all.
I know him : he is masterful to a degree, but he
has good sense ; have a talk to him when he is in
a good humour.' Alexyéi Stepanitch did not see the
need of all this caution and manœuvring : he said
that his parents would be delighted, and asked what
possible flaw could be found in Sofya Nikolayevna.
'Two terrible flaws,' said the shrewd old lady : 'she
has only twopence to her fortune, and her grandfather was a simple sergeant in a Cossack regiment.'

The significance of her words was entirely lost upon Alexyéi Stepanitch, but the old lady was not wrong in her presentiment, and her warning came too late.

Within a week Alexyéi Stepanitch got leave of absence. He called on Sofya Nikolayevna to say 'good-bye,' and she treated him kindly, wishing him a pleasant journey, and hoping he might find his parents in good health and happy to see him. Her kind words encouraged him to hope, and off he went home. The old people were glad to see him, but they were puzzled by the time of his visit and looked at him inquiringly. His sisters—who lived near Bagrovo and came there in hot haste on a summons from their mother—kissed their brother and made much of him, but kept on smiling for some reason. The youngest sister, Tatyana, was his favourite, and he revealed his passion to her ears first. Being a rather romantic girl and fonder of her brother than the elder sisters were, she listened to him with sympathy, and at last went so far as to confide in him a great secret : the family knew already of his love-affair and were opposed to it. It had happened in this way.

Two months before, Ivan Karatayeff had travelled to Ufa on business and brought back this piece of news to his wife. Alexandra Karatayeff—I have spoken already of her character—boiled over with rage and indignation. She took the lead in the family, and could twist them all, except, of course, her father, round her little finger. She set one of her brother's servants to spy on his master, and made him report to her every detail concerning his love-affair and his life at Ufa ; and she found a female friend in the town, who first rummaged and ferreted about, and then, with the help of a discarded attorney's clerk, sent her a long letter composed of town talk and servants' gossip. As her chief authorities were the servants of the late Mme Zubin, it is easy to guess the kind of portrait which these enemies drew of Sofya Nikolayevna.

It is a well-known fact that in the good old days of the Empress Catherine—perhaps it is the case still—there was little love lost between a man's wife and his sisters; and the case was worse when the sisters had only one brother, because his wife must become the sole and undisputed mistress of the household. A great deal of selfishness under-lies human nature; it often works without our knowledge, and no one is exempt from it; honour-able and kind people, not recognizing selfish motives in themselves, quite honestly attribute their actions to other and more presentable causes; but they deceive themselves and others uninten-tionally. Where there is no kindness of heart or refinement of manners, selfishness shows itself without any concealment or apology; and so it was with the womankind of Stepan Mihailovitch. It was inevitable that they should all resent their brother's marriage, irrespective of his choice. 'Alosha will change towards us and love us less than before; his bride will be a cuckoo in the nest and push out the birds born there '—such would certainly have been the language of the sisters, even if Alexyéi Stepanitch had chosen a bird of his own feather; but Sofya Nikolayevna was worse than anything they could imagine. Alexandra summoned her sister Elizabeth and hurried to Bagrovo to communicate to her mother and

sisters—of course, with suitable embellishments—
all the information she had received of her brother's
goings on. They believed every word she said, and
their opinion of Sofya Nikolayevna was to the
following effect. In the first place, the Zubin girl
—this was her regular name in the secret
meetings of the family council—was of mean birth :
her grandfather had been a Ural Cossack, and
her mother, Vera Ivanovna Kandalintsoff, had
belonged to the merchant class ; the alliance was
therefore a degradation to an ancient and noble
family. In the second place, the Zubin girl was
a mere pauper : if her father died or was dismissed
from his post, she would depend on charity for her
bread, and all her brothers and sisters would be
a stone round her husband's neck. Thirdly, the
Zubin girl was proud and fashionable, a crafty
adventuress who was accustomed to lord it over
the town of Ufa ; and she would turn up her nose
with no ceremony at plain people living in the
country, however long their pedigree. Fourthly
and lastly, the Zubin girl was a witch who used
magic herbs to keep all the men running after her
with their tongues hanging out ; and their poor
brother was one of her victims ; she had scented
out his future wealth and his easy temper, and had
determined to marry into a noble family by hook
or by crook. Alexandra managed the whole affair ;
her glib and wicked tongue frightened them all and
soon proved to them, beyond all possibility of
doubt, that such a marriage was a terrible misfortune for them. ' Likely enough, she will get
round Stepan Mihailovitch himself, and then we're
all done for ; we must leave no stone unturned to
prevent the marriage.' It was clearly of the first

importance to impress upon Stepan Mihailovitch the worst possible opinion of Sofya Nikolayevna ; but who was to bell the cat ? Their conscience was not clear, and they dared not go to work openly. If their father suspected that they had any concealed purpose, he would not believe even the truth in that case ; once before, when there had been some talk of choosing a daughter-in-law, he had seen through their repugnance to the scheme and had told them so plainly.

They had recourse therefore to the following stratagem. Arina Vassilyevna had a married niece living near; her name was Flona Lupenevsky; she was short and stout, a notorious fool and gossip, and not averse to strong liquors. She was instructed to come to Bagrovo as if on an ordinary visit, and to bring in, among other topics, the love-affairs of Alexyéi Stepanitch ; she was, of course, to represent Sofya Nikolayevna in the most unfavourable light. Alexandra spent a long time coaching this lady in what she was to say and how she was to say it. When she had learnt it as well as she could, Mme Lupenevsky turned up at Bagrovo and had dinner there ; after dinner, hosts and guests slept for three hours and then assembled for tea. The master of the house was in good humour and himself gave his guest an opening to begin the performance. ' Come now, Flona,' he said, ' tell us the news you got from the travellers to Ufa '—her sister, Mme Kalpinsky, had just been there with her husband—' I warrant they brought home a good budget, and you will add as much more out of your own head.'

' You will always have your joke, dear uncle,' said the lady ; ' but they brought plenty of news, and I have no need to invent.' Then off she started on a string of silly gossip, true and untrue, which I shall spare my readers. My grandfather pretended to disbelieve her throughout, even when she was telling the truth ; he made fun of her stories, threw her out on purpose, and teased her till all the hearers laughed heartily. The stupid woman, who had taken a stiff glass on waking to give her courage, got vexed at last and said with some heat : ' Uncle, why do you keep on laughing and believe nothing I say ? Wait a moment ; I have kept one special bit of news for the end, and that won't make you laugh, though you can't help believing it.' The family exchanged glances, and my grandfather laughed. ' Come out with it ! ' he said coolly ; ' I shan't believe it ; and, if I don't laugh at it, it's because I'm bored by your stories.' ' O uncle, uncle,' she began, ' you're quite in the dark about my dear cousin, Alexyéi Stepanitch. He's a perfect wreck : the witch of Ufa, the daughter of a great man there, Governor or Commander-in-Chief, I don't know which, has used devilish arts to fascinate him. She's a perfect beauty, they say, and has captivated all the men, young and old ; she has bewitched them with magic herbs, and they all run after her. And my poor cousin, Alexyéi Stepanitch, is so bad that he can neither eat nor drink nor sleep. He's constantly sitting beside her, he can't take his eyes off her, he just looks and sighs ; and at night he's always walking past her house, carrying a gun and a sword and keeping guard over her. They say that the Zubin girl is very sweet upon him ; of course he's handsome and well-born ; she knows what she's about and means to marry him. It's natural enough :

she has no money, and her father is a Cossack's
son who rose from the ranks; though he has
worked his way up and held great posts, he has
put nothing by; he has spent every penny on dinners and fine parties and dresses for his daughter.
The old man is at death's door, and there is a
swarm of children—half a dozen of them by his
two wives. They will all settle on your shoulders,
uncle, if my cousin marries her; she has no portion
but the clothes she wears; they have silk to their
backs, but nothing to put in their bellies. And
Alexyéi Stepanitch, they say, is changed out of all
knowledge : he looks terrible; the very servants
weep to see him and dare not inform you. Believe
me, uncle, every single word is gospel truth.
Question his servants, and they won't deny it.'

At this, Arina Vassilyevna began to cry and her
daughters to rub their eyes. My grandfather was
rather taken aback, but soon recovered himself.
Then he smiled and said coolly : ' Plenty of lies
there, and perhaps a grain of truth. I have heard
myself that the young lady is pretty and clever;
and that's all the magic there is about it.[1] It's
little wonder if Alexyéi's eyes were dazzled. All
the rest is rubbish. Mlle Zubin has no idea of
marrying Alexyéi; he is no match for her; she
will find a better man and a more pushing man to
marry her. And now, that's enough : not a word
more on the subject ! Let us go and drink tea out

[1] In general, my grandfather had little belief in witch-
craft. A wizard once told him that a gun was charmed
and would not go off. He took out the shot secretly and
fired at the wizard, who got a great fright. But he recovered and said that my grandfather himself was ' a man
of power '; and this was generally believed, except by
Stepan Mihailovitch. (*Author's note.*)

of doors.' As a matter of course, neither Mme Lupenevsky nor any one else dared to refer again to the news from Ufa. The visitor departed in the evening. After supper, when Arina Vassilyevna and her daughters were about to take a silent farewell of Stepan Mihailovitch, he stopped them and said : ' Well, Arisha, what do you think about it ? Though that stupid Flona added plenty of lies, yet it seems to me there is truth in the story too. The boy's letters have been quite different of late. The thing needs some looking into. The best plan would be to summon Alosha here ; we shall learn all the truth from him.' At this point Alexandra offered to send a special messenger to Ufa to find out the truth through a relation of her husband's : ' She is a very honest woman,' she said, ' and nothing would make her tell a lie.' Her father agreed not to send for his son till the fresh report arrived. Alexandra started at once for her own house, which was not more than 30 *versts* from Bagrovo, and returned in a week, bringing with her the letter I have mentioned already, which she had received long before from her gossiping female friend at Ufa. This letter was shown and read aloud to Stepan Mihailovitch ; and though he put little faith in the women as detectives and informers, some statements in the letter seemed to him probable, and he was displeased. He said positively, that if Mlle Zubin did wish to marry Alosha, he would forbid it, on the ground of her birth. ' Write by the next post to Alosha,' he said, ' and tell him to come home.' A few days passed, and were used by the women to prejudice Stepan Mihailovitch as strongly as possible against the marriage ; and then, as we know already, the

young man turned up at Bagrovo without having
received the letter.

Alexyéi Stepanitch heard the whole of this story
from Tatyana, and it made him very serious and
uneasy.   He was not by nature strong-willed, and
had been brought up in blind obedience to his
family and his father.   In his alarm, he did not
know what to do.   At last he decided to speak to
his mother.   Arina Vassilyevna was devoted to
her only son ; but as she was accustomed to look
on him as still a child and convinced that this child
had taken a fancy to a dangerous toy, she met his
avowal of strong feeling with the words one would
use to a child who begged to hold the hot poker ;
and when this treatment brought the tears to his
eyes, she tried to comfort him in the way that a
child is comforted for the loss of a favourite toy.
He might say what he chose, he might try as he
pleased to refute the slander brought against Sofya
Nikolayevna—his mother either did not listen at
all or listened without attending.   Two more days
passed by ; the young man's heart was breaking ;
though his love and longing for Sofya Nikolayevna
increased every hour, it is probable that he would
not easily have plucked up courage to broach the
subject to his father ; but Stepan Mihailovitch
took the first step.   Early one fine morning, he
was sitting as usual on his stoop, when Alexyéi
Stepanitch, looking rather pale and worn after an
almost sleepless night, came out to join his father.
The old man was in a cheerful mood ; he greeted
his son affectionately, and then, looking attentively
at his face, he read what was going on within.   He
gave him his hand to kiss, and then said, not in
anger but with energy : ' Listen to me, Alexyéi !

I know the burden on your mind, and I see that
this fancy has taken a strong hold of you. Just
tell me the story now, the whole truth and nothing
but the truth.' Alexyéi Stepanitch felt more fear
than love for his father, and was not in the way of
speaking to him frankly ; but his love for Sofya
Nikolayevna lent him courage. He threw himself
at his father's feet and repeated the whole story,
omitting no details and keeping nothing back.
Stepan Mihailovitch listened with patience and
attention. When any of the family appeared in
the distance and evidently meant to come and say
' good morning,' he waved his blackthorn staff
with a significant gesture, and then nobody, not
even Aksyutka with the tea, dared approach before
he summoned them. Though his son's story was
ill-arranged, confused, long, and unconvincing, yet
Stepan Mihailovitch with his clear head made out
the gist of the matter. But unfortunately he did
not and could not approve of it. Of the romantic
side of love he had small appreciation, and his
masculine pride was offended by his son's suscepti-
bility, which seemed to him degrading weakness
in a man, and a sign of worthlessness ; and yet at
the same time he saw that Sofya Nikolayevna was
not in the least to blame, and that all the evil he
had heard about her was merely malicious false-
hood, due to the ill-will of his own womankind.
After a little reflection, he said, with no sign of
anger, even affectionately, but firmly : ' Listen to
me, Alexyéi ! You are just at the time of life when
a pretty girl may easily take a man's fancy. In that
there is no harm whatever ; but I see that you
have gone too far, and that does not do. I don't
blame Sofya Nikolayevna in the least ; she seems

to me a very worthy girl; but she's not a good match for you, and she won't suit us. In the first place, her nobility dates from yesterday, while you are the descendant of an ancient and noble line. Then she is accustomed to town life, highly educated, and independent; since her stepmother died she has ruled a household; and, though poor herself, she is used to luxury; but we are plain country people, and you know yourself how we live. And you ought to know your own character; you're too compliant. But her cleverness is the chief objection to her; to marry a wife cleverer than one's self is a mistake; she is sure to rule her husband; and you are so much in love that you are certain to spoil her at first. Well, as your father, I now bid you clear your head of this notion. I confess I don't believe myself that Sofya Nikolayevna would accept you. Choose your shoe of the right size, and it won't pinch your foot. We will find out a wife for you here—some gentle quiet girl, well-born and with some money. Then you can give up your office and live here in comfort. You know, my boy, we're not rolling in wealth. We get enough to eat, but very little money comes in. As to the Kurolyessoff legacy, about which people made such a noise, I never give it a thought; we can't count on it: Praskovya Ivanovna is young enough to marry and have children of her own. Now, mind what I say, Alosha: throw all this off like water off a duck's back, and don't let me hear again of Sofya Nikolayevna.' Then Stepan Mihailovitch gave his hand graciously to his son, who kissed it as respectfully as usual. The old man ordered tea to be served and the family to be summoned; he was more than usually cheerful

and friendly to them all, but Alexyéi Stepanitch
was terribly depressed. No anger on his father's
part would have produced such an effect; that
was soon over and was always followed by indulgence and kindness, but the old man's quiet deter-
mination deprived him of all hope. There was a
change in his expression, so sudden and complete,
that his mother was frightened to see it and plied
him with questions—' Was he unwell ? What had
happened to him ? ' His sisters noticed the change
also, but they were more cunning and held their
tongues. None of this was lost on Stepan Mihailovitch. He looked askance at Arina Vassilyevna
and muttered through his teeth, ' Don't worry the
boy ! ' So they took no more notice of him but
left him in peace, and the day went on with its
usual routine.

The conversation with his father made a deep
impression on Alexyéi Stepanitch ; one may say
that it crushed him. His appetite and sleep failed,
he lost interest in everything, even his bodily
strength was affected. His mother shed tears,
and even his sisters were uneasy. Next day his
mother found it difficult to get from him any
account of the interview with his father. To all
inquiries he returned the same answer : ' My father
won't hear of it ; I am a lost man, and life will
soon be over for me.' And within a week he did
really take to his bed ; he was very weak and often
half-conscious; and though his skin was not hot,
he was constantly delirious. No one could understand what was the matter with him ; but it
was simply a nervous fever. The family were
terribly alarmed. As there were no doctors in the
neighbourhood, they treated him with domestic

remedies; but he grew steadily worse till he was
so weak that his death was expected hourly. His
mother and sisters screamed and tore their hair.
Stepan Mihailovitch, though he shed no tears and
was not always sitting by the bedside, probably
suffered more than any one : he understood
perfectly what had caused this illness. But youth
at last asserted itself, and the turn came after
exactly six weeks. Alexyéi Stepanitch woke up to
life an absolute child, and life was slow in resuming
its normal course with him; his convalescence lasted
two months, and all the past seemed to have been
blotted out from his memory. Everything that he
saw, both indoors and out, pleased him as much
as if it were new and strange. At last he got
perfectly well ; his face filled out and got back the
healthy colour which it had lost for more than a
year ; he went out fishing and shooting quails, ate
and drank heartily, and was in good spirits. His
parents felt more joy than they could express, and
were convinced that the illness had expelled all
former thoughts and feelings from his head and
heart. And perhaps this would really have been
the case, if they had taken him away from Ufa,
kept him a whole year at home, and found a pretty
girl for him to marry. But their fears were lulled
to rest by his present condition, and they sent him
back to the same place and the same duties after
six months. This settled his fate once and for all.
The old passion revived and blazed up with far
greater power. I do not know whether love came
back to his heart all at once or by degrees ; I
only know that he went seldom at first to the
Zubins' house, and then oftener, and at last as
often as he could. I know also that his old friend.

Mme Alakayeff, continued her visits to Sofya
Nikolayevna, sounding her cautiously as to her
sentiments and bringing back favourable reports,
which confirmed her own hope that the proud
beauty was not indifferent to her humble worshipper. A few months after Alexyéi Stepanitch had
returned to Ufa, a letter from him suddenly arrived
at Bagrovo, in which he declared to his parents,
with his usual affection and respect, but also with
a firmness not characteristic of him, that he loved
Sofya Nikolayevna more than his own life and could
not live without her ; he had hopes of her accepting
him, and asked his parents to give him their blessing
and their consent to the match. This letter was a
great surprise and shock to the old people. Stepan
Mihailovitch knitted his brows but did not express
his feelings by a single word. The family all sat
round in perfect silence till he dismissed them by
a gesture. When he was alone, my grandfather
sat there a long time, tracing patterns on the floor
of his room with his blackthorn staff. He soon
realized that it was a bad business, that they had
been mistaken, and that no fever would cure the
lad of his passion. His impulsive and kindly nature
shook his resolve and made him inclined to give
his consent, as may be inferred from what he said
to his wife. When they were alone together next
morning, he said : ' Well, Arisha, what do you
think of it ? If we refuse, we shall see no more of
Alosha than of our own ears. He will die of grief,
or go off to the wars, or become a monk—and that's
the end of the Bagroff family ! ' But Arina Vassilyevna had been primed already by her daughters,
and she answered, as if her son ran no risk : ' As
you please, Stepan Mihailovitch ; your will is

mine too. But how can you hope they will respect
you in future, if they resist your positive commands
now ? ' This mean and cunning trick was successful : the old man's pride was touched, and he
resolved to stand firm. He dictated a letter, in
which he expressed surprise that his son should
begin the old business over again, and repeated
what he had already said by word of mouth. In
short, the letter contained a positive refusal.

Two or three weeks passed, and brought no reply
from Alexyéi Stepanitch. Then there came one
stormy autumn morning, when my grandfather
was sitting across his bed in his own room ; he
was wearing his favourite dressing-gown of fine
camel's hair over a shirt buttoning up at the side,
and had slippers on his bare feet. Arina Vassilyevna was sitting near him with her spinning-
wheel, spinning goat's down and carefully drawing
out the fine long threads with which she intended
to make cloth—cloth to provide her son with light,
warm, comfortable garments. Tanyusha was sitting by the window, reading a book. Elizabeth,
who was on a visit to Bagrovo, was sitting on the
bed near her father, telling him of her troubles—
her husband's poor prospects, and the shifts they
had to practise at home to make ends meet. The
old man listened sadly, with his hands on his knees,
and his head, now turning white, bent down over
his breast. Suddenly the door opened ; and Ivan,
a tall handsome lad, wearing a travelling jacket,
entered the room with a quick step and delivered
a letter which he had brought from the post-town
twenty-five *versts* away. The stir among the party
showed that the letter was eagerly expected.
' From Alosha ? ' asked the old man quickly and

uneasily. 'From my brother,' answered Tanyusha, who had gone to meet Ivan, taken the letter quickly from him, and looked at the address. 'You have lost no time, and I thank you. A dram for Ivan! Then go and have your dinner and rest.' The spirit-case was opened at once; Tanyusha took out a long cut-glass decanter, filled a silver cup with brandy, and handed it to Ivan. Ivan crossed himself and drank it, then coughed, bowed, and left the room. 'Read it aloud, Tanyusha,' said her father; she did his reading and writing for him. She placed herself by the window; her father left his bed and her mother her spinning-wheel, and all crowded round the reader, who had unsealed the letter by this time but dared not take a preliminary peep. After a moment's silence, the letter was read slowly and audibly. It began with the form of address usual in those days: 'Dear and honoured Father, and dear and honoured Mother,' and then went on in this fashion:

'In answer to my last letter, I had the misfortune to receive a refusal of my request, my dearest parents. I cannot go against your will; I submit to it, but I cannot long drag the burden of my life without my adored Sofya Nikolayevna; and therefore a fatal bullet shall ere long pierce the head of your unhappy son.' [1]

The letter produced a powerful effect. My aunts began to whimper; my grandmother, who was taken utterly by surprise, turned pale, threw out

[1] I know the letter nearly by heart. It probably still exists among the old papers of one of my brothers. Some expressions in it are clearly borrowed from the novels which Alexyéi Stepanıtch was fond of reading. (*Author's note.*)

her hands, and flopped down on the ground like a corn-sheaf. Even in those days fainting-fits were not unknown. Stepan Mihailovitch never stirred ; but his head bent a little to one side, as it used to do when a fit of anger was coming on, and began to tremble slightly ; and the same tremulous motion went on from that hour till his death. The daughters rushed to their mother's aid and soon brought her back to her senses. At once, Arina Vassilyevna threw herself at her husband's feet, raising the cry of mourning for the dead ; and her daughters followed her example. Taking no notice of the storm-signals on his brow, and quite forgetting that she herself had egged him on to disappoint his son, she cried at the top of her voice : '*Batyushka* Stepan Mihailovitch ! have pity and do not be the death of your own child, our only son ! Give Alosha leave to marry ! If anything happens to him, I will not live one hour longer !' The old man never stirred. At last he said in an unsteady voice : ' Enough of that howling ! Alosha deserves a good whipping. But we'll leave it till to-morrow; morning brings good counsel. Now go and order dinner to be served.' Dinner my grandfather regarded as a sedative at every domestic crisis. Arina Vassilyevna tried to begin again—' Mercy ! Mercy ! '— but Stepan Mihailovitch called out loudly, ' Leave the room, all of you ! '—and in his voice was audible the roar that goes before a storm. The room was cleared instantly, and no one ventured near him before the dinner-hour.

It is hard to imagine the thoughts that passed through his mind in the interval, the struggle that took place in that iron heart between love and prudence, and the final defeat of the stubborn spirit ; but when Mazan's voice was heard outside the door, announcing dinner, my grandfather came out of his room quite composed. His face was rather pale, but his wife and daughters, who were standing, each by her own chair, till he appeared, could not see the faintest sign of anger ; on the contrary, he was quieter and more cheerful than he had been in the morning, and made a hearty meal. Arina Vassilyevna had to harden her heart and suit her conversation to his mood; she dared not even sigh, far less ask questions ; in vain she tried to guess what was passing through her husband's mind ; the little chestnut-brown eyes in her fat face might ask what questions they pleased, but the dark-blue eyes of Stepan Mihailovitch, for all their frank good-humoured expression, gave no answer. After dinner he lay down as usual, and woke in a still more cheerful mood, but not a syllable did he utter about his son or the letter. Yet it was clear that no wrath was brooding in the old man's heart. When he said ' good-night ' to his wife after supper, she ventured to say, ' Please say something about Alosha.' He smiled and answered : ' Did I not say that morning thoughts are best ? Go to sleep, and God bless you ! '

Morning did indeed bring good counsel and kindly action. My grandfather got up at four o'clock when Mazan was kindling his fire, and his first words were : ' Tanaichonok, you are to take a letter at once to Ufa for Alexyéi Stepanitch. Get ready immediately, and no one is to know your errand or where you are going. Put the young brown horse in the shafts, and the roarer abreast of him. Take six bushels of oats with you and

a loaf of bread. Ask the housekeeper for two
roubles in copper for your expenses. See that all
is ready when my letter is written, and don't lose
a moment ! ' When my grandfather demanded
haste, he always got it. Then he opened the oak
desk which served him as a writing-table, got
writing materials, and with some effort—for ten
years past he had written nothing but his signature
—he wrote as follows in a stiff old-fashioned hand :

' DEAR SON ALEXYÉI,

' Your mother, Arina Vassilyevna, and I,
give you our permission to marry Sofya Nikolayevna Zubin, if that be God's will, and we send
you our blessing.

' Your father,

' STEPAN BAGROFF.'

Half an hour later, long before it was light,
Tanaichonok had reached the top of the long hill
and passed the stackyard, and was trotting briskly
along the road to Ufa. At six o'clock Stepan
Mihailovitch ordered Aksyutka to bring the
samovar but to wake no one in the house. In spite
of this, the mistress was called, and told in confidence that Tanaichonok had started very early
with a pair of horses from the stable ; he was carrying a letter from the master, but his destination
was unknown. She did not venture to join her
husband at once : she waited an hour or so, and
appeared when he had finished his tea and was
chatting with Aksyutka, the maid, who had been
plain as a child and was now still plainer in middle
life. ' Well, what did they wake you for ? ' said
Stepan Mihailovitch, holding out his hand to his
wife. ' I dare say you had a bad night.' Arina

Vassilyevna kissed his hand respectfully: 'No,' she said, 'no one called me, I woke of myself; and I had a good night, for I hoped you would be kind to our poor boy.' He looked attentively at her; but her face was accustomed to wear a mask, and he could not read her thoughts. 'In that case,' he said, 'I have good news for you. I have sent a special messenger to Ufa and written to Alexyéi that he has permission from us both to marry Sofya Nikolayevna.'

Arina Vassilyevna had been horrified by her son's tragic intentions, and had sincerely begged and prayed her stern husband to consent to the marriage. Yet, when she heard how Stepan Mihailovitch had decided, she felt more fear than joy; or rather, she did not dare to feel joy, because she feared her daughters. She knew already what Elizabeth thought of the letter, and guessed what Alexandra would say. For these reasons she received the decision, which her husband hoped would delight her, rather coldly and strangely; and this did not escape him. Elizabeth expressed no satisfaction whatever, but merely respectful submission to her father's will; but Tanyusha, who took her brother's letter quite seriously, rejoiced with all her heart. Elizabeth was not alarmed even at first by her brother's threat; she shed tears and interceded for him, merely because it would not look well to act differently from her mother and youngest sister. She wrote at once to Alexandra, who was furious when she heard of the decision and came with all speed to Bagrovo. She too treated her brother's letter as an empty threat, a trick suggested by Sofya Nikolayevna; and the two together soon converted their mother and even

Tanyusha to this belief. But the matter was settled, and open rebellion was now out of the question. Stepan Mihailovitch had thought that Sofya Nikola-yevna would refuse his son ; but no one else at Bagrovo believed this. But it is time now to leave Bagrovo and see what was going on at Ufa.

I shall not take upon myself to decide positively whether Alexyéi Stepanitch really intended to shoot himself, if his parents were obdurate, or took a hint from some incident in a novel and tried to excite their fears by suggesting the awful result of their refusal. Judging by the later development of his character—and I knew it well—I cannot think him capable of either course of action. Therefore, as I suppose, the young man was not playing a trick in order to frighten his parents ; on the contrary, he sincerely intended to blow out his brains, if he was forbidden to marry Sofya Nikolayevna. But at the same time I do not think he could ever have brought himself to carry out his fatal purpose, although your mild quiet people, who are often called faint-hearted, are sometimes more capable of desperate actions than men of bold and energetic temperament. The idea of suicide was certainly borrowed from some novel : it was quite out of keeping with the character of Alexyéi Stepanitch, his view of life, and the circle of ideas in which he had been born and brought up. However that may be, when he had launched the fatal letter, he became greatly agitated and was soon laid up with fever. His friend and con-fidante, Mme Alakayeff, knew nothing of the letter ; she came to see him daily and soon per-ceived that his illness and his love-affair were not enough to account for his excessive agitation. She was sitting beside him one day, knitting a stocking and talking about trifles, in order to amuse the invalid and distract his mind from his hopeless passion ; he was lying on the sofa, with his hands behind his head, looking out of the window. Suddenly he turned as white as a sheet. A cart with a pair of horses had turned off the street into the courtyard, and he recognized the horses and Tanaichonok. He sprang to his feet, cried out, ' A message from my father, from Bagrovo ! ' and made for the door. Mme Alakayeff seized his arm, and, with the help of a servant, prevented him from hurrying to the steps ; it was wet and cold autumn weather. Meanwhile Tanaichonok came quickly into the room and delivered the letter. Alexyéi Stepanitch broke the seal with trembling fingers, read the few lines, burst into tears, and fell on his knees before the ikon. Mme Alakayeff was puzzled until he handed her the letter ; but when she had read it, she too shed tears of joy. The young man was beside himself with happiness. He now confessed the nature of the letter he had written to his parents, and she shook her head when she heard it. Tanaichonok was called in and closely questioned ; when he told how he had been sent off, they saw that Stepan Mihailovitch had settled the matter by himself, without the knowledge of his womankind and probably against their wishes.

Mme Alakayeff was entirely taken by surprise : even when she had read the letter over again she could not believe her own eyes, because she knew Stepan Mihailovitch of old and quite realized the opposition of the family. But when the first excitement of surprise and joy was over, the two began to discuss how they should set to work. So long as opposition from their own side made the marriage seem remote and impossible, they had been sanguine as to the feelings of the lady; but now a doubt seized on Mme Alakayeff. When she recalled and examined all the favourable signs, she felt that perhaps she had attached more importance to them than they deserved; and like a sensible woman, she made haste to moderate the young man's confident hopes, prudently calculating that if he were seduced by them, he would find it harder to bear the sudden collapse of those radiant dreams. A refusal now seemed to her quite possible, and her fears had effect upon her companion. Still, she did not back out of her promise to help him: on the contrary, she went next day and laid his proposal before Sofya Nikolayevna.

Simply, clearly, and with no exaggeration, she described the constant and ardent attachment of Alexyéi Stepanitch—all the town had long known it, and certainly Sofya Nikolayevna did; she spoke warmly of the fine character of her young relative, his kind heart, his rare modesty; she gave true and exact details of his financial position and prospects; she told the facts about his family, not forgetting to state that he had received by letter yesterday his parents' blessing and their full consent to seek the hand of a lady so worthy and highly respected as Sofya Nikolayevna; she added, that the young man had caught a fever in the excitement of waiting for his parents' reply, but found it impossible to postpone the decision of his fate, and therefore had asked her, as his kinswoman and a friend of Sofya Nikolayevna's, to find out whether a formal proposal for her hand, laid before her father, would be distasteful to her or not.

Sofya Nikolayevna had long been accustomed to act for herself : without confusion and without any of the affectation and prudery expected of women in those days, she replied as follows :

'I thank Alexyéi Stepanitch for the honour he has done me, and you, dear lady, for your interest in the matter. I say frankly that I noticed long ago his partiality for me and have long expected that he would make me a proposal; but I have never decided whether I would accept or reject it. His last visit to his parents, the suddenness—you told me this yourself—of his long and dangerous illness at home, and the change in him when he came back to Ufa—these were signs that his parents disapproved of me as a daughter-in-law. This, I confess, I did not expect ; it seemed more natural to fear opposition on the part of my father. Later I saw that Alexyéi Stepanitch had revived his former feeling for me ; and now I suppose that he has been able to induce his father and mother to consent. But you must admit yourself, my dear lady, that the matter now assumes quite a new aspect. To enter a family where one is not welcome is too great a risk. Certainly, my father would not oppose my choice ; but can I venture to conceal the truth from him ? If he were to learn that an obscure country squire thought twice before admitting me to the honour of alliance with his family, he would consider it a degradation, and nothing would induce him to consent. I am not in love with Alexyéi Stepanitch : I only respect his good qualities and his constant affection, and I believe he might make the woman he loved happy.

Allow me, therefore, to think it over ; and also, before I speak of this to my father and trouble him in his feeble state with such news, I wish to speak myself to Alexyéi Stepanitch. Let him come and see us, when he is well enough.'

Mme Alakayeff reported this answer exactly to the young man. He did not think it promising, but she disagreed with him and tried to soothe his anxiety.

After parting on very friendly terms with her visitor, Sofya Nikolayevna sat for a long time alone in her drawing-room, and thought hard. Her bright lively eyes were clouded ; sombre thoughts raced through her brain and were reflected on the mirror of her beautiful face. All that she had said to Mme Alakayeff was perfectly true : the question, whether she should marry Alexyéi Stepanitch or not, was really not settled. But the proposal had now been made, and it was necessary to make the great decision, so critical in every woman's life. Sofya Nikolayevna had an unusually clear head ; in later years, the trials of life and her own passionate temperament may have warped her judgement, but she was able then to see everything exactly in its true light. Her prospects were not bright. Her father was a hopeless invalid, and Zanden, their best doctor, declared he could not live more than a year. His property consisted of two villages near Ufa, Zubkova and Kasimofka—forty serfs in all and a small amount of land ; he had also scraped together a sum of 10,000 roubles which he intended as a portion for his daughter. To see her married was his constant and eager desire ; but strange things do happen, and Sofya Nikolayevna had never before received a formal offer. He would leave behind him six orphans, the children of his two marriages, and separate guardians would have to be appointed. The three youngest would go to their grandmother, Mme Rychkoff ; their mother's fortune consisted of a small estate of fifty serfs. Sofya Nikolayevna's own brothers were at a boarding school in Moscow ; she would be left absolutely alone without even distant relations to take her under their roof. In short, she had not where to lay her head. To face poverty and want, to live on the charity of strangers and in complete dependence upon strangers—such a fate might distress any one ; but to a girl who had lived in comfort and held a high position in society, a girl proud by nature and flattered by general attention and popularity, a girl who had experienced all the burden of dependence and then all the charm of authority—such a change might well seem intolerable. And here was a young man, good-looking, honest, modest, the heir of an ancient line and an only son, whose father possessed 180 serfs and who was himself to inherit wealth from an aunt ; and this young man worshipped her and offered her his hand and heart. At first sight, hesitation seemed out of the question. But, on the other hand, they were ill-matched in mind and temperament. No one in the town could believe that Sofya Nikolayevna would accept Alexyéi Stepanitch, and she realized the justice of public opinion and could not but attach importance to it. She was considered a marvel of beauty and intelligence : her suitor was certainly pretty in a boyish way—which was no recommendation to Sofya Nikolayevna—but rather simple and stupid, and passed with every one for a plain country lad. She was quick

and enterprising : he was timid and slow. She
was educated and might almost be called learned,
had read much, and had a wide range of intellec-
tual interests : he was quite ignorant, had read
nothing but a few silly novels and a song-book,
and cared for little beyond snaring quails and
flying his hawks. She was witty and tactful and
shone in society : he could not string three words
together ; clumsy, shy, abject, and ridiculous, he
could only blush and bow and squeeze into a corner
or against a door, to escape from the talkative and
sociable young men whom he positively feared,
though he was in truth far cleverer than many of
them. She had a firm, positive, unbending temper :
he was humble and wanting in energy, easily
silenced and easily discomfited. Was he the man
to support and defend his wife in society and in
domestic life ?

Such were the contradictory thoughts and ideas
and fancies which swarmed in the young girl's mind,
mingling and jostling one another. Long after
darkness had come down, she was still sitting there
alone. At last a feeling of extreme misery, a
terrible certainty that her reason was utterly
baffled and growing less and less able to solve her
problem, turned her thoughts to prayer. She
hurried to her room to beg for the light of reason
from on high, and fell on her knees before the ikon
of Our Lady of Smolensk, who had once before by
a miracle lightened her darkness and pointed out
to her the path of life. For a long time she prayed,
and her hot tears fell. But by degrees she felt a
kind of relief, a measure of strength, a power of
resolve, though she did not know yet what her
resolve would be ; and even this feeling helped

her. She went downstairs to look at her father in his sleep; then she came back to her own room, lay down, and went peacefully to sleep. When she woke next morning, she was perfectly composed; she reflected for a few minutes, gave a thought to her hesitation and perplexity of the night before, and then kept quietly to her purpose, which was, first to have a conversation with her suitor, and then to settle the matter definitely, in accordance with the impression left on her mind by their interview.

Alexyéi Stepanitch, wishing to know his fate as soon as possible, sent for the doctor and begged to be put on his legs without delay. The doctor promised to let him out soon and kept his promise for once. Within a week Alexyéi Stepanitch, though still pale, thin, and feeble, was sitting in Sofya Nikolayevna's drawing-room. Touched by the loss of colour and change in his young face, she was not quite as outspoken and rigorous as she meant to be. In substance she repeated to him what she had said to Mme Alakayeff, but she added two points—that she would not part from her father while he lived, and that she would not live in the country. She wished to live in a town, in Ufa for choice, where she was acquainted with many worthy and cultivated people, and hoped to enjoy their society after her marriage. She ended by saying that she would like to see her husband in the public service and holding a position in the town, which, if not brilliant, should at least secure deference and respect. To all these conditions and anticipations of a wife's rights, Alexyéi Stepanitch replied, with abject humility, that her will was law to him, and that his happiness

would consist in the fulfilment of all her wishes.
Such an answer no man should have given : it
proved that his love was not to be depended on,
and that he could not assure a woman's happiness ;
yet it pleased Sofya Nikolayevna, clever as she
was. Reluctantly I must confess that love of
power was one of her ruling passions ; and the
germs of this passion, now that she had been
released from the cruel oppression of her step-
mother, were sprouting actively at this time. Love
of power did really, though she herself did not
know it, help her to her decision.

She expressed a wish to see the letter of consent
which he had received from his parents ; and he
produced it from his pocket. She read it and was
convinced that she was right in guessing that his
wishes had at first been opposed. The young man
was incapable of dissimulation, and also so much
in love that he could not resist a kind look or word
from his idol. So, when Sofya Nikolayevna
demanded perfect frankness, he made a clean breast
of everything ; and I believe that this frankness
finally settled the question in his favour. Sofya
Nikolayevna was clever, but still she was a woman ;
and she was filled with the idea of reshaping and
remoulding in her own way this good-tempered
young man, so modest and sincere and uncorrupted
by society. How delightful to think of the gradual
awakening and enlightenment of this Orson !
Orson had no lack of sense ; and feeling, though
wrapt in unbroken slumber, was there too. Orson
would love her still better, if that were possible, in
gratitude for his transformation. This vision took
hold of her eager imagination ; and she parted
very graciously from her adorer, promising to

talk the matter over with her father and communicate the result through Mme Alakayeff.
Alexyéi Stepanitch was 'swimming in bliss '—
to use an expression of that day. That evening
Sofya Nikolayevna again had recourse to prayer,
and prayed for a long time with great mental
strain and fervour. She was exhausted when she
went to sleep ; and she had a dream which she
interpreted, as people often do, as a confirmation
of her purpose. Men are clever enough to interpret
anything according to their desires. This dream
I forget ; but I remember that it was capable,
with much more probability and much less forcing,
of the opposite interpretation. Next morning
Sofya Nikolayevna lost no time in telling her
father, who was now in a very feeble state, of the
proposal she had received. M. Zubin did not know
Alexyéi Stepanitch, but had somehow come to
think of him as a person of no importance ; and
he was not pleased, in spite of his eager desire to
see his daughter settled before he died. But she
proved to him, with her usual eagerness and convincing eloquence, that it was unwise to show the
door to such a suitor. She urged all the advantages
of the match which we know already, and above
all that, far from parting with him, she would
continue to live in the same house. She painted
her helpless condition when it should please God
to remove her father, till the sick man shed a tear
and said : ' Do as you please, my dear clever child.
I consent to everything. Bring your future husband to see me soon : I wish to become better
acquainted with him. And I insist on receiving
a proposal in writing from his parents.'
Sofya Nikolayevna then sent a note to Mme

Alakayeff, asking Alexyéi Stepanitch to call on her
father at a fixed hour.   He was still ' swimming in
bliss,' which he shared only with his old friend and
supporter ; but he was much disconcerted by this
invitation which he had never expected from such
a confirmed invalid.   M. Zubin, in the absence of
the Lieutenant-Governor the most important and
powerful personage in the whole district of Ufa !
M. Zubin, whom he had always approached with
reverence and awe !   His name seemed now more
formidable than ever.   What if he frowned on this
proposal for his daughter's hand from one of the
humblest of his subordinates ?   Might he not treat
it as insolence, and thunder out : ' How dared you
think of my daughter ?   Are you a fit match for
her ?   Off with him to prison and to judgement ! '
However wild these notions may appear, they did
really pass through the young man's head, and
he often told the story afterwards himself.   Plucking up his spirits and encouraged by Mme Alakayeff, he put on his uniform, which hung loosely
on his limbs from loss of flesh, and set off to wait
on the great man.   With his three-cornered hat
under his arm, and clutching his troublesome
sword in a trembling hand, he entered M. Zubin's
study, so nervous that he could hardly breathe.
M. Zubin who had once been clever, lively, and
energetic, now lay on his couch hardly able to
move and shrunk to a mere skeleton.   The visitor
bowed low and remained standing by the door.
This in itself was enough to annoy the invalid.
' Step this way, M. Bagroff, and take a chair
near my bed ; I am too weak to talk loud.'
Alexyéi Stepanitch, with a profusion of bows, sat
down on the edge of a chair close to the bed.   ' I

understand that you seek my daughter's hand,'
the old man went on. The suitor jumped up,
bowed, and said that he did in fact venture to seek
this happiness.

I could report the whole of this interview in
detail, as I have often heard it fully described by
Alexyéi Stepanitch himself; but part of it would
be a repetition of what we know already, and I am
afraid of wearying my readers. The important
points are these. M. Zubin questioned the young
man about his family, his means, and his intentions
with regard to his profession and place of residence;
he said that Sofya Nikolayevna would have nothing
but her portion of 10,000 roubles, two families of
serfs as servants, and 3,000 roubles in cash for
initial expenses; and he added : ' Though I am
quite sure that you, as a dutiful son, would not
have made such a proposal without the consent of
your parents, yet they may change their minds;
and social usage requires that they should write to
me personally on the subject; and I cannot give
you a positive answer till I receive a letter to that
effect.' Alexyéi Stepanitch got up repeatedly,
bowed, and sat down again. He agreed to everything and promised to write that very day to his
parents. In half an hour the invalid said that
he was tired—which was perfectly true—and
dismissed the young man rather dryly. The
moment he left, Sofya Nikolayevna entered her
father's study; he was lying with closed eyes, and
his face expressed weariness and also anxiety.
Hearing his daughter's approach, he threw an
imploring glance at her, pressed his hands to his
breast, and ejaculated : ' Is it possible, Sonitchka,
that you intend to marry him ! ' But Sofya Niko-

layevna had anticipated the result of the interview
and was prepared for an even worse impression.
' I warned you, father,' she said in a gentle but
firm voice, ' that Alexyéi Stepanitch, owing to
utter ignorance of society, awkwardness, and
timidity, was bound to appear to you at first somewhat of a simpleton ; but I, who have seen him
often and had long conversations with him, will
vouch for it that he is no fool and has more sense
than most people. I beg you to have two more
interviews with him ; and I am sure you will
agree with me.' M. Zubin looked long at his
daughter with a keen and penetrating gaze, as if
he wished to read some secret hidden in her heart ;
then he sighed heavily and consented to do what
she asked.

By the next post Alexyéi Stepanitch sent a very
affectionate and respectful letter to his parents.
He thanked them for having given him life a second
time, and humbly begged them to write at once to
M. Zubin and request the hand of his daughter for
their son ; he added that this was the regular
custom, and without such a letter the father
would not give a positive answer. The fulfilment
of this simple request gave some trouble to the old
people at Bagrovo. They were no hands at
composition, and for want of previous experience
had no idea how to set about it, while they were
exceedingly loath to commit themselves before the
Governor's Deputy and their future relation, who
was sure to be a skilful man of business and a
practised writer. It took them a whole week to
compose their letter ; at last it got written somehow and was dispatched to Alexyéi Stepanitch.
It was not a skilful production, having none of

those polite phrases and professions of affection which are indispensable in such cases.

While waiting for the answer from home, Alexyéi Stepanitch received two more invitations from M. Zubin. The second visit did not remove the unfavourable impression produced by the first. On the next occasion, however, Sofya Nikolayevna was present. Returning from a call earlier than usual, she walked into her father's room, as if she did not know that her suitor was sitting there. Her presence made all the difference. She could make him talk and knew what he could talk about, so as to display to advantage his natural good sense, high principle, and goodness of heart. M. Zubin was obviously pleased : he spoke kindly to the young man and invited him to come to the house as often as he could. When they were alone, the old man embraced his daughter with tears, called her by many fond names, and said she was a witch whose spells could draw out a man's good qualities, even when they were so deeply hidden that no one suspected their existence. She too was much pleased ; for she had not dared to hope that Alexyéi Stepanitch would do so much to support her favourable opinion and justify the character she had given him.

The letter containing the formal proposal arrived at last, and Alexyéi Stepanitch delivered it in person to M. Zubin. Alas ! without the magic presence and aid of Sofya Nikolayevna the suitor failed again to please his future father-in-law, who was also far from satisfied with the letter. Next day he had a long conversation with his daughter, in which he set before her all the disadvantages of marrying a man inferior to herself in intelligence,

education, and force of character ; he said that the
Bagroff family would not take her to their hearts—
they would be much more likely to hate her,
because coarse and cruel ignorance always hates
refinement ; he warned her not to rely on the
promises of a lover ; for these as a rule are not
kept after marriage, and Alexyéi Stepanitch, even
if he wished, would not have the power to keep
them. To all this sage advice, drawn directly
from the experience of life, she had an answer of
surprising adroitness ; and at the same time she
depicted in such lively colours the advantages of
marrying a man who, if he lacked energy and
refinement, was at least kind-hearted, honourable,
loving, and no fool, that her father was carried
away by her confidence and gave his full consent,
She clasped her father in her arms and kissed his
washed hands, then she gave him the icon and
received his blessing,[1] kneeling by his bed and
weeping. ' Father,' she cried in her excitement,
' with God's help, I hope that in a year's time
Alexyéi Stepanitch will be a different creature :
the reading of good books, the society of clever
people, and constant conversation with his wife—
these will make up for defects of education ; his
bashfulness will pass away, and the power to take
a place in society will come of itself.' ' May it be
so ! ' he answered. ' Now send for the priest. I
wish that we should pray together for your happiness.'

That same evening Alexyéi Stepanitch was
invited to the house, with Mme Alakayeff and
some old friends of the Zubins—M. Anitchkoff

---

[1] The sacred picture is often held by the person giving
the blessing.

and the Misailoffs ; and the favourable answer was given.   The young man's bliss no words can describe : Sofya Nikolayevna, even in extreme old age, used to speak of his joy at that moment. He threw himself at M. Zubin's feet and kissed his hands, cried and sobbed like a child, and nearly fainted from the effect of this immense good-fortune which down to the last moment had seemed beyond his reach.   She too was deeply moved by such a frank expression of ardent and entire devotion.

The official betrothal came two days later, and all the town was invited to the ceremony.   There was general surprise, because many had disbelieved the reports of the engagement.   But all sceptics were convinced at last, and came to express their congratulations and good wishes.   Alexyéi Stepan-itch was radiant with happiness ; he was quite unaware of any hidden meaning in congratulations, of any mockery in looks and smiles.   But Sofya Nikolayevna let nothing pass unnoticed : she saw everything and heard everything, though in speaking to her, every one was cautious and polite. Though she knew beforehand the view society would take of her action, she could not help being vexed by this expression of their opinion.   But no one detected her vexation ; for she was cheerful and affectionate with every one and especially with her suitor, and seemed perfectly happy and content with her choice.   The pair were soon summoned into M. Zubin's study, and the betrothal took place there before a few witnesses.   While the priest read the prayers, the old man shed tears ; when the rite was over, he told the bridegroom to kiss the bride and embraced them both himself

with a great effort ; then he gazed earnestly at
Alexyéi Stepanitch and said, ' Love her always as
you do now ; God is giving you such a treasure
. . .' and then he broke down. The engaged
couple and the witnesses returned to the drawing-
room, where all the men embraced the bridegroom
and kissed the bride's hand, while all the ladies
embraced the bride and had their hands kissed by
the bridegroom. When this fuss was over, the
pair were made to sit on a sofa side by side, and
exchange kisses again ; and then the company,
holding glasses in their hands, repeated their
congratulations and good wishes. Anitchkoff
acted as host, and Mme Alakayeff as hostess.
Alexyéi Stepanitch, who had never in his life drunk
anything but water, was forced to take a glass of
wine, and the unfamiliar stimulant had a strong
effect upon him, weakened as he was by recent
illness and prolonged agitation. He became uncommonly lively, laughed and cried, and talked
a great deal, to the amusement of the company
and the mortification of the bride. The guests
soon grew merry : glass followed glass, and a fine
supper was served. All ate and drank heartily,
and at last the party broke up amid noise and
merriment. The bridegroom's head was beginning
to ache ; and Mme Alakayeff took him home in
her carriage.

M. Zubin felt that he was in great danger and
therefore wished to have the wedding as soon as
possible ; but as he also wished his daughter's
outfit to be rich and splendid, it was necessary to
postpone the ceremony for some months. Her
mother's diamonds and emeralds had to be sent to
Moscow, to be reset and restrung in the newest

fashion; silver had to be ordered from Moscow, and some dresses and presents; the other dresses, curtains for the state bed, and a sumptuous black-brown fur cloak which cost 500 roubles then and could not be bought now for 5,000—all these were made in Kazan; a quantity of table-linen and Holland sheets were also provided. Ten thousand roubles, the amount fixed for the dowry, was a great sum in those days; and, as many valuable things were provided as well, the inventory of the bride's outfit assumed such splendid proportions, that when I read it now I can hardly believe in the simple life of our ancestors at the end of last century.

The first business after the formal betrothal was to send complimentary letters to all relations on both sides. One of Sofya Nikolayevna's gifts was her remarkable skill in letter-writing; and her letter to her future husband's parents was such that Stepan Mihailovitch, though no letter-writer himself, set a high value on it. First he listened to it with great attention: then he took it out of Tanyusha's hand, praised the distinct handwriting, and read it through twice himself. 'Well, she's a clever girl,' he said, 'and I make sure she has a warm heart.' This enraged the family, but they had the sense to keep silent. Alexandra alone could not restrain herself: her gooseberry eyes flashed with rage as she said: 'She can write a fine letter, father, I admit; but all is not gold that glitters.' The old man scowled at her and said in his dangerous voice: 'How do you know? You're snarling at her already, and you've never even seen her! Take care! Keep your tongue from wagging, and don't stir up the rest!' All sat as

silent as mice, and of course hated Sofya Nikolayevna worse than ever. Meanwhile Stepan
Mihailovitch under the influence of that warm and
affectionate letter, took the pen himself and wrote
as follows, in defiance of all established etiquette :

' MY DEAR, PRECIOUS, SENSIBLE DAUGHTER-IN-
LAW TO BE,

' If you, without seeing us, have learnt to love
and respect us old people, we feel the same for you.
And when, by God's blessing, we meet, we shall
love you still better ; and you will be to us as our
own daughter, and we shall rejoice in the happiness
of our son Alexyéi.'

On her side, Sofya Nikolayevna valued the old
man's simple words as they deserved ; from what
she had heard, she had already taken a fancy to
him. As she had no relations living, the bridegroom had no letters to write ; but she asked
Alexyéi Stepanitch to write a letter of intimation
to M. Anitchkoff, the friend at Moscow whom she
had never seen and who had taken her brothers
under his care. The bridegroom of course gladly
consented. Not having much confidence in his
power to express himself on paper, she asked to
see the letter before it was sent. When she read it,
she was horrified ! Alexyéi Stepanitch, who had
heard a great deal of M. Anitchkoff as a wit, took
it into his head to adopt an elaborate style. Therefore he had recourse to some novel of the day,
and filled two sides with phrases which, in other
circumstances, would have made Sofya Nikolayevna laugh outright ; as it was, the blood rushed
to her face, and then the tears poured from her
eyes. When she grew calmer, she wondered how

she was to get out of such an awkward situation.
She did not wonder long however. She wrote a
rough draft of a letter herself, and then said to her
betrothed that, not being in the habit of writing
to strangers, he had written in a way that might
not please M. Anitchkoff; and therefore she had
written a rough draft, which she asked him to copy
out and send off. She felt shame and pain, and
was hurt on his account ; her voice shook, and she
nearly broke down. But he welcomed her suggestion with enthusiasm ; when she read him the
letter, he was charmed with it, praised her wonderful skill, and covered her hands with kisses. This
was the first step in disrespect for her future
husband, the first step towards realizing her dream
of complete domination over him ; and she did not
find it easy to take.

Knowing that his parents had little money and
were forced to be chary in spending any, Alexyéi
Stepanitch wrote to ask for a very moderate sum ;
and to strengthen his request, he asked Mme
Alakayeff to write to his father, to assure him that
the request was reasonable and that some expense
was inevitable in view of the marriage. He asked
only 800 roubles, but Mme Alakayeff stated the
necessary sum at 1,500. The old people replied
that they had not got such a sum ; they sent him
all they had—300 roubles, and suggested that, if
the other 500 were necessary, he should borrow
them ; but they promised to send him a team of
four horses with a coachman and postilion, and
provisions of all kinds. They did not even answer
Mme Alakayeff : so indignant were they with her
for demanding such a huge sum. It could not be
helped : Alexyéi Stepanitch thanked them for their

kindness and borrowed 500 roubles ; when even
this proved insufficient, Mme Alakayeff gave him
500 more, without the knowledge of his parents.

Meantime, as the engaged couple met more
often and were together longer, they became more
intimate.   Sofya Nikolayevna for the first time
saw her lover as he really was, and realized for the
first time what a heavy task lay before her.   She
had made no mistake in thinking that he possessed
natural intelligence, a very kind heart, strict
principles of honour, and perfect integrity in
official life ; but otherwise she found such a limita-
tion of ideas, such a pettiness of interests, such an
absence of self-esteem and independence, that her
courage and firmness in the execution of her
purpose were more than once severely shaken.
More than once, in despair, she took the engagement ring off her finger, laid it before the ikon of
Our Lady of Smolensk, and prayed with tears that
her feeble intelligence might be enlightened by
divine wisdom.   As we know already, she was
accustomed to act thus at each crisis in her life.
When she had prayed, she felt braver and calmer.
Interpreting this feeling as heavenly guidance, she
would put her ring on again and go back, composed
and cheerful, to join her lover in the drawing-room.
Her father felt that he was losing strength daily ;
and she was able to assure him that she was
constantly discovering fresh merits in her lover,
that she was quite content and looked forward to
happiness in her marriage.   By this time disease
had dulled M. Zubin's perspicacity : he not only
believed that she was sincere, but was convinced
himself that his daughter would be happy. ' Thank
God ! ' he used to say ; ' now I can die happy.'

And now the wedding-day drew near. The bride's outfit was all ready. The bridegroom too made his preparations, being guided by the advice of Mme Alakayeff, who assumed the entire management of him. The old lady, in spite of her shrewdness, was surprised at his profound ignorance of the customs of polite society. But for her, he would have been guilty of many blunders which would have made his bride blush for shame. Thus he intended to give her as a birthday present a kind of cloth for a dress which would have only been suitable as a present to her maid ; and he thought of driving to the church in an old shandrydan without springs, which would have made all the town laugh ; and so on. The things were not of importance in themselves ; but it would have tried Sofya Nikolayevna too hard to see her bridegroom the laughing-stock of Ufa society. All such things were put right by Mme Alakayeff, or rather by the bride herself, for the two women discussed every point together. Sofya Nikolayevna told her lover in time, that he must not think of giving her a present for her birthday, because she loathed birthday presents in general. For the wedding, she made him get a new English carriage which had lately been ordered from Petersburg by a local landowner, whose name was Murzahanoff.[1] and who had managed to run through his fortune in a few months. The price paid for the carriage was 350 roubles ; Sofya Nikolayevna bought it herself as a present from her father to the bridegroom, and begged him not to trouble the dying man by thanking him. And the other difficulties were got over in the same fashion.

[1] The Russianized form of an oriental name. Mirza Khan.

Then the bride and bridegroom wrote, for themselves and M. Zubin, to Stepan Mihailovitch and Arina Vassilyevna, pressing them to honour the wedding by their presence ; but the old people, as a matter of course, declined the invitation. They had lived so long in their country solitude that town society seemed to them something strange and formidable. None of the daughters wished to go either ; but Stepan Mihailovitch thought this awkward, and desired Elizabeth and Alexandra to attend the wedding. The latter was accompanied by her husband, Karatayeff ; but Yerlykin was detained by his duties at Orenburg.

The presence of these uninvited and unexpected guests was the cause of much annoyance to Sofya Nikolayevna. Her future sisters-in-law were clever and cunning women : they were determined to dislike her, and their behaviour to her was cold, unfriendly, and even rude. Though Sofya Nikolayevna knew very well the sort of attitude they were likely to adopt, yet she thought it her duty to be friendly and even cordial to them at first ; but when she saw that all her efforts were vain, and that the better she treated them the worse they treated her, she retired behind a wall of cold civility. But this did not protect her from those mean hints and innuendoes which it is impossible not to understand and not to resent, though it is awkward to do either, because you lay yourself open to the retort—‘ If the cap fits, wear it ! ’ This odious form of attack, now banished to the servants’ hall by the advance of refinement, was formidable in those days, and much used in the houses of rural landowners, many of whom differed little from their own servants in their manners and customs. But is it true that it has really been banished ? Does it not still live on among us, concealed under more decent and artistic forms ?

The good people of Ufa made fun, as might be expected, of the country clothes and manners of the two ladies. As to Karatayeff, who had now adopted all the Bashkir habits and began drinking Bashkir decoctions at eight in the morning, when he was first introduced to Sofya Nikolayevna, he kissed her hand with a sounding smack three times over, and cried out with real Bashkir enthusiasm, ' My word ! what a dazzler brother Alexyéi has hooked ! ' The coarse jests and compliments of the man were as distressing as the malicious sallies of the women ; and both forced Sofya Nikolayevna to swallow many tears. But worse than all was the blindness of Alexyéi Stepanitch : he seemed perfectly satisfied with the relations between his sisters and his bride, and this was not only a mortification for the present but also a peril for the future. These venomous creatures, who were staying with their brother, began at once to drop their poison into his simple soul, and did it so artfully that he did not suspect their manœuvres. Allusions to the young lady's pride, to the poverty which she hid under jewels and fine clothes, to her caprices and his meek submission to them, were dinned into his ears all day long. Much passed unnoticed, but much also went straight to the mark and made him thoughtful and vaguely uneasy. All their attacks, whether secret or open, were accompanied by a pretence of sympathy and sisterly affection. ' What makes you look so worn, my dear boy ? ' Elizabeth would ask ; ' Sofya Nikolayevna wears you out with all her com-

missions. You've just got back from the other end
of the town, tired and hungry, and off you run
again, without eating a morsel, to dance attendance
on her. As your sisters, we can't help being sorry
for you ' ; and then sham tears, or at least some
play with the pocket-handkerchief, completed the
crafty sentence. Then Alexandra would make a
furious entry into the conversation. ' No, my dear,
I really cannot stand it ! I know you will be angry,
and perhaps you will cease to love us ; but I can't
help it, I must tell you the truth. You are quite
changed : you're ashamed of us and have forgotten
us altogether ; your one wish is to mumble that
girl's hand ; your one fear, to get into her black
books. You have become her lackey, her slave !
Then it cuts us to the heart to see that old witch,
Mme Alakayeff, ordering you about like a servant
and making you fetch and carry for her ; and she 's
not content with that, but finds fault with you and
urges you to greater activity.' Alexyéi Stepanitch
could think of no answer to all this, except that he
loved his sisters and would continue to do so, and
—it was time to go and see Sofya Nikolayevna ;
whereupon he took his hat and hurried off. ' Oh,
go by all means ! ' Alexandra called after him,
' and go quickly ; or else she will be angry and
perhaps* withhold her hand from your lips ! '
Scenes like this took place again and again and
undoubtedly left their impression.

Sofya Nikolayevna could not help noticing that
his sisters' visit had brought about a certain change
in her lover. He seemed depressed, was less exact
in keeping his engagements, and spent less time
with her. The reason for this she herself understood
very well ; and Mme Alakayeff, who had become

a very intimate friend and also knew all that went
on in the Bagroffs' lodgings, did not fail to provide
her with detailed information. Her impulsive
nature made her unwilling to let things drag on.
She reasoned justly, that she ought not to give
time for the sisters' influence to take root at leisure,
that she must open her lover's eyes and put the
strength of his character and affection to a decisive
test. If they proved too weak, it was better to
part before marriage than to unite her fate to such
a feeble creature, who was, to use her own expression, ' neither a shield from the sun nor a cloak to
keep out the rain.' She summoned him early one
morning and ordered that no visitors should be
admitted to the drawing-room where they were
sitting. Then she turned to Alexyéi Stepanitch,
who was looking pale and frightened, and addressed
him as follows :

' I wish to have a frank explanation with you
and to make a clean breast of what I am feeling :
and I ask you to do the same. Your sisters detest
me and did their best to rouse your parents against
me. That I know from yourself. But your love
overcame all obstacles : your parents gave you
their approval, and I resolved to accept you and
brave the hatred of all your family. I hoped to
find protection in your love for me and in my
endeavour to prove to your parents that I don't
deserve their displeasure. But now I see that I
was mistaken. You saw yourself how I received
your sisters, how friendly I was and how hard I
tried to please them ; and though their rudeness
made me draw back, yet I never once failed in
politeness to them. And what has been the result ?
It is only a week since they came, and you treat

me differently already : you make me promises and then forget to keep them ; you spend less time with me ; you are depressed and anxious, and even less affectionate to me than you used to be. Don't defend yourself, or deny it ; that would not be honourable on your part. I know that you love me still, but you are afraid to show it : you fear your sisters, and that is why you are depressed and even avoid opportunities of being alone with me. You know yourself that all this is quite true. Well then, tell me, how can I hope that your love will stand firm ? It is a strange kind of love that turns coward and hides, because your sisters disapprove of your bride, as you knew they did long ago. Suppose your parents disapprove of me and turn up their noses at me ? What then ? Then you will really cease to love me. No, Alexyéi Stepanitch, honourable men do not behave so to the woman they love. The knowledge that your sisters disliked me should have made you twice as attentive and twice as devoted in their presence ; and then they would not have dared to utter a syllable ; but you have suffered them to use insulting language in your presence. I know just how they speak to you. From all this I conclude that your love is not love at all, but love-making, that I cannot rely on you, and that we had better part now than be unhappy for life. Consider carefully what I have said ; I shall give you two days to think it over. Come to the house as usual, but I shall not see you alone and shall not refer to this interview. After two days, I shall ask for an honest answer to these questions : "Have you sufficient firmness to be my defender against your relations and any one else who chooses to insult me?

Can you shut your sisters' mouths and prevent them from uttering in your presence a single insulting word or allusion against me ? " To break her engagement a week before her marriage is a great misfortune for any girl ; but it is better to bear it once for all than to suffer all one's life. You know that I am not in love with you, but I was beginning to love you ; and I believe my love would have been stronger and more constant than yours. Now, good-bye ! For to-day and to-morrow we are strangers.'

Long before she ended, Alexyéi Stepanitch had been in tears, and he tried several times to interrupt ; but before he could open his mouth, she had left the room and shut the door behind her. It was some time before he recovered from this tremendous blow. But at last the terrible thought of losing his adored mistress presented itself to him with appalling reality, and summoned up that energy and vigour of which the mildest and gentlest of men are capable, though they cannot keep it up for long. He hurried home ; and when his sisters, with no pity for his evident disturbance and distress, greeted him with the usual malicious jests, he flew into such a rage and attacked them with such fury that they were frightened. The wrath of a gentle patient man is a formidable thing. Among other things, he told his sisters that if they ventured to say another insulting word about his bride or about himself, he would instantly move to other lodgings, from which, as well as from M. Zubin's house, they would be excluded ; and he would write to his father and tell him the whole story. That was enough. Alexandra had a clear recollection of her father's warning—' Keep your

tongue quiet, and don't stir up the rest of the family!'
She knew very well what a thunder-cloud her
brother's complaint would call up, and what
alarming consequences she might expect.   Both
the sisters fell on their brother's neck and begged
forgiveness with tears ;   they solemnly declared
that it should never happen again ;   they were
really very fond of Sofya Nikolayevna, and it was
only out of pity for his health and fear that he was
doing too much that they had ventured on those
foolish jests.   They called on Sofya Nikolayevna
that same day and paid court to her with the
utmost servility.   The meaning of all this was not
lost upon her, and she felt she had prevailed.

The position of her lover really deserved pity.
His feelings, which had been calmed and composed
to some extent by frequent interviews with Sofya
Nikolayevna, her simple friendly behaviour to him,
and the near prospect of the marriage, had then
been rather alarmed and abashed by the sneers of
his sisters ;   and now they flamed up so fiercely,
that at the present moment he was capable of any
self-sacrifice or any desperate action, a true knight-
errant !   His state of mind was clearly reflected on
his handsome young face during those two endless
days.   The lovers met several times, and Sofya
Nikolayevna could not look on his face without
pain ;   but she had the firmness to support the test
she had imposed.   The agitation and pity which
she felt was a surprise to herself.   She felt that she
did really love this simple, modest young man, who
was absolutely devoted to her and would not have
hesitated to put an end to his existence if she made
up her mind to refuse him.   At last the two long
days were over.   Early on the third day, Alexyéi

Stepanitch sat in the drawing-room, waiting for his mistress to appear. The door opened softly, and in she came, more beautiful, more charming than ever. She was smiling, and her eyes expressed such tenderness that when he looked at her and saw her kind hand stretched out towards him, the excess of his emotion deprived him for an instant of the power of speech. He soon recovered, and then, instead of taking her hand, fell at her feet and poured forth a torrent of burning heartfelt eloquence. She interrupted him and raised him to his feet. Then she said : ' I see and feel your love, and I share it ; I believe all your promises ; I put my fate in your hands without fear.' She had never been so affectionate to him before, and she used words of tenderness which he had never before heard from her lips.

Only five days remained before the marriage. All their preparations were complete, and the lovers were free to spend most of their time together. For five whole months Sofya Nikolayevna had been true to her intention of educating her future husband over again. She never lost a suitable moment, but did her best to impart those ideals which he did not possess, to clear up and develop feelings of which he was dimly conscious, and to root out the notions which he had derived from his early surroundings. She even made him read, and discussed with him the books he had read, explaining what puzzled him, filling up gaps in his memory, and illustrating fiction from real life. But it is probable that she got on faster with her task during these five days than in the course of five long months ; for the recent incident which I have described had raised her lover's mind to a higher level of refinement, and he was in an unusually receptive and impressionable mood. How far the teacher succeeded on the whole in impressing her ideas upon the pupil, I cannot venture to decide. It is hard to know how much weight to attach to the opinions of the two persons concerned ; but it is certain that in later years they both maintained—and they appealed to the evidence of disinterested persons in confirmation of the statement—that a great change took place in Alexyéi Stepanitch, and even a complete transformation. I am very willing to believe it ; but I have a proof that his proficiency in social etiquette left something to be desired. I know that he made his bride very angry the day before the marriage, and that her vehemence left a strong and painful impression on his mind. It happened in the following way. Two ladies were calling on Sofya Nikolayevna when a servant brought in a paper parcel and handed it to his mistress, with the explanation that Alexyéi Stepanitch had sent it by his coachman and wished her at once to make a cap for his sister Alexandra. Her lover had left her half an hour before without saying one word about this commission, and Sofya Nikolayevna was exceedingly annoyed. The ladies, who were of some importance, had supposed at first that the parcel contained a present from the bridegroom ; and now they did not try to conceal their amusement. Sofya Nikolayevna lost patience : she ordered the parcel to be returned, with a message that Alexyéi Stepanitch had better apply to a milliner ; it was no doubt a mistake to have brought the thing to her. The explanation was quite simple. On going home, he had found his sister in a great difficulty,

because the milliner, who had engaged to make
her a cap for the wedding, had fallen ill and
returned the materials. As he had seen with his
own eyes the skill with which Sofya Nikolayevna
could trim hats and caps, he offered to help his
sister out of her trouble, and told his servant to
carry the parcel to his bride, with a humble request
that she would trim a cap for Alexandra. But the
servant was busy, and instead of going himself,
sent the coachman; and the humble request
became in the coachman's mouth an imperious
demand. Alexyéi Stepanitch hastened back to
explain matters, and carried with him the same
unlucky parcel. Sofya Nikolayevna had not yet
cooled down, when she saw him coming into the
room with the odious parcel under his arm; and
she flared up worse than ever, and said many
violent and unkind things which she had better
have left unspoken. The culprit, utterly dumbfounded, tried to defend himself, but did it very
badly; he was seriously hurt by this onslaught.
She sent the materials for the cap to some milliner
she knew of; and then, repenting of her violence,
she tried to put matters right. But to her surprise,
Alexyéi Stepanitch could not get over it: he felt
that he had been unjustly treated, and she had
frightened him. He became very depressed, and
her efforts to calm and cheer him were unsuccessful.

The wedding day, the 10th of May, 1788,
arrived, and the bridegroom paid an early visit to
his bride. After her excitement of the previous
day, she was distressed to see that Alexyéi
Stepanitch still wore the same pained expression.
She felt hurt; for she had always supposed that he
would be in an ecstacy of joy on the day when he

led her to the altar ; and here he was, looking
grave and even depressed ! She expressed her
feelings, and that made matters worse. Of course,
he assured her that he considered himself the
happiest man in the world, and so on ; but the
pompous and trivial phrases, which he had repeated
many a time before and she had heard with satisfaction, were now distasteful to her ear, because
they lacked the fire of inward conviction. They
soon parted, to meet next in church, where the
bridegroom was to be in waiting for her at six in
the evening.

Sofya Nikolayevna was assailed by a terrible
misgiving—would she be happy in her marriage ?
A host of dark forebodings passed before her
heated imagination. She blamed herself for her
hot temper and violent language ; she recognized
that the offence was trifling, and that she must
expect many slips of the kind on her lover's part,
and must take them calmly. They had happened
often enough before ; but on this occasion, the
unlucky combination of circumstances and the
presence of the two unfriendly visitors had pricked
her vanity and irritated her natural impetuosity.
Conscious that she had frightened her lover, she
repented of her fault ; but at the same time she
was aware in the depth of her heart that she was
quite capable of committing the same fault again.
And now she realized afresh all the difficulty of the
tremendous task she had undertaken—the refor-
mation and regeneration of a man of twenty-seven.
Her whole life—and it might be long—must be
spent with a husband whom she loved indeed but
could not entirely respect ; there would be constant collision between utterly different ideas and

opposite qualities, and they would often misunderstand one another. Doubts of success, doubts of her own strength, doubts of her power to command the qualities of firmness and calmness so foreign to her nature—these rose before her for the first time in their appalling truth, and she shrank back in terror. But what could she do ? If she broke off the marriage at the eleventh hour, what would be the consequences ? It would be a terrible blow to her dying father, who took comfort in the conviction that his daughter would be happy in the care of a kind husband ; her rivals in society and enemies would mock at her ; she would be the talk of the town and the laughing-stock of the district, perhaps even a mark for calumny ; and, above all, she would kill, literally kill, her devoted lover. And all for what ? Merely because she was afraid she might lack firmness to carry out a purpose which she had deliberately formed and which was beginning to take shape with triumphant success. ' No ! that shall never be ! God will help me ; Our Lady of Smolensk will be my intercessor and will give me strength to conquer my impetuous nature.' Thus Sofya Nikolayevna thought, and thus she decided. She wept and prayed and regained her stability.

The Church of the Assumption was quite close to the Zubins' house, and there was then an empty space round it. Long before six o'clock, it was surrounded by a crowd of curious spectators. The high steps projecting from the house into the street were blocked by the carriages of the privileged persons who had been invited to escort the bride. The bride was dressed, and her little brother, Nikolinka, whose birth had cost his mother her

life three years before, put on the stockings and
shoes, according to established custom, though of
course the maids lent their assistance. By six the
bride was ready ; she received her father's blessing
and came into the drawing-room. The rich bridal-
dress lent an added lustre to her beauty. The
bridegroom on his way to church had to pass
right under the drawing-room windows, and Sofya
Nikolayevna saw him drive past in the English
carriage drawn by the four fine horses bred at
Bagrovo ; he had his head out and was looking up
at the open windows ; she smiled and nodded.
Next came the bridegroom's sisters with Mme
Alakayeff, and all the men who were escorting him
to church. She did not wish to keep him waiting,
and insisted, in spite of various hindrances, that
they should start at once. Sofya Nikolayevna
was calm and composed when she entered the
church , she gave her arm cheerfully and smilingly
to the bridegroom ; but she was vexed to see that
his face still wore the same sad expression ; and it
was generally remarked that they both looked
depressed during the ceremony. The church was
brilliantly lighted and full of people ; the cathedral
choir did not spare their voices. Altogether, it
was a dignified and splendid ceremony. When the
rite was over, the young couple were escorted to
the Zubins' house by the bridegroom's sisters, the
whole train of friends and relations on both sides,
and all the important people of Ufa. Dancing
began at once and went on till an early but
sumptuous supper was served. Privileged guests
paid a visit to M. Zubin in his study and con-
gratulated him on his daughter's marriage. The
usual festivities took place on the next and follow-

ing days—balls, dinners, and calls, in fact the regular routine which we see nowadays even in Moscow and Petersburg.

The shade of sadness soon vanished from the faces of the young couple. They were perfectly happy. Kind people could not look at them without pleasure; and every one said, ' What a handsome couple ! ' A week later, they prepared for a visit to Bagrovo; the bridegroom's sisters had gone back there three days after the wedding, and Sofya Nikolayevna had sent by them an affectionate letter to the old people.

Startled by their brother's explosion, Elizabeth and Alexandra had been cautious of late. They refrained from all hints and sneers and grimaces in his presence, and were even polite to Sofya Nikolayevna. She, of course, was not taken in by this ; but their brother entirely believed in the sincerity of their devotion to his bride. At the wedding and the festivities which followed, they were, naturally, somewhat out of place, and therefore hastened their departure. On arriving at Bagrovo, they determined to do nothing rash and to hide their hostility towards Sofya Nikolayevna from their father ; but to their mother and two sisters they described the marriage and events at Ufa in such a way as to fill their minds with a strong prejudice against the bride ; and they did not forget to mention their brother's threats and his fury excited by their attacks upon Sofya Nikolayevna. It was agreed to treat her kindly in the presence of Stepan Mihailovitch, and to say nothing bad about her directly ; at the same time they were to use every opportunity to excite by indirect means his displeasure against their enemy.

It was a highly delicate operation ; and Elizabeth and Alexandra could not trust it in any hands but their own.

My grandfather questioned them minutely about the wedding, the people they had seen there, the health of M. Zubin, and so on. They praised everything, but the poison under their praises could be smelt and tasted, and they failed to deceive their father. By way of a joke, and perhaps also for the sake of comparison, he turned to Karatayeff and said : ' Well now, friend Ivan, what say you of the daughter-in-law ? As a man, you are a better judge of the point than the women are.' Karatayeff, disregarding a signal from his wife, burst out with enthusiasm : ' I do assure you, *batyushka*, that such another dazzler '—he always used this phrase of a beautiful woman—' as brother Alexyéi has bagged is not to be found in the whole world. A look from her is as good as a shilling. And her cleverness ! it 's past all telling. But there 's one thing, *batyushka* : she 's proud : she can't stand a joke. When you try to have a little fun with her, she gives you a look that makes you bite off the end of your tongue.' ' I see, my friend, that she made short work with your nonsense,' said the old man with an amused look ; then he laughed and added, ' Not much amiss there, so far.' In fact, Stepan Mihailovitch, from what he had heard and the bride's letters and Karatayeff's description, had formed in his own mind a highly favourable opinion of Sofya Nikolayevna.

The expected visit of the young couple produced bustle and confusion in the quiet or, one might say, stagnant waters of life at Bagrovo. They had to bestir themselves, to clean things up, and bring

out their best clothes. The bride was a fine town
lady, poor perhaps, but accustomed to live in
luxury ; she would be critical and contemptuous
—so they all thought, and so they all said,
except the master of the house. As there were
no separate rooms in the house unoccupied,
Tanyusha had to turn out of her bedroom, one
corner of which overlooked the garden and the
clear waters of the Boogoorooslan with its green
bushes and loud nightingales. Tanyusha was very
unwilling to move to the bath-house, but there
was no other place ; all her sisters were put up in
the house, and Karatayeff and Yerlykin slept in
the hayloft. The day before the visitors' arrival
brought their state-bed and bed-hangings and
curtains for the windows, and with them a man
who knew how to put everything up properly.
Tanyusha's room was completely furnished in a
few hours. Stepan Mihailovitch came to see it
and expressed his admiration, but the women bit
their lips with envy. At last a messenger galloped
up and announced that the couple had stopped at
the village of Noikino, eight *versts* from Bagrovo ;
they were to change their dress there and would
arrive in two hours. This caused a general stir.
The priest had been summoned hours before ; but
as he had not yet arrived, Stepan Mihailovitch sent
a mounted messenger to hasten his steps.

Meantime the following scene was taking place
in the Mordvinian village of Noikino. The
travellers were making their way along side roads
and had always to send a man ahead to arrange
about fresh horses. The people of Noikino had all
known Alexyéi Stepanitch from childhood, and
had a great regard and respect for his father. Every

one of the six hundred inhabitants of the village,
men and women, old and young, gathered before
the cottage where the young people were to make
their halt.   Sofya Nikolayevna had probably
never seen people of this tribe close at hand ; and
therefore the dress of the women and the uncommonly tall stout girls—their white shifts
embroidered with red wool, their black woollen
girdles, and the silver coins and little bells which
hung from their heads over their breasts and
backs—was very interesting to her.   But when
she heard them all break out into joyful greetings
and compliments and good wishes, childish enough
and expressed in bad Russian, but coming from the
heart, then she both laughed and cried.   ' What
a fine wife God has given you, Alosha ! How glad
our father Stepan Mihailovitch will be ! Good
luck ! Good luck ! '   But when the bride, arrayed
in her fine city clothes, came out to take her seat
in the carriage, there was such a roar of enthusiastic
applause that the horses actually shied.   The
travellers made a present of ten roubles, to be spent
on whisky, to the whole village, and went on their
way.

The stack-yard at Bagrovo was at the top of a
hill, and now the high carriage was seen emerging
from behind it.   The cry, ' They're coming !
They're coming ! ' flew from room to room, and
house-servants and labourers soon gathered in the
large court-yard, while the young people and
children ran to meet the carriage.   The master and
mistress, attended by all their family, came out
upon the steps.   Arina Vassilyevna wore a silk
jacket and skirt and a silk handkerchief adorned
with gold sprigs upon her head ; Stepan Mihailo-

vitch was clean-shaved and wore an old-fashioned
frock-coat and a stock round his neck. Husband
and wife stood on the top step ; and he held in his
hands an ikon representing the Presentation of the
Virgin, while she carried a loaf of bread and a
silver salt-cellar. Their daughters and two sons-
in-law were grouped round them. The carriage
drove up to the steps. The young couple got out,
knelt down before the old people, and received
their blessing ; then they exchanged embraces
with each member of the family. Hardly had the
bride completed this ceremony and turned again
towards her father-in-law, when he caught her by
the hand and looked keenly at her eyes from which
the tears were falling. His own eyes grew wet ;
he clasped her in a tight embrace, kissed her, and
said, ' I thank God. Let us go and thank Him
together ! ' He took her by the hand and led her
through the crowd of people into the parlour.
There he made her sit near him ; and the priest,
who was waiting for them with his robes on,
pronounced the solemn words :

' We praise thee, O God : we acknowledge thee
to be the Lord.'

FRAGMENT IV

THE YOUNG COUPLE AT BAGROVO

STEPAN MIHAILOVITCH joined fervently in the prayers, and so did his daughter-in-law. When the service was over, all kissed the Cross, and the priest sprinkled the young pair and the rest of the company with holy water. Then the kissing and embracing began over again, with the phrases customary on such occasions—' We beg that you will look on us as relations and love us,' and so on— said of course by those to whom the bride was still a stranger. Stepan Mihailovitch said nothing: he only looked affectionately at the tearful eyes and flaming cheeks of Sofya Nikolayevna, listened attentively to every word she spoke, and noted her every movement. Then he took her by the hand and led her to the drawing-room, where he sat down on the sofa and made the pair sit near him. Arina Vassilyevna seated herself next her son at the other end of the sofa, while her daughters with their husbands sat round the central group. It should be said that Stepan Mihailovitch never sat in the drawing-room: he entered it very seldom and never stayed long. There were only two parts of the house which he used—his own room, and the outside stoop, a very simple contrivance of beams and boards; there he was thoroughly at home, but in the drawing-room he was never quite at his ease. For once he put constraint upon himself and carried on a friendly conversation with his daughter-in-law. He began by asking about her

father's health, and expressed sincere regret on
hearing that he grew weaker daily : ' In that
case, my dear,' he said, ' I must not keep you too
long at Bagrovo.' It need not be said that the
bride was at no loss for words : she was not merely
polite, but cordial and eager to make a good
impression. Arina Vassilyevna, naturally a very
simple woman, took her tone from her husband, as
far as her intelligence and her dread of disobeying
her daughters would let her. She was friendly to
her son's wife and had taken a real liking to her
at first sight ; but the others were silent, and it
was not hard to guess their feelings from their
faces. After half an hour the bride whispered to
her husband, who rose at once and went to the
bedroom which had been specially prepared for
them near the drawing-room. Stepan Mihailovitch
looked on with surprise ; but the bride's lively
talk engaged his attention, and he was so much
interested by it that he was startled when presently
the folding doors of the bedroom opened and his
son came in, holding a large silver salver, so loaded
with presents for the family that it actually bent
under their weight. Sofya Nikolayevna sprang to
her feet ; she took from the salver and presented
to her father-in-law a piece of fine English broadcloth, and a waistcoat of watered silk, richly laced
with gold thread and embroidered all over with
spangles ; and she told him quite truly that she
had worked it all with her own hands. Stepan
Mihailovitch looked uneasily at his son standing
with the salver in his arms, but he accepted the
presents graciously and kissed his daughter-in-
law. Next, Arina Vassilyevna was presented with
a silk handkerchief covered with gold embroidery,

to wear over her head, and a complete length of excellent China silk, which even then was considered a rarity ; each sister-in-law received a piece of costly silk, and each of their husbands a piece of English broadcloth ; but these presents were naturally rather less valuable. All got up, kissed the hands of the donor, and bowed their thanks. Meanwhile the door leading to the parlour was cracking with the pressure of curious spectators of both sexes, and the well-oiled heads of the maids kept peeping timidly out of the bedroom door, which they had to themselves, because none of the outdoor servants dared to enter the elegant apartment of the young couple. In the parlour there was a great noise ; for the men-servants were prevented by the intruders from laying the table, and were unable to turn them out. Stepan Mihailovitch guessed what was going on ; he got up and glanced through the door ; one look and one quiet word was enough : ' Off,' he said, and the parlour was empty in a moment.

The dinner passed off in the usual fashion. The young pair sat side by side between the old couple ; there were a great many courses, one richer and more indigestible than another ; the cook, Stepan, had been lavish with his spice, cloves, and pepper, and especially with his butter. The bride ate the dainties pressed upon her by Stepan Mihailovitch, and prayed that she might not die in the night. There was little talking, partly because every mouth was otherwise occupied, and also because the party were not good at conversation. Indeed they were all uncomfortable in their own ways. Yerlykin in his sober intervals drank nothing but water, and hardly spoke at all at such times, which gained him a reputation for exceptional intelligence ; and Karatayeff dared not open his mouth in the presence of Stepan Mihailovitch except to answer a question, and went no farther than repeating the last words of other people's remarks. If they said : ' the hay crop will be good, if we get no rain,' or ' the rye made a good start till that sudden frost came '—Karatayeff came in like an echo, ' if we get no rain,' ' till the frost came ' ; and his repetitions were sometimes ill-timed. As the hosts had not thought of procuring sparkling wine from Ufa, the health of the bride and bridegroom was drunk in strawberry wine, three years old and as thick as oil, which diffused about the room the delicious perfume of the wild strawberry. Mazan, with long boots smelling of tar on his feet, and wearing a long coat which made him look like a bear dressed up in sacking, handed round the loving-cup ; it was ornamented with a white pattern and had a dark-blue spiral inside its glass stalk. When the young pair had to return thanks, Sofya Nikolayevna was not much pleased to drink from the cup which had just left Karatayeff's greasy lips ; but she made no wry faces. Indeed she was intending to drain the cup, when her father-in-law stopped her : ' Don't drink it all, my dear,' he said ; ' the liquor is good and sweet but strong ; you are not accustomed to it, and your little head would ache.' She declared that such a noble drink could not hurt her, and begged to be allowed a little more, till Stepan Mihailovitch allowed her one sip from the cup which he held in his hands.

It was clear to all the family that the old man was pleased with his daughter-in-law and liked all that she said. And she could see this herself, though she had been surprised twice over by a shadow of displeasure passing over his face. But more than once during the meal she had encountered his expressive look, as his eyes rested with satisfaction on her. At last the long and solemn dinner came to an end. Sofya Nikolayevna, unlike the rest, had found this rustic feast very wearisome, but she had done her best to enliven it by cheerful conversation. When they rose from table, his son and daughters kissed their father's hand, and Sofya Nikolayevna tried to do so too, but the old man embraced and kissed her instead. It was the second time this had happened, and Sofya Nikolayevna, with her natural impulsiveness, asked him in a lively affectionate tone : ' Why do you not give me your hand, *batyushka* ? I am your daughter too, and I wish to kiss your hand out of love and respect, like the rest.' The old man looked at her keenly and attentively ; then he said in a kind voice : ' I love you, my dear, but I am not a priest,[1] and no one kisses my hand except my own children.'

The party went back to the drawing-room and sat down where they were before. The maid Aksyutka brought in coffee, which was only served on very solemn occasions ; the old man did not drink it, but all his family were very fond of it ; they always called it ' coff,' never ' coffee.' When it was swallowed, Stepan Mihailovitch rose and said : ' Now it is time to have a good sleep, and the young people too would be none the worse for a rest after their journey ' ; then he went off to his own room, escorted by his son and daughter-in-

---

[1] Devout Russians kiss a priest's hand.

law. ' This is my den, my dear,' said the old man
cheerfully ; ' sit down and be my guest. As your
husband knows, it was an exception for me to sit
in the drawing-room with you all, with this
bearing-rein on as well,' and he pointed to his
stock : ' and in future, if any one wants my
society, I shall welcome them here.' Then he
kissed her, gave his hand to his son to kiss, and let
them go. When alone, he undressed and lay down
to rest from the unusual bodily exertions and mental
excitement of the day. He was soon sound asleep ;
and his powerful snoring echoed through the house
and swayed to and fro the curtains which Mazan
had drawn round his old master.

His example was followed by the rest. Yerlykin
and Karatayeff went off to the stable to lie down
on the hay-mow ; both their faces showed that
they had done well at dinner, and Karatayeff had
also drunk too much. The daughters assembled
in their mother's room which was separate from
their father's ; and now began such a debate and
discussion, carried on in whispers, that not one of
the party even lay down to sleep that afternoon.
Poor Sofya Nikolayevna was their theme, and her
sisters-in-law simply tore her to pieces ; they were
enraged beyond all bounds by their father's
evident partiality for her. But there was one kind
heart there—Aksinya, the eldest sister, who was
now a widow for the second time ; she stood up
for Sofya Nikolayevna and brought down their
wrath on her own head : they turned her out of
the room and banished her for the future from
their family councils ; and to her old nickname of
' Miss Simplicity,' they now added another
offensive title which she still bore in advanced old

age. Yet, for all the persecution of her sisters, her
kind heart never swerved from its devotion to her
sister-in-law.

Meanwhile the young pair went off to their own
fine bedroom. With the help of her own maid
Parasha, a brisk black-eyed girl, Sofya Nikolayevna unpacked the large number of boxes and
trunks which the English coach had brought from
Ufa. Parasha was able already to run through a
list of outdoor servants and old people among the
peasants who deserved special notice ; and her
mistress, who had brought with her a goodly store
of trifles, fixed the present to be given to each,
taking account of their age and services and the
respect which their owners had for them. The
husband and wife were not tired and did not think
it necessary to rest. Sofya Nikolayevna changed
into a simpler dress, and left Parasha to finish the
unpacking and arrangement of the bedroom, while
she went out with her young husband, who was
very anxious, in spite of the heat, to show her all
his favourite haunts—the beech-wood, the island
with its lime-trees just coming into leaf, and the
transparent waters of the river where it made a
bend round the island. And how delightful it was
there at that season, when the freshness of spring
combines with the warmth of summer ! Alexyéi
Stepanitch was passionately in love with his
adored wife, and time had not yet blunted the
edge of his happiness ; but he was disconcerted
to find that she was not charmed either by wood
or island, and indeed took little notice of either.
She sat down in the shade on the bank of the rapid
river, and began at once to speak to her husband
of his relations. She discussed their reception.

' I like your father so much,' she went on, ' and
I could see at the first glance that he liked me ;
perhaps your mother liked me, but she seemed
afraid to show it. Aksinya seems the kindest of
them, but she is afraid of something too. Oh, I
understand it all perfectly ; I know in what
quarter the damp wood is smouldering. I did not
miss a single word or a single glance ; I know
what I am bound to expect. God will judge your
sisters, Elizabeth and Alexandra ! ' But Alexyéi
Stepanitch was hardly listening to her words. The
fresh shade, the green of the boughs bending over
the stream, the low ripple of the running water,
the fish jumping, his adored wife sitting beside him
with one arm round his waist—in such surroundings how was it possible to find fault or make
objections or express discontent ? How was it
possible even to take in what was said ? And in
fact Alexyéi Stepanitch did not take in what his
young wife was saying to him : he was so happy
that nothing but silence and oblivion of the world
around him could serve as a full expression of his
intoxicating bliss. But Sofya Nikolayevna went
on : she said a great deal, with warmth and
feeling ; and then she noticed that her husband
was not listening and was nearly asleep. She
sprang up at once, and then followed a scene of
conflict and mutual misunderstanding, more pronounced than any they had ever had before,
though there had been premonitory symptoms
once or twice already. Sofya Nikolayevna kept
nothing back this time : the tears rushed from her
eyes as she poured forth a torrent of reproaches
for his indifference and inattention. Alexyéi
Stepanitch was puzzled and distressed : he felt as

if he had fallen from the skies or awakened from a delightful dream. Thinking to calm his wife, he assured her with perfect sincerity, that there was nothing wrong at all, that it was all her imagination, and that all the family loved her; how could any one help loving her, he asked. That he was honestly convinced of this was clear as day; and his eyes and face and voice all expressed his devoted love for his wife; yet Sofya Nikolayevna, for all her cleverness and lively sensibility, did not understand her husband, and found in his words only a fresh proof of the same indifference and inattention. Statements and explanations went on with increasing heat, and I do not know how far they would have gone; but suddenly Alexyéi Stepanitch caught sight of his sister Tatyana's maid crossing the high gangway and hastening towards them. He guessed that they were being searched for because his father had got up, and told his wife at once what he feared. She regained her self-control in a moment, caught his arm, and hastened home with him; but he was not in good spirits as he walked beside her.

Preparations had been made beforehand at Bagrovo to celebrate the day of the young people's arrival by an entertainment given to the outdoor servants and all the serfs on the estate; and if serfs from neighbouring estates chose to come on foot or on wheels, they were welcome too. A quantity of beer had been brewed, and some twenty buckets of strong home-made spirits distilled; and drinking vessels of all kinds were ready. Before he lay down after dinner, Stepan Mihailovitch had asked whether many had come from the neighbouring villages. When he was told that the whole population, from the old men and women to the babies, had assembled, he smiled and said, ' Well, we shall not stint them ; tell the house-keeper and steward to have everything ready.' He did not sleep long, but he woke in even better spirits than when he lay down. ' Is all ready ? ' he asked at once, and was told that all was ready long ago. The old man dressed quickly ; instead of his ceremonial frock-coat, he put on his familiar dressing-gown of fine camel's hair, and went out to the stoop to superintend the entertainment in person. On the broad lawn, which was not fenced off from the road, tables had been put up on trestles, and the tables were laden with barrels of beer, casks of whisky, and piles of buns to eat with the liquor ; these buns, made of wheat-flour, were cut in halves. The outdoor servants stood in a group apart near the house ; a great crowd of serfs and their wives stood farther off, and beyond them a still greater crowd of Mordvinians of both sexes. Stepan Mihailovitch threw a hasty glance over the scene, saw that all was in order, and went back to his stoop. The family had collected round him, and he was just going to ask where the young couple were, when they appeared together. He greeted his daughter-in-law even more affectionately than before, and treated her with no more formality than if she had been his own daughter. ' Now then, Alosha,' he said, ' take your wife's arm and lead her round to greet the people ; they are all anxious to see her and kiss the hand of their young mistress. Let us start ! ' He went in front himself ; then came Alexyéi Stepanitch, leading his wife, and last, at a little distance, Arina Vassilyevna with her daughters and their husbands.

The sisters-in-law, except Aksinya, found it hard
to restrain their wrath. The signs of growing
affection on their father's part, his mention of
Sofya Nikolayevna as 'the young mistress,' the
triumph of this hated intruder, her beauty and
pretty clothes, her ready easy tongue, her charming
respect and affection for her father-in-law—all
these things rankled in their jealous bosoms. They
felt at once that they had sunk in importance.
'It matters less to us,' whispered Alexandra : 'we
are severed branches ; but I can't look at Tanyusha
without crying. She is nothing now in the household but Sofya Nikolayevna's maid. And you,
mother—no one will respect you any more :
the servants will all look to her for orders.'
Her voice shook, and the tears gathered in her
round rolling eyes. Meanwhile Stepan Mihailovitch had got to the outdoor servants and was
calling the peasants to come nearer : 'Why don't
you all stand together ? You all belong to the
same family. Well,' he went on, 'here you see
your young mistress ; the young master you know
already. When the time comes, serve them as
faithfully and zealously as you have served me and
Arina Vassilyevna, and you will earn their love and
favour.' All the people bowed to the ground. The
bride, unaccustomed to such demonstrations, felt
disconcerted, not knowing where to go or what to
do. Noticing this, her father-in-law said : 'Don't
be frightened ! Their heads may bend, but they
won't come off. Well, my friends, first kiss your
young mistress's hand, and then drink to her
health.' The people all got up and came near
Sofya Nikolayevna. She looked round and signed
to her man Theodore and handy Parasha, who

were standing on one side, holding the presents.
In a moment they handed her a large parcel and a
well-filled box. It felt strange to her to stretch
out her hand to be kissed while standing motionless
as a statue ; and she began to kiss them all herself.
This ceremony was repeated, as each received a
gift from her hands. But Stepan Mihailovitch
interfered at this point : he saw that at that rate
he would not get his tea till supper-time. ' My
dear,' he said, ' you can't possibly kiss them all
once, let alone twice ! There are too many. The
old people are a different matter ; but it will be
enough if they kiss your hand.' This simplified
and shortened the rather tiresome ceremony, but
even so it lasted a long time. Stepan Mihailovitch
sometimes spun it out himself, because he could
not refrain from naming some of the people and
praising them to her. Many of the old people
spoke some simple words of love and devotion,
some shed tears, and all looked at the bride with
pleasure and cordiality. Sofya Nikolayevna was
much moved. ' These good people are ready to
love me, and some love me already,' she thought ;
' how have I deserved it ? ' At last, when young
and old had kissed her hand and she had kissed
some of them, and when all had received handsome
presents, Stepan Mihailovitch took her hand and
led her to the crowd of Mordvinians. ' I am glad
to see you, neighbours,' he cried in a hearty cheerful voice ; ' and thank you for coming. I ask your
goodwill for this young lady who is coming to live
near you. You are welcome to eat and drink what
God has given us.' The Mordvinians showed their
pleasure by shouting, ' Many thanks, Stepan
Mihailovitch ! Thank God, for giving such a wife

to your son! You deserve such luck for your
goodness, Stepan Mihailovitch.'

When the drinking began, Stepan Mihailovitch,
surrounded by his family, hastened back to his
beloved stoop. He was conscious that his tea-
time was long past : it was now past seven, and
tea was invariably served at six. The long shadow
of the house was sloping towards the south, and
its edges touched the storehouse and stable ; the
samovar had long been hissing on a large table close
to the stoop, and Aksyutka was in attendance.
While the rest sat down round the table, Stepan
Mihailovitch stuck to his favourite place : he first
spread out his invariable woollen mat to sit on, and
then sat down on the stoop. Tatyana, assisted by
Aksyutka, poured out tea. Then Sofya Nikolayevna asked leave of her father-in-law to sit
beside him, and he consented with obvious satisfaction. She sprang up from the table, carried
her half finished cup of tea to the stoop, and sat
down beside the old man. He caressed her and
ordered a mat to be put down for her, that she
might not spoil her dress. Then they began a
lively cheerful talk ; but at the tea-table angry
looks and even whispers were exchanged, in spite
of the presence of the young husband. He could
not help noticing this, and his spirits, which had
not been high before, fell yet lower. Suddenly
the old man's loud voice rang out : ' Come and
join us, Alosha ; it 's livelier over here.' Alosha
started ; but the change of place seemed to im-
prove his spirits. When tea was over, they remained where they were and went on talking till
supper, which was served at nine—an hour later
than usual. All the time the loud singing and

hearty laughter of the revellers rang out far and wide as the darkness slowly gathered round ; but they all departed to their own homes as soon as the family had finished supper. On saying 'goodnight' Sofya Nikolayevna asked her father-in-law to give her his blessing, and the old man at once signed her with the Cross and kissed her with a father's tenderness.

The young couple were escorted to their room by the lady of the house and her eldest daughter, who sat there a few minutes ; and then it was the turn of Alexyéi Stepanitch to escort his mother and sister to rest. Sofya Nikolayevna hastily dismissed her maid and sat down by one of the open windows fronting the river, which was fringed at that point by a thick border of osier and alder. It was a lovely night : the freshness from the river and the scent of the young leaves came through the open windows, together with the trills and calls of the nightingales. But Sofya Nikolayevna had something else to think of. As a clever woman who knew in advance what awaited her in her husband's family, she had naturally formed a plan of action beforehand. She had always lived in a town and had no conception of the sort of life led by landowners of moderate means on their scattered estates in that vast country. She had not expected much, but the reality was far worse than she had imagined. Nothing was to her taste, neither house, nor garden, nor wood, nor island. In the neighbourhood of Ufa she had been accustomed to admire noble views from the mountainous bank of the river Byélaya ; and this little village in a hollow, the time-stained and weatherbeaten wooden house, the pond surrounded by swamps, and the unending clack of the mill—all this seemed to her actually repulsive. And the people were no better : from her husband's family to the peasants' children, she could love none of them. But there was one exception, and that was Stepan Mihailovitch. But for him, she would have been in despair. She had formed a favourable opinion of him from the beginning ; then, when she first saw him, she was frightened by his rough exterior ; but she soon read in his intelligent eyes and kindly smile, and heard in his voice, that this old man had a tender heart which beat kindly to her, that he was ready to love her and would love her. Knowing from the first that all her hopes depended upon him, she had firmly resolved to gain his love by all means ; but now she had learnt to love him herself, and her deliberate plan coincided with the impulse of her heart. In this respect Sofya Nikolayevna was satisfied with herself : she saw that she had reached her goal at once. But she was distressed by the thought that by her impetuosity she had hurt her kind husband. She waited impatiently for him, but as if to spite her, he did not return. Had she known where he was, she would have hurried off in search of him long ago. She longed to throw herself into his arms and beg his forgiveness with tears, and to remove the last trace of dissatisfaction from his mind by a torrent of loving words and caresses. But Alexyéi Stepanitch still did not return ; and the happy moment, when she was penitent and loving and filled with a passionate desire to atone for her faults, went by to no purpose. An impulse soon passes, and Sofya Nikolayevna first grew alarmed and then angry at her husband's long

absence. When he came in at last, looking rather
upset and distressed, instead of rushing into his
arms and begging to be forgiven, his wife called
out to him in an excited and somewhat irritated
voice, as soon as he crossed the threshold : ' Where
on earth have you been ? Why did you leave me
alone ? I am quite worn out with waiting for you
two whole hours ! ' ' I sat a quarter of an hour or
so with my mother and sisters,' he answered. ' And
that was time enough for them to complain of me
and invent calumnies against me, and you believed
them ! Why are you so depressed and sad ? '
Sofya Nikolayevna's face expressed strong emotion,
and her beautiful eyes filled with tears. The young
husband was startled and even alarmed ; he was
beginning to dread her tears. ' Sonitchka,' he
said, ' calm yourself ; no one complained of you ;
why should they, when you have injured no one ? '
This was not quite a true statement. If nobody
had complained openly or attacked her in plain
terms, they had implied by hints and allusions that
his wife was singling out her father-in-law to pay
court to, with the object of trampling on the rest
of the family ; but they saw through her tricks,
and so would her husband some day when he found
himself under her feet ! Alexyéi Stepanitch did
not believe these innuendoes ; but the feeling of
sadness, which had never left him since the scene
on the island, became heavier and lay like lead on
his kind heart. He only said, ' It is no use talking
like that,' and left the room. But instead of
returning at once to his bedroom, he spent some
time in walking alone up and down the parlour
which was now dark and empty. Through the
seven open windows he looked at the Jackdaw

Wood sleeping in darkness, and at the dark line
of trees by the river, the scene of his childhood's
amusements and occupations ; and he listened
to the sound of the mill, the whistles of the nightingales, and the screeching of the owls. Feeling
somewhat relieved, he went off to the bedroom,
entirely unconscious of the reception he was to
meet there.

But Sofya Nikolayevna soon grew calmer :
the voice of penitence began to speak again in
her heart, though not with the same force as
before ; she changed her tone and turned to her
husband with a genuine feeling of love and pity ;
she caressed him and begged his forgiveness. She
spoke with unfeigned warmth of her happiness in
finding that she loved his father, and begged him
to be perfectly frank with her : frankness, she said,
was essential between them. Her husband was
soothed and comforted ; and in the fullness of his
heart he told her all he had determined to keep
secret at all costs, lest he should make a quarrel
between his wife and his sisters. He lay down and
went to sleep at once, but Sofya Nikolayevna lay
awake for long, and her brain worked busily. At
last she remembered that she had to get up early,
because she intended to join her father-in-law on
the stoop at sunrise, long before the family assembled ; she wished to cheer the old man by her
presence and to speak her mind to him at leisure.
At last, with a strong effort, she fell asleep.

Sofya Nikolayevna woke with the first rays of
the sun. Though she had not slept long, she rose
fresh and vigorous. She dressed quickly, kissed
her husband and told him she was going to his
father, and he might sleep on another hour or so,

and then hurried off. Stepan Mihailovitch, after sleeping longer than usual, had just washed himself and gone out to the stoop. It was a lovely May morning, with all the charm of late spring, fresh and yet deliciously warm; all living things sang together for joy, and the long morning shadows still hid the coolness and moisture from the conquering rays of the sun. The feeling of the morning took hold of Sofya Nikolayevna and breathed life into her, though she was not accustomed to be moved by natural beauty or the charms of the country. Her father-in-law was surprised and pleased to see her. Her fresh face and shining eyes, her neat hair and pretty dress, made it impossible to guess that she had sprung out of bed after little sleep and had spent but little time over her toilet before she hurried out. Stepan Mihailovitch liked people to be lively and quick and clever : and all these requirements he was pleased to find in Sofya Nikolayevna. He kissed her and said good-humouredly : 'What made you get up so early? You can't have had your sleep out. I'm sure you're not accustomed to rise so early; you will have a headache.' 'No, *batyushka*', she replied, embracing the old man with genuine tenderness; 'I am used to early rising. From childhood I have had much to do and many cares, with a sick father and a whole family to look after. Of late I have been spoilt and have lain in bed longer. But I woke early this morning, and Alexyéi told me '—here the old man frowned— 'that you were up already; so I came out here, hoping that you would not drive me away but allow me to give you your tea.' The words were ordinary enough, but they came from the heart and were spoken so earnestly that the old man was touched. He kissed her forehead and said : ' Well, in that case, thank you, my dear child. You shall give me my tea, and we will have a leisurely talk together.' Aksyutka had already set the samovar on the table. Stepan Mihailovitch gave orders that no one else should be called, and Sofya Nikola-yevna began to arrange about the tea. All her actions were as quick and neat as if she had done nothing else all her life. The old man was pleased, as he watched that young and pretty figure, so unlike what he was accustomed to, and those busy active fingers. The tea was made strong, and served exactly as he liked it : that is, the teapot, covered with a napkin, was placed on the top of the samovar ; his cup was filled close up to the brim ; Sofya Nikolayevna handed it without spilling a single drop in the saucer ; and the fragrant beverage was so hot that it burnt his lips. The old man took his cup and tasted the tea. With surprise and pleasure he said : ' I declare you are a witch : you know all my tastes and fancies. Well, if you make yourself as pleasant to your husband, he will be a happy man.' He generally drank his tea alone, and the family did not begin theirs till he had finished ; but this morning, when he had got his second cup, he told his daughter-in-law to pour one out for herself and drink it sitting beside him. ' I never drink more than two, but I will take a third cup to-day ; the tea tastes better somehow,' he said in the kindest of tones. And indeed, the pleasure which Sofya Nikolayevna felt in her occupa-tion was so visible on her expressive face that it could not but communicate itself to the susceptible nature of Stepan Mihailovitch ; and his spirits rose

unusually high. He made her take a second cup
and eat a scone, of the kind for which the ovens at
Bagrovo were long famous. The tea was cleared
away, and a conversation began, most lively and
animated, most frank and affectionate. Sofya
Nikolayevna gave free course to her eager feelings ;
she talked easily and charmingly ; her conquest
of the old man was complete. In the middle of
their talk he suddenly asked, ' What of your
husband ? Is he asleep ? ' 'Alexyéi was waking
when I left him,' she said quickly ; ' but I told him
to sleep on.' The old man frowned severely and
was silent. After a moment's reflection, he spoke,
not angrily but seriously. ' Listen to me, my dear
little daughter-in-law ; you are so clever that I can
tell you the truth without beating about the bush.
I don't like to keep a thing on my mind. If you
take my advice—well and good ; if you don't—
well, you are not my daughter and can please
yourself. I don't like your calling your husband
" Alexyéi," as his parents might ; he has got
another name ; [1] " Alexyéi " is a name you might
address to a servant. A wife must treat her husband with respect, if she wishes other people to
respect him. There was another thing yesterday
I did not like : you sent him to fetch the presents,
and he stood there holding the tray like a footman.
Then again just now, you said you had " told "
him to go to sleep. A wife ought not to give orders
to her husband ; if she does, mischief comes of it.
That may be the fashion with you in the town,
but according to our old-fashioned country
notions, all that is a great mistake.' Sofya Nikola-

---

[1] i. e. Stepánitch, son of Stephen, which should be used
in public by the wife.

yevna listened respectfully, and then she spoke, so frankly and feelingly, that every word made its way to the old man's heart : 'I thank you, *batyushka*, for not keeping back from me what displeased you. I shall gladly do what you wish, and I begin to see myself that I was wrong. I am still young, *batyushka*, and I have had no one to guide me : my own father has not left his bed for six years. I caught up that way of addressing my husband from others ; but it shall never happen again, either in your presence or behind your back. *Batyushka*,' she went on, and the large tears welled from her eyes, 'I have come to love you like a father ; treat me always as a daughter : stop me, scold me, whenever I do wrong, but forgive me and do not keep displeasure in your heart against me. I am young and hasty, and I may go wrong at every step. Remember that I am a stranger in this house, where nobody knows me and I know nobody. Do not you fail me.' Then she fell on his neck and embraced him like a daughter, kissing his breast and even his hands ; and the old man's own eyes filled with tears. He let her keep hold of his hands and said, 'Well, that is all right.' As we know already, Stepan Mihailovitch had a natural sagacity which divined the presence of evil and was attracted by goodness ; and he never made a mistake in either case. He had taken a fancy to his daughter-in-law at first sight ; and now that he understood her and appreciated her, he loved her for better and for worse. That love was exposed to many trials in later years, and any other man might have wavered, but he never wavered in his love for her to his last breath.

Alexyéi Stepanitch soon appeared, and was

followed by all the family. Her daughters had urged Arina Vassilyevna to go out long before, but she did not dare to appear, because, when Stepan Mihailovitch gave orders 'that no one should be called,' it was taken to mean that he did not wish to see anyone. She only came out now because her husband had told Mazan to summon all the family. There was no trace of tears on Sofya Nikolayevna's face; and she greeted the newcomers with more than usual cordiality. Nor could one tell from Stepan Mihailovitch that anything unusual had happened; but the bride could not conceal her high spirits, and the two sisters-in-law noticed this at once and guessed the alarming truth pretty accurately.

Stepan Mihailovitch had settled that the young couple were to visit their relations in order of seniority; and it was therefore arranged that they should go to Aksinya's house next day. Aksinya herself went home that afternoon, accompanied by her sister Elizabeth, who was to help her in entertaining the guests. The distance was only 50 *versts*, and the strong Bagrovo horses could go all the way without baiting. The start was fixed for six o'clock next morning.

Stepan Mihailovitch did not in the least conceal his feeling towards his daughter-in-law. He kept her beside him and talked with her repeatedly, asking questions about her family affairs, or making her speak of her life at Ufa; and he listened to her with attentive interest, now and then giving his opinion in some pithy phrase. She eagerly caught up his pertinent remarks; but it was clear that she was moved, not by obsequious concurrence with the old man's ways of thinking, but by a full

comprehension of his words and a conviction of
their truth. Then in his turn he initiated her into
the past and present history of her new relations ;
and his whole description was so simple and true,
so frank and lifelike, that she realized it as few
could have done, and was charmed by it. Never
in her life had she met his equal. Her own father
was intelligent and kind, emotional and unselfish ;
but at the same time he was weak, falling in with
the prevailing tone of his surroundings, and bearing
the stamp of the evasive time-serving official who
had worked his way up from a clerk's stool to the
position of Governor's Deputy. Here she saw
before her an old man of little education and un-
couth exterior, and report said of him that he was
ruthless when angry ; and yet he was sensible
and kind, honest and inflexible in his clear judgement of right and wrong—a man who was upright
in all his actions and truthful in every word he
spoke. Her quick intellect conceived a noble type
of manly worth, which set aside her old ideas and
opened up new possibilities. And what happiness
that this man was her husband's father ! On him
depended her peace of mind in her husband's
family, and perhaps even the happiness of her
marriage !

Dinner was a much more lively and cheerful
affair than on the previous day. The bride sat as
before between her husband and her father-in-law ;
but Arina Vassilyevna now took her usual place
opposite Stepan Mihailovitch. Immediately after
dinner, Aksinya left, accompanied by her sister
Elizabeth. As the old man was lying down to rest
as usual, he said, ' Well, Arisha, I think God has
given us a splendid daughter-in-law ; it would be

a sin not to take her to our hearts.' 'True indeed, Stepan Mihailovitch,' she answered; 'if you approve of Sofya Nikolayevna, of course I do.' The old man made a wry face but said nothing; and she hurried away, fearing to make a slip of the tongue, and anxious to report to her daughters the remarkable words of Stepan Mihailovitch, which must be accepted as law and obeyed, in appearance at least, to the letter.

Though she had slept little at night, Sofya Nikolayevna could not sleep after dinner. She went out with her husband, and they walked, by his wish, to the old beech-wood where the jack-daws built, and down the course of the river. There was no repetition of the old disagreements. She had been charmed and captivated by her father-in-law, and she now tried to convey to her husband the feelings of her own eager impression-able mind. As all people of her temperament are apt to do, she transferred to her handsome young husband some part of the merits she had found in his father, and loved him more than ever. He listened with surprise and pleasure to the enthu-siasm of his beautiful wife, and said to himself, 'Thank God that my father and she have become such friends! There will be no further trouble.' He kissed her hands, and said that he was the happiest man on all the earth, and she a peerless goddess before whom all should bow down. He did not quite understand his wife nor appreciate her estimate of his father, so acute and profound; he only felt, as he had always felt, perfectly con-vinced that Stepan Mihailovitch was the kind of man whom all must respect and even fear. This time Sofya Nikolayevna found no faults: his

feelings were her feelings and his language hers :
she praised the deep river and the beech-wood
with all its uneven stumps ; even of her sisters-in-
law she spoke kindly.

When he woke up in the afternoon, Stepan
Mihailovitch at once summoned all the family.
It was a long time since he had been seen in such
a bright and gentle mood : whether it was due to
a good sleep or to happy feelings, it was clear to
every one that the old master was satisfied and
cheerful beyond his wont. After their father's
pronouncement, Alexandra and Elizabeth were on
their guard, while Tanyusha (as she was always
called) and her mother were very willing to be
more friendly and conversational. At a sign from
his wife, Karatayeff began with more boldness
to echo what was said, even when he was not
addressed ; but his brother in law, the General,
persisted in his gloomy silence and frowned
significantly. The conversation became unusually
brisk and animated. The old man expressed a
wish to have his tea early, in the shade near the
stoop, of course ; and the privilege of pouring it
out was conferred on Sofya Nikolayevna exclu-
sively. Tanyusha was quite willing to hand over
the office. After tea Stepan Mihailovitch ordered
two cars to be brought round, took his daughter-
in-law in one, and drove off with all his family to
the mill. It should be said that a mill was a special
hobby of my grandfather's, and that he understood
the working of it thoroughly. The mill itself was
not much to look at, and the weed grew round it
in an untidy way ; but the stones did their work
thoroughly well. He liked to show off his mill, and
now displayed it in detail to his daughter-in-law,

taking pleasure in her utter ignorance and astonishment, which sometimes turned to fear, when he suddenly turned on a strong current of water upon all the four wheels, till the machinery began to move and swing and rattle, the stones to whirl round, creaking and whizzing, and the building, filled with flour-dust, to quiver and shake under foot. All this was an entire novelty to Sofya Nikolayevna, and she did not like it at all, though out of politeness she asked many questions and expressed surprise and admiration at everything. He was much pleased, and kept her there a long time. When the pair went out upon the dam, where Alexyéi Stepanitch and his sisters were fishing, they were hailed with laughter by the anglers : they were both covered with flour. Stepan Mihailovitch was accustomed to this ; besides he had given a shake and a brush to his clothes on leaving the mill ; but Sofya Nikolayevna had no suspicion that she was so completely and artistically powdered. When he looked at her, her father-in-law himself laughed heartily ; and she laughed more than any one, and was very merry, regretting only that she had no looking-glass to consult, to find out if her ball-dress became her. Seeing the anglers intent upon their sport, Stepan Mihailovitch next drove his companion round the pond and over the bridge ; and after visiting the stream higher up, he came back along the dam to the place where the anglers were engaged, while Arina Vassilyevna, who was very stout, sat on the ground and watched them. The whole course of their drive was over bog and swamp ; it was hardly safe to cross the crazy little bridge, and difficult to make way over the dam which was made of manure

and sank under the wheels. Though Sofya
Nikolayevna found all this distasteful, it was
impossible for Stepan Mihailovitch to detect it.
He saw neither mire nor swamp, and he was im-
pervious to the unpleasant smell from the stagnant
water and the material of the dam. He had
planned and constructed it all himself, and he
enjoyed it all. It grew damp at sunset, and all set
off for home in good spirits. The anglers carried
their spoil with them, perch and other kinds. The
bailiff was waiting for his master by the stoop;
and orders were given about work on the land,
while the bride put her dress in order. Meanwhile
the fish was boiled or fried in sour cream, while the
largest perch were baked in their skins and scales;
and all these were pronounced very good at supper.

So the second day passed, and the party broke
up soon, because the young couple had to make
an early start next morning for their visit. When
alone with her mother and youngest sister, Alexandra threw off the mask with relief and gave full
play to her infernal temper and cruel tongue. She
saw perfectly that all was lost and all her forebodings realized : that her father was taken in the
toils and infatuated with the adventuress, and
there was nothing to be done now except to dismiss
the pair to Ufa as soon as possible and devise some
scheme in their absence. She abused her mother
and sister for being too affectionate. 'But for
me,' she said, ' you would have been taken in too
by that dressed-up doll, that pauper with a Cossack
for her grandfather.'

At six exactly next morning the young couple
started in their English coach drawn by six of the
fine horses bred at Bagrovo. Sofya Nikolayevna

was up in time to give his tea to her father-in-law ; and he embraced her at starting, and even signed her with the Cross, because she was to be absent for the night. They drove down the river and across it, and then uphill to the little town of Boogoorooslan. Without a halt our travellers crossed the river Great Kinel, and the horses trotted at the rate of ten *versts* an hour along the rutty road on the flat side of the river, where the grass grew tall and thick and there was no sign of habitation. It was long since Alexyéi Stepanitch had been across the Kinel ; and he was delighted by the greenness and fragrance of the steppe. Bustards constantly rose off the road, and solitary snipe kept up with the carriage, wheeling over it and flying on ahead, or perching on the guide-posts and filling the air with their notes. Alexyéi Stepanitch was very sorry that he had not taken his gun. In those days the steppe was alive with birds of every kind, and the sound of their myriad voices was so attractive to him, and indeed absorbed his attention so completely, that his ears were generally deaf to the lively and clever conversation of his wife. She soon noticed this and became thoughtful ; her high spirits gave place to displeasure, and she began to talk to her maid Parasha, who was with them in the coach. After crossing a district of high level land, they arrived at their destination exactly at noon. The little wooden house, an even greater contrast than Bagrovo to the houses of Ufa, stood on the flat bank of the Little Kinel, divided from it only by a kitchen-garden containing a few sunflowers and young vegetables and rows of peeled pea-stakes. I still recall with pleasure this unpretending spot,

which I first saw ten years after this time ; and
I understand why my father liked it and my mother
was bound to dislike it. It was a bare empty place,
quite flat and fully exposed to the sun, without
a bush or a tree ; the level steppe with its marmot-
burrows lay all around ; and the quiet river flowed
by, deep in places and overgrown with reeds. It
had nothing striking or picturesque to attract any
one ; yet Alexyéi Stepanitch preferred it even to
Bagrovo. I don't agree with him, but I had a
strong liking for that quiet little house on the river-
bank, the clear stream, the weed swaying in the
current, the wide stretch of grassy steppe, and the
ferry which started from close to the door and
took you across to a yet wilder steppe, where the
prairie-grass stretched straight southwards to what
seemed an illimitable distance.

The hostess, with her two little boys and a
daughter of two years old, met her guests at the
door ; her sister Elizabeth and her husband were
there also. In spite of the unpromising aspect
of the simple rooms, everything was very clean
and nice, much more so indeed than at Bagrovo.
Though ' Miss Simplicity,' as her sisters called her,
was a widow with small children, there was a neat-
ness and order in the place which showed that it
was managed entirely by a female hand. I have
said already that Aksinya was a kind woman and
had taken a fancy to her sister-in-law ; it was
therefore very natural that she should do honour to
her guests and receive them with cordiality in her
own house. This had been foreseen at Bagrovo,
and Elizabeth had been sent on purpose to restrain
the excessive friendliness of her sister by means of
her superior intelligence and higher position in

society, due to her husband's rank. But that
simple soul held out against her clever cunning
sister : to all her urgent admonitions her answer
was short and plain : ' Do as you please at Bagrovo;
you may hate and abuse Sofya Nikolayevna, but
I like her ; she has always been polite and kind
to me, and therefore I intend to make her and my
brother happy in my house.' And she carried out
her purpose with sincere affection and satisfaction,
showing every attention to her sister-in-law and
pressing her good things on both guests. But the
proud Elizabeth and even her husband—though
he drank so much towards evening that he had to
be shut up in an empty bath-house—were much
colder and more distant in their behaviour than at
Bagrovo. Sofya Nikolayevna took no notice of
them, and was charming to her hostess and the
children. After dinner the party rested for a little
and then went out for a walk by the river ; they
crossed by a ferry to the far bank and drank tea
there. Sofya Nikolayevna was asked to fish, but
she declined, saying that she hated fishing and was
quite happy sitting with her sisters-in-law. But
Alexyéi Stepanitch, much pleased to see how well
his wife got on with his eldest sister, eagerly
accepted the proposal and sat till supper-time on
the bank, hidden in the thick reeds ; he landed
several of the large bream which abounded in the
quiet waters of the Kinel. The servants used
constantly to fish, for their own amusement and
for that of their young masters. The guests determined to start next morning at six, and were half
inclined to depart even earlier, so as not to keep
Stepan Mihailovitch waiting for his dinner. Their
hostess and her sister were to wait till the evening,

spending a night at Boogoorooslan to rest the horses, and reaching Bagrovo the following day.

Sofya Nikolayevna was still a little vexed with her husband. For all her intelligence she could not understand how a man who loved her dearly could also love his damp Bagrovo, with its stump-strewn woods, unsavoury dam, and stagnant pools ; how he could gaze with delight at the tiresome steppe with its stupid snipe ; and, above all, how he could desert his wife for hours for the sake of a fishing-rod and those bream which smelt so damp and disgusting ! So she felt almost offended when Alexyéi Stepanitch tried to communicate to her his delight in nature and in sport. She was wise enough, however, not to start upon explanations or reproofs this time ; the scene on the island was still fresh in her memory.

The young couple passed a peaceful night in Aksinya's own bedroom which she had given up to them ; and she had done it up for them to the best of her ability, undeterred by the caustic remarks of her sister. They left the house half an hour earlier than the time originally fixed ; and nothing particular happened on their way back, except that Alexyéi Stepanitch was not quite so much absorbed by the steppe and the snipe, and did not call out quite so loud when bustards rose off the road, so that he could listen with more attention to his wife and look at her more tenderly. They reached Bagrovo before they were expected. But preparations were making for dinner, and Alexandra had had time to say : ' Poor papa will have to wait for dinner to-day ; but how can you expect town-people to get up so early several days running ? ' The old man saw through this perfectly.

He astonished them all by saying very good-humouredly, ' Well, never mind ; we can wait for our guests.' This caused a sensation, because Stepan Mihailovitch had never in his life sat down to dinner later than twelve o'clock, though sometimes, when he felt hungry, he had it earlier, and the slightest delay or unpunctuality made him exceedingly angry. ' You see what Sofya Nikolayevna can do,' whispered Alexandra to her mother and youngest sister ; ' if *she* keeps him waiting, there is no complaint ; but if you had come back from Nyeklyoodovo late for dinner, you would never have heard the end of it, nor should we.' The malicious whisper was hardly ended when the carriage dashed up to the steps ; while the tired horses snorted, the old man kissed his daughter-in-law and praised her for being in time ; then his voice rang through the house, ' Mazan, Tanaichon-ok, dinner at once ! '

The day passed off as before. After tea Stepan Mihailovitch, whose affection for his daughter-in-law seemed to grow with every hour, ordered the drove of horses to be driven in from the steppe. He wished to show it to Sofya Nikolayevna, who happened to say that she had never seen such a thing and would like to see it. When the animals were driven into the yard, the old man took his daughter-in-law round himself, pointing out the best brood-mares, the yearlings and two-year-olds and young geldings, all fat and healthy from the steppe where they grazed together all summer. He gave her two fine mares with foals at foot, and hoped she would have good fortune with their stock. Sofya Nikolayevna was much pleased by the foals, and liked to watch them as they started and bounded and then nuzzled against their mothers ; and she expressed much gratitude for the gift. Then Stepan Mihailovitch gave strict orders to his head groom, Spirka : ' See,' he said, ' that extra care is taken of Sofya Nikolayevna's mares ; and we shall put a special mark on the foals by splitting one ear rather lower ; and later we must make a brand with the young mistress's name on it.' Then he turned to her : ' I wish you were a lover of horses, my dear,' he went on ; ' Alexyéi does not care for them in the least.' The old man was very fond of them himself ; and though he was not rich, by endless trouble he had got together a large stud and owned a breed which was the admiration of fanciers and good judges. He was pleased by her interest in his stud ; though her only motive was to please him, he believed that she meant what she said, and carried her off to see how the carriage-horses, his own and those of his guests, were fed ; of the latter there were often a large number in the stables at Bagrovo.

I am afraid of wearying the reader by such a minute description of the young couple's visit, and shall only say that the next day, which was the fifth, was spent just like the preceding day. According to the order of seniority the next formal visit should have been to the Yerlykins ; but as their estate was 170 *versts* from Bagrovo and much nearer Ufa, it was settled to take them on the return journey to the town. There was this other reason, that General Yerlykin, Elizabeth's silent gloomy husband, having broken out at Aksinya's house, had started on one of his regular drinking bouts, which generally lasted at least a week, so that his wife had been forced to leave him with some friends at Boogoorooslan, and give out that he was ill. Alexandra was therefore to receive the next visit, and started off home with her husband on the previous day; with her father's consent, she invited the oldest and youngest of the sisters for the occasion, while Elizabeth remained behind, ostensibly to be near her sick husband, though her real object was to bring her influence to bear on her parents. The Karatayeffs lived about 50 *versts* from Bagrovo; the distance was the same as to Aksinya's house, but the road ran in the opposite direction, due north, and passed through woods and hills in the second half of the journey. The visitors started after an early lunch. As the road was little used and heavy for the horses, they halted half-way for two hours in the open field, and reached Karatayevka about tea-time. The house was infinitely worse than Aksinya's : the small dark windows caught the eye at once ; the floors were uneven, riddled with rat-holes, and so dirty as to defy soap and water. Sofya Nikolayevna felt fear and disgust as she entered this inhospitable and repulsive dwelling. Alexandra was haughty in her reception of them ; she was profuse in sarcastic apologies of this kind : ' We are glad to see our guests and bid them welcome ; my brother, I know, will not be critical, but I doubt if Sofya Nikolayevna will deign to enter our poor house after her father's grand mansion at Ufa. Of course *we* are poor people, with no official rank ; living on our own property, *we* have no lucrative salaries to maintain us.' But Sofya Nikolayevna gave as good as she got : she replied that the way people lived depended as much on their tastes as on their money, and that it was all one to her where her

husband's relations lived and how they lived.
When supper was over, the young couple were
shown to their bedroom, which was the so-called
drawing-room. As soon as the candle was out,
a great disturbance began in the room; the
pattering and noise increased, and swarms of
rats soon assailed them with such boldness that
the poor bride lay awake all night, shaking
with fear and disgust. Alexyéi Stepanitch was
forced to light a candle and arm himself with a
window-prop for the defence of the bed, on which
the rats kept jumping up as long as it was dark.
He felt neither fear nor disgust; it was no novelty
to him; at first he was rather amused by the
ceaseless activity and bold springs of the repulsive
creatures, and then he fell asleep, lying across the
bed and still holding the window-prop. But his
wife woke him again and again and only fell asleep
herself at sunrise, when the enemy sought the
concealment of his trenches. She got up with a
headache, but her hostess only laughed at the
fright the rats had given her, and added that they
only attacked strangers, and the people of the
house were used to them. Tanyusha was afraid
of rats herself; and she and Aksinya could not
look unmoved at the signs of suffering on their
sister-in-law's face. They expressed sympathy
with her, and Aksinya even scolded Alexandra for
not taking the ordinary precautions by placing the
bed in the centre of the room, attaching curtains
to it, and tucking the ends under the mattress; but
the hostess said with an angry laugh, 'It is a pity
they did not bite off her nose.' 'You had better
look out!' said her sister; 'if this gets to our
father's ears, you will catch it.'

Karatayevka was situated on the slope of a hill,
above a little spring-fed stream which was dammed
up at the end of the village and turned a small
mill. The position was not bad, but the owners
and all their ways were so objectionable that the
place had no attractions for any one. M. Karatayeff, who was afraid of Stepan Mihailovitch at
Bagrovo and of his wife at home, would have liked
to pay some attentions to Sofya Nikolayevna when
his wife was out of the room ; but he only found
courage to ask leave from time to time to kiss her
hand, and generally added that she was the most
beautiful creature in the world. When he repeated
his request, it was refused. His was a strange
existence. Most of his summer was spent in
visiting wandering Bashkir tribes, and drinking
koumiss every day till he was intoxicated ; he
spoke the Bashkir language like a native ; he rode
on horseback whole days without dismounting,
and had become as bow-legged as a Bashkir ; he
had their skill with the bow and could smash an
egg at long range with the best of them. All the
rest of the year he spent in a kind of lumber-room
warmed by a stove, near the house-door ; he wore
a skin coat, and kept the little window always open
even in the hardest frosts ; and there he remained
all day with his head stuck out of the window,
humming Bashkir songs and taking a sip now and
then of Bashkir mead or some decoction of herbs.
Why Karatayeff looked out of his window over the
empty yard with a rough path running across it,
what he saw and noted there, what thoughts passed
through the brain at the top of that big body—
these are problems which no ingenuity can solve.
Sometimes, it is true, his philosophic meditations

were disturbed : when some plump woman or girl appeared from the servants' quarters and walked mincingly along the path towards the cattle-shed, then a pantomime of nods and signals took place between the window and the yard ; but soon the fair vision turned out of sight and vanished like a ghost, and Karatayeff was left staring into empty void.

Sofya Nikolayevna was eager to escape from this horrible place : after an early dinner, during which the horses were already standing at the door, they said ' good-bye ' at once and started. The hostess kissed her sister-in-law on both cheeks and on the shoulders, and thanked her significantly for her kind visit ; and Sofya Nikolayevna just as significantly thanked the lady for her kind hospitality.

When alone with her husband in the carriage, Sofya Nikolayevna gave vent to her anger. Aksinya in her simplicity had let out accidentally that the hostess had purposely taken no precautions against the rats ; and the bride, though she had refrained from an outburst in her enemy's house, was unable any longer to control her excitable nature. Forgetting that Alexandra was her husband's sister, and that Parasha was in the carriage with them, she was lavish in her terms of abuse. Alexyéi Stepanitch, a straightforward and kindly man himself, could not believe that there was any intention on the part of his sister : attributing what had happened to mere careless-ness, he was hurt by his wife's violent language, which was really inexcusable under any provoca-tion. The young husband was angry for the first time with his young wife : saying that she should be ashamed to speak so, he turned from her and was silent. Such was their state of mind when they arrived at Mertovshchina, where Mme Myortvavo, a remarkably intelligent old lady, was then living with her daughter Katherine, who had lately been married to Peter Chicbágoff. Sofya Nikolayevna was warmly attached to both the Chichagoffs. She did not in the least expect to find them there, and soon forgot all her displeasure in this agreeable surprise ; she became very lively and cheerful, but no one could fail to notice that Alexyéi Stepanitch remained silent and sad.

Chichagoff's history, and especially his second marriage, is quite a romance ; and I shall tell it as briefly as I can, because we shall often come across this family in future, and especially because the life of the young Bagroffs was a good deal influenced by this pair. Peter Chichagoff was a man of exceptional ability or, I should rather say, exceptional acuteness, and had received what was for those days an advanced education in many subjects : he knew several languages, could draw and understood architecture, and wrote both in prose and verse. In his hot youth he fell in love at Moscow with a young lady of the Rimsko-Korsakoff family, and went so far as to misrepresent his position, in order to win her hand. This was discovered after the marriage, and he was banished to Ufa. His wife soon died. Within a year he consoled himself and fell in love with Katherine Myortvavo, who was attracted by his gay and amiable temper, his intelligence and acquirements ; his face was so very plain that it could exercise no attraction. She was no longer a girl and had too strong a character to be controlled by her mother

and brothers : they let her marry Chichagoff, and
he was pardoned soon afterwards but not allowed
to leave the Government of Ufa. Sofya Nikolayevna liked him for two reasons : because he was
the husband of her dearest friend, and perhaps still
more for his own cleverness and wide information.
Mme Myortvavo had just settled to leave Ufa and
live in the country, and the Chichagoffs had come
on purpose to help her in building a house and a
church. After a week's experience of her husband's
relations, this meeting was a spring in the desert
to Sofya Nikolayevna ; it was like a breath of
fresh air in which her heart and quick intelligence
expanded ; she talked on with her friends till
near midnight. But Alexyéi Stepanitch would
have sat there in silence and solitude, had not the
old lady grasped the situation and entertained
him by her pleasant talk. After supper, however,
he said ' good night,' and went off to the bedroom
allotted to the visitors ; when Sofya Nikolayevna
came she found him fast asleep. They started for
Bagrovo early next day without disturbing their
hosts.

During their drive Alexyéi Stepanitch was still
sullen and silent. In reply to direct questions from
his wife, his answers were so cold and short that
she gave up speaking to him. Her lively and impatient temper resented this treatment, but she did
not care to clear up matters in Parasha's presence,
preferring to wait till the after-dinner rest when
she would be alone with her husband. For the
present she started a conversation with her maid
about their life at Ufa, while Alexyéi Stepanitch
squeezed into a corner of the carriage and either
fell asleep or pretended to. They reached Bagrovo

two hours before dinner. Stepan Mihailovitch
was obviously pleased to see his daughter-in-law
again, and even said that he had missed her. ' My
dear,' he added, ' you really must not stay here too
long, or I shan't be able to let you go ; as it is, I
shall miss you, likely enough.' He made her give
him a minute account of their expedition. He
praised Mme Myortvavo whom he knew well, and
said that he would send her an invitation next day
to come with her daughter and son-in-law and dine
at Bagrovo ; he fixed on the following Sunday,
which was four days ahead, for the entertainment.
' You must visit the Kalpinskys and Lupenevskys the day after to-morrow,' he said ; ' and then
you can invite them too for Sunday ; and then,
three days later, you had better be off home to Ufa.
Your father has never been parted from you before,
and must miss you terribly ; and I am sure, my
dear, that you are even more anxious to see him,
poor suffering old man ! '

Stepan Mihailovitch was not long in finding out
that something disagreeable had happened on this
expedition. In the course of conversation, he said,
' Well, were the Karatayeffs glad to see you ? '
The answer was of course in the affirmative ; but
Sofya Nikolayevna happened to mention that she
had been kept awake all night by rats. This
surprised the old man : he had only been there
once long ago, and had heard of nothing of the kind.
But here Arina Vassilyevna unsuspiciously joined
in, in spite of the warning signs of her daughter
Elizabeth ; she suffered for it afterwards, poor
lady, at the hands of her daughters. ' O yes, yes,
batyushka Stepan Mihailovitch ! ' she cried ; ' the
rats there are perfectly awful ! Without bed-

curtains, it's impossible to get a wink of sleep.'
' Had you no curtains to your bed, then ? ' asked
the old man, and there was an ominous change in
his voice as he spoke. ' No,' was the only possible
answer. 'An excellent hostess!' he said, and looked
at his wife and daughter in such a way that a cold
shiver ran down their backs.

The Karatayeff party had not yet returned, but
were expected by tea-time. Dinner was not a
cheerful meal : all were out of spirits, and each
had his or her reasons. Arina Vassilyevna and
Elizabeth were conscious of the approaching storm,
and feared that the thunderbolt might smite them
also. It was long since Stepan Mihailovitch
had been in a rage, and the prospect was more
alarming to them because they had become unused
to such outbreaks. Sofya Nikolayevna noted the
frown on her father-in-law's face ; she did not
objoot to his giving a good fright to his daughter,
whom she detested as her avowed enemy ; but
she feared she might somehow get involved herself.
She had no unkind intention in speaking about the
rats : she never supposed that her father-in-law
would take any special notice of this circumstance
or attach serious importance to it. Nevertheless,
a stone lay on her heart also : she could not
determine how to act towards her husband. He
had been angry with her for the first time, when
she used insulting language about his sister : was
it best to wait till he appealed to her voluntarily,
or to put an end to the uncomfortable situation by
begging him to forgive her ? Her love and her
tender caresses might then cause him to forget her
regrettable impulsiveness. And she certainly
would have chosen this course : for she was

passionately in love with her kind young husband. She blamed herself severely : she ought to have foreseen everything and been prepared for everything. She knew that Alexyéi Stepanitch would not hesitate to die for her, but she knew also that she ought not to demand of him what he could not give—a tender and constant observation, and a full comprehension of all the trifling occurrences that might give her pain. And this was hard for her, with her hot blood and sensitive nerves, her eager excitable brain and impressionable nature. Such were the poor woman's thoughts and feelings as she walked up and down her room waiting for her husband ; his mother had stopped him on the way there after dinner and asked him to come to her bedroom. The minutes seemed to her like hours. The thought that he was loitering on purpose, fearing a scene and unwilling to be alone with her ; the thought that without relieving her heart of its many troubles and without a reconciliation with her husband, she would see him again in the presence of her enemies and must play a part the whole evening—this thought oppressed her heart and threw her into a fever. Suddenly the door opened, and Alexyéi Stepanitch walked in. There was no hesitation in his movements ; he was no longer timid and sad, but fearless and even displeased. He began at once to reproach her for complaining to his father and getting Alexandra into trouble. ' They are all trembling and crying now, and God only knows what will come of it,' he said, primed with all that his mother and sister had been impressing upon him. ' It is wrong and a sin on your part to cause trouble and quarrels in your husband's family.

I told you what my father is like when he is angry;
and you, knowing this and seeing his love for you,
took advantage of it!' Sofya Nikolayevna's
patience snapped instantly, and she fired up at
once; love was silent, and of pity and contrition
not a trace was left; and her poor husband discovered that Stepan Mihailovitch was not the only
person who could fly into a passion. An irresistible
flood of complaints, accusations, and reproaches
poured down upon him. He was utterly crushed
and confounded; he could make no defence, and
was all but a monster in his own eyes. Soon he was
kneeling at her feet and begging forgiveness with
tears. It was not surprising that Alexyéi Stepanitch was powerless before that volcanic eruption
of feeling and intelligence, that heartfelt conviction
and wonderful power of eloquence. A man
entirely in the right, a man much more resolute
than Alexyéi Stepanitch, would have pleaded
guilty before the youth and beauty of a woman
whom he loved. And Alexyéi Stepanitch was
certainly not in the right.

When the storm had calmed down in the bedroom of the young couple, it was still brewing at
the other end of the house, in the smallish room
which belonged to Stepan Mihailovitch. Sleep had
not brought peace to him or smoothed the frown
from his high forehead. He sat for some time
across his bed in gloomy silence, and then called
out, ' Mazan!' Mazan had long been lying outside
the door, breathing heavily according to his wont,
and looking in through a chink; he had been
placed there as a sentry, while the family were
sitting in the parlour full of gloomy apprehensions.
He called out at the top of his voice, ' What is

your pleasure, sir ? '—and hurried into the room.
' Has my daughter Alexandra arrived ? Yes ?
then bring her here.' Alexandra entered on his
heels, for on such occasions delay was more
dangerous than anything. ' How dared you,
Madam,' began the old man in the voice she knew
and dreaded—' how dared you set rats on your
brother and his wife ? ' ' I am sorry, father,'
humbly answered Alexandra, while her knees
trembled beneath her, and fear kept down her own
infernal temper. ' I put my guests on purpose in
the drawing-room, and I never thought of putting
curtains to their bed. I was so busy and so glad
to see them that it slipped my memory.' ' You
were so glad to see them ! Do you expect me to
believe *that* ? How did you dare to act so to your
brother and to me ? How did you dare to bring
shame on your father in his old age ? ' The affair
would perhaps have gone no farther than angry
words and loud threats and possibly a rap from
his fist ; but Alexandra, stung by the thought
that she was suffering on account of Sofya Nikolayevna, and hoping that the storm would still
blow over, forgot that any sort of answer was a
new offence. She could not resist saying, ' I am
punished for nothing on her account.' A fresh
and terrible fit of rage seized Stepan Mihailovitch,
that rage which invariably ended in painful and
shocking violence. Words of fury were on the
point of rushing from his lips, when Arina Vassilyevna, with her daughters, Aksinya and Tanyusha,
ran into the room, and fell at the old man's feet
with tears and cries ; they had been standing
outside the door and had seen what was coming.
Karatayeff had been standing there with them ;

but he ran out of the house and into the wood,
where he slashed furiously at the innocent birch-
branches with his stick, punishing them for the
wrong done to his wife. Elizabeth did not venture
to enter the room, knowing that her own conscience
was not clear, and that her father was quite aware
of the part she had played. '*Batyushka* Stepan
Mihailovitch!' cried Arina Vassilyevna, 'your
will is law, you are our master, do what pleases
you! Only do not shame us and disgrace your
family in the sight of your daughter-in-law! You
will frighten her out of her life; all this is new to
her.' The words seemed to have some effect on the
old man. He was silent for a moment; then he
pushed Alexandra from him with his foot, crying,
'Begone, and don't venture to show yourself till
I send for you!' No one waited for any further
orders : in a moment the room was cleared, and
all was silence round Stepan Mihailovitch; but
his blue eyes long remained dark and clouded, and
his chest rose and fell with his heavy breathing, as
he restrained the passionate anger which had been
aroused and not satisfied.

The samovar had long been hissing on the
drawing-room table, not in the shade of the stoop,
because heavy rain had just ceased falling and it
was damp out of doors. Nature seemed to
sympathize with what was passing in the house of
Bagrovo. Soon after dinner two clouds of intense
blackness had met in the zenith and long remained
there motionless, emitting from time to time
flashes of lightning and shaking the air with peals
of thunder. At last the rain came down in torrents,
the clouds shifted to the east, and the setting sun
shone out. Fields and woods smelt sweeter,

refreshed by the rain, and the birds began to sing louder ; but alas ! the storms of human passion are not followed by such a calm.

Alexandra pretended illness, but the other daughters came with their mother to the drawing-room ; Karatayeff also was there, but Yerlykin was still absent from the house, on the pretext of ill-health. Stepan Mihailovitch had tea in his room and gave orders that he was not to be disturbed. The door of the young couple's room was locked ; after a short delay, tapping was tried and brought them out at once. Sofya Nikolayevna looked cheerful, and her husband really was more cheerful than before ; but it was easy to guess from their faces that something unusual had been happening in their room. Of what had passed in the bedroom of Stepan Mihailovitch, they knew nothing. As for Arina Vassilyevna and her daughters, they looked like people who had just been pulled out of the water or snatched from the fire. It is a pity that there was no one to observe the scene ; for it is certain that the different expressions on the faces of the company would have afforded an entertaining spectacle. All attempts to keep up a conversation were unsuccessful. The absence of the father and of one daughter puzzled Sofya Nikolayevna beyond endurance : she invented some pretext for going to her own room, where she summoned Parasha and got to the bottom of the mystery. They knew all about it in the maids' room : not only had Mazan and Tanaichonok been listening all the time, but the old lady and her daughter were in the habit of keeping nothing back from their waiting-women. Thus Parasha was able to give her mistress an

exact and detailed report. Sofya Nikolayevna
was much disturbed. She had never expected such
alarming consequences ; she heartily regretted
having told her father-in-law about those wretched
rats ; and she was sincerely sorry for Alexandra.
She went back to the drawing-room and asked leave
to visit the invalid, but was told she was asleep.
During her absence, Alexyéi Stepanitch had heard
the whole story. After a hasty supper they
separated to their rooms at ten o'clock. When
alone with her husband, Sofya Nikolayevna, with
much agitation and many tears, fell on his neck,
and again asked his forgiveness with heartfelt
penitence, blaming herself much more than she
really deserved. But he did not understand the
delicacy of feeling which prompted her genuine
grief and drew tears from her. He was only sorry
to see her distress herself about trifles; and he
tried to console her by saying that all's well that
ends well, that the family were accustomed to
such scenes, that his father would wake in a good
temper to-morrow and forgive Alexandra, and all
would go on as well as before. Only he begged her
not to have any explanations with any of the
family, and not to ask pardon, as she wished to do,
for her unintentional slip ; and he advised her not
to visit his father in the morning but to wait till he
sent for her. Sofya Nikolayevna understood her
husband's character better than she had ever done
before ; and the knowledge hurt her deeply. While
he slept peacefully all night, she never closed an
eye.

Stepan Mihailovitch was the worse for his fit of
anger and also disliked the thought that his
daughter-in-law might have heard of it. His

honest nature resented every underhand action
and deliberate unkindness ; and also he saw, in
what his daughter had done, disregard to his own
authority and position. He was on the brink of an
illness ; he ate no supper, stayed indoors instead
of going to sit on the stoop, and when he should
have seen his bailiff, sent his orders by a servant.
But the benign darkness of night which gives light
to the eye of our mind, the stillness, and then sleep,
which calms the passions of men and rains down
blessings upon them—all these did their kindly
office. Early next day he summoned Arina
Vassilyevna and gave her his instructions to convey
to his daughters—they were intended mainly for
Alexandra, but in part also for Elizabeth—that
Sofya Nikolayevna was not to know of any un-
pleasantness, and they were to behave accordingly.
In a short time the samovar was placed on the
table, and all the family summoned.   Arina
Vassilyevna fortunately had time to send a message
by her son to Sofya Nikolayevna, begging her to
do her best to cheer up the master of the house :
' He is not quite well,' she said, ' and in low spirits
for some reason.'   In spite of her sleepless night
and the aching of her own heart, Sofya Nikolayevna
carried out this request to admiration ; all the
party, and she herself more than any, were anxious
it should be done.

Sofya Nikolayevna was an astonishing woman !
Lively, impressionable, and excitable, she could
be carried away in a moment by impulses of the
head or heart, and was capable of very sudden
and complete transformations of behaviour.   In
later years stupid people accused her of insincerity
on this ground, but no one else did.   It was really

a kind of artistic power, which enabled her to adapt herself instantly to a new atmosphere and a new position, and to act absolutely in accordance with her immediate purpose ; and this purpose, being entirely sincere, acted like a spell on others. In this case she laid herself out to calm the agitation of her father-in-law, for whom she had conceived a warm affection, and who had championed her cause at the cost of his peace of mind and at the risk of his health ; and she wished to relieve her husband and his family, who had been terrified and assailed owing to her slip of the tongue. Her imagination and feelings were so completely mastered by this purpose, that she exercised a kind of magical power over the party and soon subdued them all by the irresistible spell of her personality. She poured out tea herself and handed the cups herself, first to her father-in-law and then to the rest ; she talked to every one so easily and pleasantly and brightly that the old man, quite convinced that she had caught no glimpse of the skeleton in the cupboard, soon relaxed his features. Of him also it was true that his cheerfulness was infectious ; and before an hour had passed, all traces of the storm of yesterday had disappeared.

Immediately after dinner the young couple started off to pay two ceremonial visits—to Ilarion Kalpinsky and his wife Catherine at Nyeklyoodovo, and to our old acquaintance Mme Lupenevsky, who lived within two *versts* of the Kalpinskys. Kalpinsky was in his own way a remarkable man : though he had received no regular education, he was very intelligent and well-read ; his origin was obscure—it was said that he was of Mordvinian descent—but he had risen to

a considerable rank in the public service, and had
made a marriage of interest with the daughter of
a country gentleman of good family. His present
pursuit was farming, and his object to save money.
He set up for a freethinker; and his few neighbours who had heard of Voltaire called him a
Voltairian. He lived at home without taking
any part in the life of the family, and reserved to
himself complete freedom in the gratification of
his somewhat epicurean tastes and habits. Though
she had heard of him, Sofya Nikolayevna had never
seen him, because he had only recently removed
to Orenburg from his public office at Petersburg.
She was surprised to find in him a man possessed of
intelligence and culture according to the standards
of the time, and dressed like a gentleman living in
the capital. She was pleased with him at first; but
he soon began to show off before such an attractive
visitor, and then his profanity and the shameless
immorality of his family life made her feel a disgust
for him which she never afterwards got over. His
wife was far more intelligent than her sister, Mme
Lupenevsky, but not her superior in any other
respect. The visit lasted for an hour, and was
followed by a visit to Mme Lupenevsky. In both
houses tea was given to the guests and home-made
jam, and the meal was seasoned with a kind of
conversation which horrified Sofya Nikolayevna.
Both families were invited to dine at Bagrovo on
the following Sunday. By one of those striking
inconsistencies in human nature which it is impossible to explain, Mme Lupenevsky fell in love
at first sight with Sofya Nikolayevna, and used
such language to her at parting that her guest
must needs either blush or laugh aloud; never-

theless her words were the expression of sincere and even enthusiastic attachment.

The pair reached home an hour before supper-time, and were welcomed with unusual cordiality and pleasure by Stepan Mihailovitch, whom they found sitting on the familiar stoop. He was much amused when he was told that Mme Lupenevsky had conceived such a passion for his daughter-in-law, kissing her repeatedly, claiming that they were kindred spirits, and lavishing terms of affection upon her. Contrary to custom, the whole family went out again to the stoop after supper, and spent a long time there in cheerful conversation with the master of the household, in the cool of the night and under the starry sky. Stepan Mihailovitch, though he could not have explained why, was fond of the faint colourless light that follows the glow of sunset.

The solemn feast on the Sunday was to be some thing beyond what had ever been seen at Bagrovo, but nothing special happened on either of the inter-vening days. Yerlykin came back from Boogoo-rooslan looking yellow and ill, as he always did after a drinking bout. Stepan Mihailovitch knew of his son-in-law's unfortunate weakness or disease, and tried to cure him by dosing him with unpala-table drinks, but without success. When sober, Yerlykin had a loathing for alcohol and could not raise a glass of wine to his lips without a shudder; but he was seized four times a year with a sudden and irresistible craving for spirits. If the attempt was made to keep drink from him, he became a most pitiable and wretched object, talking con-stantly and weeping, and begging abjectly for the poison; and if it was still refused he became frantic and even capable of attempts at suicide. Sofya Nikolayevna, who had heard the whole story, was exceedingly sorry for him. She spoke kindly to him and tried to make him talk to her. But it was no good : the General persisted in his sullen silence and gloomy pride. Instead of being grateful to her sister-in-law, Elizabeth resented these advances to her husband, and expressed her resentment in bitter terms. But Stepan Mihailovitch noticed this and addressed a stern reproof to his clever daughter, who did not love her sister-in-law any the better in consequence.

Stepan Mihailovitch twice took his daughter-in-law out to see his crops of rye and spring-sown wheat, and drove with her to all his favourite water-springs in the hills, and the ' Sacred Wood ' where the trees had been protected from the axe by a religious service. The old man believed that all these sights were interesting and agreeable to her ; but in fact she positively disliked them all. Her sole support was in the thought that she would soon leave Bagrovo and would do her best never to set eyes on it again. If any one had told her that she would spend most of her life there, grow old there, and even die there, she would not have believed it : she would have said that death was preferable, and would have meant what she said. But whatever God decrees, to that man can become accustomed, and that he can endure.

Sunday came and the guests began to assemble. Mme Myortvavo came, and the Kalpinskys and Lupenevskys, and two old bachelors, the judge and the mayor of Boogoorooslan. Another guest was Afrosinya Andréyevna (her surname, which was never used, I forget), a spare little old lady

and a great talker ; she had a small estate near
Bagrovo. She was famous for her powers of
invention, and Stepan Mihailovitch liked at times
to listen to her, as a grown man sometimes listens
with pleasure to a fairy tale intended for children.

But Afrosinya Andréyevna deserves that the
reader should have at least a bowing acquaintance
with her. At one time in her life she had spent ten
years in Petersburg to watch a lawsuit ; when she
won it, she came back to her little estate in the
country. She brought back with her from Petersburg a store of anecdotes whose extravagance made
Stepan Mihailovitch laugh till he cried. For
instance, she used to represent herself as a bosom
friend of the Empress Catherine, adding by way of
explanation that two people could not live ten
years in the same town without being thrown
together. ' I was in church one day '—she talked
this way when she was in the vein—' the people
were going out, and the Empress walked past me,
and I made a low curtsey and ventured to congratulate her on the festival ; and then Her Majesty
was so very kind and condescending as to say :
" How are you, Afrosinya Andréyevna ? How is
your suit going ? Why don't you come to see me
of an evening and bring your knitting with you ? We
could chat together and pass the time pleasantly."
Of course I never missed an evening after that.
I got to know the people about the court, and every
one in the palace without a single exception knew
me and liked me. Suppose a royal footman was
sent anywhere, to buy something it might be, he
never failed to look in at my house and tell me all
about it. As a matter of course, I always offered
him a glass of something good ; I kept a bottle of

whisky in the cupboard on purpose. I was sitting by my window one evening when I saw a royal footman in red uniform, with a coat of arms on it, ride past at a gallop; he was soon followed by a second and a third. That was too much for me : I threw up the window and called out, "Philip Petrovitch! Philip Petrovitch! what are you galloping for, and why don't you pay me a visit?" "No time, Afrosinya Andréyevna!" was his answer; "a terrible thing has happened : candles will soon be wanted at the palace, and we've run out of them!" "Stop!" I cried out; "I have 5 lb. of candles laid in ; you can come in and take them." Philip Petrovitch was delighted ; I carried out the candles with my own hands and relieved the people from their difficulty. So you see, *batyushka* Stepan Mihailovitch, they simply couldn't help being fond of me.'

Stepan Mihailovitch had many traits of character peculiar to himself ; and this was one—though he was a sworn foe to deliberate lying of every kind, and detested the most trifling deception and even the kind of evasion which is sometimes quite excusable, yet he liked listening to the harmless fabrications and fictions of simple people, who were innocently carried away by the vividness of their imagination till they actually came to believe in their own incredible romancing. He liked talking to Afrosinya Andréyevna, not only at a merry party, but also when they were alone together, if he was in the right mood for it ; and she spent whole hours in pouring out for his benefit the story of her life in Petersburg, which consisted entirely of such incidents as that which I have already quoted.

But it is time to go back to the guests arriving

at Bagrovo. The mayor's *kaftan* [1] and the judge's
uniform were equally remarkable ; but the best
sight of all was Kalpinsky : on each side of him
stood a female scarecrow in the person of his wife
and of her sister, while he himself wore an embroidered coat of French cut, a pair of watch-
chains, a number of rings, silk stockings, and shoes
with gold buckles. All the family wore their best
bib and tucker, and even Stepan Mihailovitch
was forced to smarten himself up. M. Chichagoff,
who had a critical satirical turn of mind, made fun
with much effect of the motley assembly and
especially of his friend Kalpinsky ; he was talking
all the time to his wife and to her inseparable
companion, Sofya Nikolayevna, who sat together
and apart from the rest. Sofya Nikolayevna had
hard work to keep from laughing : she tried not to
listen, and begged Chichagoff either to hold his
tongue or to start a conversation with Stepan
Mihailovitch, whom he would find worthy of
respect. He did so, and soon took a great fancy
to the old man ; and his feeling was reciprocated.
But Stepan Mihailovitch disliked Kalpinsky, both
as an upstart and also as an unbeliever and loose-
liver.

The splendour of the banquet may be imagined.
Stepan Mihailovitch for once resigned all his
favourite dishes—haggis, roast ribs of pork, and
porridge made of green rye. A *chef* had been procured, of special skill in the culinary art. Materials
of all sorts were provided in abundance—a six-
weeks-old calf, a pig fed to monstrous proportions,
fat sheep, and poultry of all kinds. It was the
custom then to place all the courses at once on the

[1] The *kaftán* is a long cloth coat belted in at the waist.

cloth ; and the table at Bagrovo could hardly
hold them all or support their weight. Cold dishes
came first—smoked hams seasoned with garlic ;
next came green cabbage soup and crayfish soup,
with forcemeat balls and rolls of different kinds ;
then fish-salad on ice, sturgeon kippered and
sturgeon dried, and a dish heaped mountain-high
with crayfish tails. Of entrées there were only
two : salted quails *aux choux*, and stuffed ducks
with a red sauce containing raisins, plums, peaches,
and apricots. These entrées were a concession to
modern fashion ; Stepan Mihailovitch did not like
them and called them ' kickshaws.' They were
followed by a turkey of enormous size and fatness,
and a hindquarter of veal ; the accessories were
preserved melons and gourds, apple chips, and
pickled mushrooms. The dinner ended up with
round jam-tarts and raised apple pies served with
thick cream. All this was washed down with
home-made liquors, home-brewed March beer, iced
kvass, and foaming mead.

Such were the meals which our heroic grandfathers and grandmothers consumed without leaving out a single course, and even managed to
digest satisfactorily ! But they took their time over
it, and the meal went on for hours. The dishes
were solid substantial affairs, as we have seen, and
there were plenty of them ; and the servants also,
both those of the house and those whom the guests
brought with them, had no idea of waiting : they
bustled about and collided with one another and
seemed likely at every moment to spill the sauce or
the gravy over some lady's dress.

The dinner was a cheerful meal. The master of
the house had Mme Myortvavo on his right, and

on his left Chichagoff, who steadily rose in his
host's good graces and was quite capable, unaided,
of enlivening the dullest of parties. The young
couple were near the head of the table, with
Mme Chichagoff and Kalpinsky ; the latter, while
paying constant attentions to the two young women
and exchanging an occasional jest with Alexyéi
Stepanitch, ate for two all the time, to make up for
the voluntary abstinence which he practised at
home in his eagerness to save money. Yerlykin
sat next to Chichagoff ; unlike the rest of the
party, he ate little and drank nothing but cold
water ; he never spoke, but looked gloomy and
profound. The lady of the house had her daughters
and nieces with other guests near her at table.
The party next adjourned to the drawing-room,
where there were two tables set out with sweet-
meats. On one stood a round cabinet of Chinese
porcelain, resting on a round metal stand which
was gilt and painted in bright colours. The
cabinet contained a number of closely fitting trays,
each of which held a different sort of preserved
fruit—raspberries, strawberries, cherries, goose-
berries, and blackberries ; and there were crystal-
lized rose-petals in a small round receptacle at the
top. This cabinet, which would be considered very
rare and precious nowadays, was a present sent
by the bride's father to Stepan Mihailovitch.
Small plates were set out on the other table, filled
with black and white currants, apricots, peaches,
dates, raisins, nuts of many kinds, and almonds in
the shell.

Stepan Mihailovitch rose from table in such
good spirits that he did not even wish to lie down
and rest. All could see—and indeed he wished it

to be seen—his pride in his daughter-in-law and his affection for her ; and her love and respect for him were as plain to see. During dinner he often turned towards her and asked her to do him some trifling service—to hand something, or pour out something. ' Please help me yourself,' he would say, ' for you and I agree in our tastes '—or, ' Just remind me of what I said to you the other day '— or, ' Do repeat what you told me yesterday ; I seem to have forgotten it.' After dinner it was the same : he often asked her to give some order, or to hand him something, and so on. The form of his address was always plain and unpretentious, sometimes even unceremonious ; but the tone of affection in which these appeals were expressed left no doubt in the mind of any spectator that he was entirely captivated by his daughter-in-law. And she, I need hardly say, replied with love and gratitude to every token of the stern old man's love for her—tokens often so slight that many would have missed them. Stepan Mihailovitch, who was thoroughly enjoying himself, tried to make Mme Lupenevsky talk : pretending ignorance, he asked in a loud voice, ' Well, Flona, what say you of my daughter-in-law ? ' The lady's enthusiasm had been raised to a higher pitch by the ale and strong waters she had been drinking. She declared most positively and solemnly that she had fallen in love at first sight with Sofya Nikolayevna, and rather preferred her to her own daughter, Lizanka ; and that Alexyéi Stepanitch was the most fortunate of men. ' It used to be quite another story,' said the old man significantly ; ' don't change back again, my dear ! ' But now Sofya Nikolayevna, perhaps from a dislike for this topic, strongly urged her

father-in-law to go and lie down, if only for a short
time. He consented, and she went with him and
drew his curtains with her own hand ; he asked her
to see to the entertainment of the party, and she
hurried back, pleased and flattered by this commission. While some lay down to rest, the others
crossed to the island and sat on the river-bank in
the shade of the trees. Sofya Nikolayevna was
reminded of the scene that had taken place there so
recently—her unreasonable excitement and the
unjust reproaches which had rankled in the mind
of her husband. Her heart was full ; and though
she saw him now, in perfect content and happiness,
laughing loudly at a story which Kalpinsky was
telling, she drew him aside, threw her arms round
him, and said with tears in her eyes, ' Forgive me,
my dear, and bury in oblivion all that happened
here on the day we came ! ' Alexyéi Stepanitch
had a strong objection to scenes , but he kissed both
her hands and said good-humouredly, ' How can
you recall such a trifle, my darling ? You are quite
wrong to trouble yourself.' Then he hurried back
to hear the end of the story, which was very
amusing as Kalpinsky told it. Though there was
really no cause for distress, Sofya Nikolayevna
felt a momentary heartache.

The master of the house soon woke and summoned all the party to join him by the stoop.
Tables and chairs were placed in the broad thick
shadow cast by the house ; and the samovar was
soon hissing. Tea was poured out by Sofya
Nikolayevna : there were rolls and scones and
cream so thick that it had a golden tinge on it ;
and for all this some at least of the guests still
found room. The Kalpinskys and Mme Lupen-

evsky went off after tea : there was positively no room for them to sleep at Bagrovo, and they had not far to go, only fifteen *versts*. The guests from Boogoorooslan also took their leave.

Mme Myortvavo and her party left early next morning, and the Yerlykins after dinner, to prepare for a visit from the young couple on their way back to Ufa. The same evening Stepan Mihailovitch announced quite frankly that the time had come for the rest of the party to disperse : he wished to spend the last days alone with his son and daughter-in-law, and to enjoy their society without interruption. As a matter of course, his wishes were carried out. Alexandra said ' good-bye ' to her sister-in-law as graciously as she could, and the sister-in-law said ' good-bye ' to her with unfeigned satisfaction. Her secret wish to spend some days without the hateful presence of Elizabeth and Alexandra had been divined by Stepan Mihailovitch ; and she blessed him in her thoughts for his power of intuition. Aksinya was quite different ; and Sofya Nikolayevna parted from her with feelings of gratitude and real affection. None of this escaped the old man's keen eyes. Tanyusha and her mother caused no constraint, partly because they were more good-tempered and friendly to their guest, and also because they often withdrew and left the others to their own devices.

The three remaining days were spent at Bagrovo in perfect peace of mind, untroubled by malevolent observation or pretences of affection or venomous innuendoes. The strain on Sofya Nikolayevna's nerves was relaxed, and she was able to take her bearings with less prejudice and study the peculiarities of the little world in which she found herself. In spite of their complete unlikeness to herself, she could now understand her mother-in-law and Tanyusha better, and make allowances for them; she could form a cooler judgement of Stepan Mihailovitch, and could understand how her husband came to be what he was. To some extent she realized that Alexyéi could not be entirely changed, and that the time was distant —perhaps it would never come—when misunderstandings between them would cease. But this last thought passed too lightly through her mind; and the old dream, that she could educate her husband over again and make a new man of him, took fresh hold of her eager imagination. What happens to most young wives in the course of life was happening now to Sofya Nikolayevna : she found in her husband a certain inferiority, certain limitations of feeling and perception; and though her love for him was none the less passionate on that account, she was beginning to feel vaguely dissatisfied with his love for her, because he found room in his heart for other things—the pond and the island, the steppe and its population of snipe, the river and those horrid fish! A feeling of jealousy, though directed to no definite object as yet, was lurking at her heart; and she felt a dim presentiment of coming disaster.

Stepan Mihailovitch also had been somewhat taken up hitherto by constant observation of the feelings and actions of his daughters; but now he was more at leisure to attend to his daughter-in-law and his son also. For all his want of education and rough-and-ready way of expressing himself, his natural sagacity and power of intuition revealed to him the whole difference of character

between the two ; and he found here matter for
serious reflection.   Their present love for one
another was a pleasant sight to him, and he felt
happy when he saw Sofya Nikolayevna's eyes
constantly fixed on her husband and her eager
desire to please him ; but his happiness had a
shade of fear and of disbelief in the solidity and
permanence of a state of things in itself so charming.
He would have liked to speak his mind on the
subject, to give them some hints or some useful
advice ; but whenever he began, he could not find
the right words for thoughts and feelings which he
could not make clear even to himself ; and he
went no farther than those trivial commonplaces,
which, for all their triviality, have been bequeathed
to us by the practical wisdom of past generations
and are verified by our own experience.   His
failure troubled him, and he said so frankly to his
daughter-in-law.   She was a clever woman, yet
she failed to understand the thoughts which the
old man was turning over in his brain, and the
feeling hidden in his heart.   To his son he said :
' Your wife is very clever and very excitable.   Her
tongue will probably run away with her at times ;
if so, don't be weak with her : stop her at once, and
make her see her mistake.   Scold her, but forgive
her at once ; if she displeases you, don't be sullen
or keep up resentment ; have it all out with her at
once.   But trust her absolutely ; she is as true as
steel.'   Again, when he was alone with Sofya
Nikolayevna, he said to her : ' My dear daughter-
in-law, God has given you many good gifts.   I have
only one thing to say to you : don't give the rein
to your impetuous temper.   Your husband is
honest and kind ; his temper is mild, and he will

never willingly hurt your feelings ; don't you hurt
his. Honour him and treat him with respect.
If you cease to respect your husband, things will
go wrong. Suppose he says or does something you
don't like, then say nothing ; don't be too exacting,
and don't expect perfection. I can see through and
through you, and I love you dearly. For God's
sake, don't fill the cup till it runs over : anything
can be overdone, even the affection between
husband and wife '.

The advice was received as always by his son
with profound respect, and by Sofya Nikolayevna
with the ardent gratitude of a daughter. There was
much talk on other subjects—their future life at
Ufa, the husband's prospects in his profession, and
the means of defraying their expenditure. Definite
arrangements were made on all points, and all
parties were satisfied.

And now the day came for their departure. The
silk curtains in the bedroom were taken down ; the
muslin and satin pillow-cases with broad lace
edging were taken off the pillows ; and all this
finery was packed up and dispatched to Ufa.
Pies of different kinds were baked for the travellers.
Father Vassili was summoned once more, and the
prayers for those ' travelling by land or by water '
were said. Fresh horses were to be in readiness
at Korovino, forty *versts* away ; to that point they
were to be taken by the Bagrovo horses, the same
fine team of six which had conveyed the pair on
their ceremonial visits. They dined together for
the last time ; and for the last time Stepan
Mihailovitch pressed his favourite dishes on his
daughter-in-law. The carriage was already standing at the steps. When the party rose from table,

they went to the drawing-room and sat there in
silence for some minutes. Then Stepan Mihailovitch crossed himself and rose to his feet; the rest
followed his example, said a prayer,[1] and began
their good-byes. All shed tears except Stepan
Mihailovitch, and even he had hard work to refrain.
He embraced his daughter-in-law and gave her
his blessing; then he whispered in her ear, ' Mind,
I look forward to a little grandson.' She blushed
up to the ears and kissed his hands without speaking; and now he did not resist her doing so. All
the outdoor servants and most of the peasants
were standing by the steps. Some of them had
half a mind to come forward and say farewell to
their young master and mistress; but Stepan
Mihailovitch, who hated good-byes and parting
scenes, called out, ' What are you up to there ?
Make your bow, and that will be enough !' Sofya
Nikolayevna had only time to exchange greetings
with one or two of the people. They took their
seats quickly, and the strong horses started off
with the carriage as if it had been a mere feather.

Stepan Mihailovitch shaded his eyes from the sun
with his hand; for some minutes he tried to make
out the moving carriage in the cloud of dust which
followed it; and when it had reached the stack-
yard at the top of the hill, he went back to his own
room and lay down to sleep.

[1] In prayers of this kind, nothing is said aloud : the
worshipper turns towards the ikons on the wall and crosses
himself.

FRAGMENT V

LIFE AT UFA

DURING the first few minutes Sofya Nikolayevna felt sorry for her father-in-law and sad to part with him. The image of the old man who had learnt to love her and was suffering now from the separation, came vividly before her. But before long the easy motion of the carriage, with the fleeting glimpses of fields and coppices and the outline of the hills along which they were driving, had a soothing effect upon her mind ; and she began to feel heartily glad that she had left Bagrovo. Her joy was too great to be concealed, though she realized that her husband would not like it. He, she thought, was milder than he had any business to be. Some explanations might possibly have followed, but were fortunately prevented by the presence of Parasha. The carriage rolled quickly through the village of Noikino, where it was saluted by hearty shouts from the Mordvinians, and then crossed the river Nasyagai by a crazy bridge. They crossed the same river again and passed through the village of Polibino, and came at last to Korovino, where a fresh team was waiting for their arrival ; their own horses were to rest there for some hours and return to Bagrovo in the evening.

Sofya Nikolayevna had provided herself with writing materials, and now she wrote a warm letter of thanks to her husband's parents. It was intended especially for Stepan Mihailovitch ; and he understood this perfectly and hid the letter in the secret drawer of the modest writing-desk which satisfied his needs ; and there Sofya Nikolayevna came upon her own letter unexpectedly eight years afterwards, when the old man was in his grave. The horses were put to, good-byes were said to the coachman and postilion—long-legged Tanaichonok was acting as postilion on this occasion—and the pair resumed their journey. Fortune was kind at this point to Sofya Nikolayevna : it proved impossible to get to the Yerly-kins' house, and thus she was saved from a most tiresome and oppressive visit. A deep river had to be crossed on the way, and the bridge had rotted and collapsed. As it would take a long time to mend it, the young couple could keep straight on towards Ufa. As they got near the town, Sofya Nikolayevna could think of nothing but her sick father, who had not seen her for more than a fortnight ; he had been left in the care of servants and must be feeling lonely and eager for his daughter's return. The travellers took a full hour to cross the river Byélaya in a crazy ferry-boat ; and the ascent of the steep hill on the other side took time. Before it was over, Sofya Nikolayevna was very impatient and in great agitation. At last she got to the house. In a fever of excitement she hurried to her father's room and softly opened the door. He was lying in his usual position ; and near him, in the very armchair which was usually occupied by Sofya Nikolayevna herself, his servant Nikolai was sitting.

This man was a Kalmuck, and I must say something of his history. In those distant times it was a common practice in the district of Ufa to buy native boys and girls, either Kalmucks or Kirghizes,

from their parents or relations, and to make use of
them later as serfs. Forty years before the date
of my story, M. Zubin had bought two Kalmuck
boys. He had them baptized, became fond of
them, and made pets of them. He had them
taught to read and write; and when they grew up,
they became his personal servants. Both of them
were intelligent and neat-handed and appeared
to be very devoted; but when Pugatchoff[1] raised
the standard of revolt, they both ran off and joined
the rebels. One of them soon lost his life; but the
other, who had been his master's favourite and
was called Nikolai, now became the favourite of
one Chika, who was prominent among the rebels
and stood high in the favour of Pugatchoff himself.
It is well known that one band of the revolters was
encamped for a long time near Ufa, on the opposite
bank of the river Byélaya. Nikolai was in this
camp and had by this time been promoted to
a position of some authority. It was said that
he was fiercer than any of them and breathed fire
and slaughter against no one so much as his old
master who had brought him up. Tradition tells
that whenever the rebels were preparing to cross
the river and fall upon the defenceless town, they
saw a great army march out to defend the heights
on the opposite bank, and an ancient warrior at
their head, riding on a snow-white horse and
holding a spear in one hand and a Cross in the other.
The cowardly band of outlaws were terrified by
this vision and desisted from all their attempts;
and they had done nothing when the news came
that Pugatchoff was defeated. Of course they
scattered at once. The revolt came to an end,

[1] See note to p. 91.

and the scattered rabble were seized and brought
to trial. Nikolai, who was one of these, was condemned to the gallows. I cannot vouch for the
truth of this ; but I have been assured that after
his trial at Ufa the noose was actually round his
neck, when M. Zubin claimed the privilege which
he possessed as a landholder, pardoned his old
favourite, and took him home, undertaking to be
responsible himself for the criminal's behaviour.
Nikolai seemed penitent and tried by zeal and
devotion to atone for his crime. By degrees he contrived to get back into his master's confidence ;
and when Sofya Nikolayevna, after her step-
mother's death, took over the management of the
household, she found Nikolai established as butler ;
he had been a favourite with her step-mother, and
this now became a passport to her father's goodwill. Nikolai had been guilty of much insolence to
his young mistress during her time of humiliation ;
but he was a very cunning fellow and quite realized
his present position. He played the part of the
repentant sinner, throwing all the guilt on the
step-mother, and blaming himself for the slavish
spirit in which he had carried out her orders. It
would have been quite easy for Sofya Nikolayevna
to get rid of him for good and all ; but her youth
and generous nature made her believe that his
repentance was genuine. She pardoned him, and
actually begged her father to leave him in his old
position. As time went on, she was sometimes
vexed by the way in which he settled things without
consulting her, and she felt doubts about his
honesty. She noticed also that his intimacy with
her father, though concealed from her, was closer
than she liked. But he was very zealous in his

attendance upon his sick master, sleeping always in
the same room, and also found time to do his work
as butler exceedingly well. She was therefore content with mild reproofs, and the man was left free
to take root at leisure in his double office. When
she became engaged, she had to see herself to the
buying of her wedding-clothes and to spend much
time with her future husband ; and so she was less
with her father and gave less attention to household affairs. Nikolai took full advantage of this
opportunity, and his power over the old invalid
increased daily. Hoping soon to get rid of his
mistress and to become master of the house himself,
he grew more insolent and less careful to conceal his
power. Sofya Nikolayevna sometimes snubbed
him sharply ; she was grieved to see her father's
increasing dependence on this man and abdication
of his own authority.

Nikolai had made full use of the few days that
preceded and followed the marriage, and of her
absence for a fortnight at Bagrovo : his master,
now at death's door, was completely under his
control. Sofya Nikolayevna guessed the true
state of affairs as soon as she saw the man lying
asleep in the armchair ; never before had he
ventured on such a liberty. She gave him a look
which sent him in some haste and confusion out of
the room. Her father was by no means as pleased
to see her as she expected ; he made haste to tell
her that Nikolai was not to blame : ' It is at my
urgent wish,' he said, ' that he sometimes takes
a seat at my bedside.' ' It is a pity you do that,
father,' she said ; ' you will spoil him altogether
and be forced to turn him off ; I know him better
than you do.' Then, without entering upon

further explanations, she expressed her joy at having found him no worse. Alexyéi Stepanitch soon came in; and then the old man, touched by his daughter's unfeigned tenderness, his son-in-law's attentive behaviour, and the love between husband and wife, listened with pleasure to their narrative and thanked God with tears for their happiness.

Sofya Nikolayevna began at once the business of instalment. She chose three rooms, quite separate from the rest, for their own occupation; and in a few days her arrangements were so complete that she could receive her own guests without any disturbance to her father. It was her intention to arrange as before about the management of the house and the attendance on her father, and to assign to Nikolai the subordinate part of carrying out her instructions; but the man had always hated her, and now felt himself strong enough to declare open war against his young mistress. While attending to the father more zealously than ever, he contrived with extraordinary cunning to insult the daughter at every turn; and to Alexyéi Stepanitch he was so insolent that the young man lost patience, in spite of his easy and unexacting temper, and told his wife that he could not possibly put up with the position. For some time Sofya Nikolayevna did not trouble her father, hoping by her own influence to keep Nikolai within the bounds of reasonable politeness; she relied upon his intelligence, and also believed that he knew her determined character and would not venture to drive her to extremities. But the malicious Asiatic —this was the servants' name for him—was convinced beforehand that he would conquer, and tried to provoke Sofya Nikolayevna into some

passionate outburst. Long ago he had been able
to instil into his master the belief that the young
lady could not endure her father's faithful servant
and would certainly try to turn him out of the
house. The invalid was horrified by this prospect,
and solemnly declared that he would prefer death
to such a deprivation. Sofya Nikolayevna tried
to hint to her father in very gentle and affectionate
terms that Nikolai forgot himself in his behaviour
to her husband, and neglected to carry out her
orders ; it seemed to be his intention to provoke
her to anger. But her father became agitated and
refused to listen : he said that he was perfectly
satisfied with Nikolai, and begged her not to
trouble the butler but to give her orders to some
other servant. Young and impulsive, and accustomed to undisputed authority in her father's
house, Sofya Nikolayevna found it hard to endure
the insulting behaviour of an unworthy menial,
yet her love for her father, and her desire to nurse
and comfort him and alleviate his sufferings as far
as possible, kept her for long from the idea of leaving him in that dying state to depend entirely
upon such a wretch as Nikolai and other servants.
She controlled her impulsiveness and injured pride ;
she gave her household orders through one of the
other servants, knowing all the time that all her
instructions were altered by her enemy at his will
and pleasure. She induced her father to order that
Nikolai should not enter the sick-room while she
was sitting there. But this arrangement soon
broke down : under various pretexts, the man
constantly came into the room ; and indeed the
invalid himself constantly asked for him. This
painful situation continued for several months.

Sofya Nikolayevna arranged her engagements in the town in accordance with her own wishes. The people whom she liked she often met, either in their houses or her own ; the rest she seldom saw, and was content to exchange formal calls with them. Her husband was acquainted already with everybody in the town ; but his wife's intimate friends now became intimate with him. He became popular with them and got on very well in his new position—I mean, in the select society that gathered round his wife.

Meanwhile, soon after her return to Ufa, Sofya Nikolayevna began to feel unpleasant symptoms of a peculiar kind, which gave great satisfaction to Stepan Mihailovitch when he heard of them. The continuation of his ancient line, the descendants of the great Shimon, was a constant theme of the old man's thoughts and wishes ; it troubled his peace of mind and stuck in his head like a nail. On receiving the good news from his son, Stepan Mihailovitch was full of happy hopes and convinced that the child would infallibly be a boy. His family always said that his spirits were unusually high at this time. He had prayers said in church for his daughter-in-law's health, forgave certain sums owed him by neighbours or dependants, asked every one to congratulate him, and made them drink till they were dizzy.

In his excitement and joy, it occurred to him suddenly to bestow a mark of his favour upon Aksyutka, the maid who poured out tea and coffee, to whom he always showed an unaccountable partiality. Aksyutka was a peasant's daughter who had lost both parents and was brought to the house at Bagrovo when she was seven years old,

merely to save her from starvation. She was
exceedingly ugly—red-haired and freckled, with
eyes of no colour in particular ; she was also bad-
tempered and a horrible sloven. This does not
sound attractive ; but Stepan Mihailovitch took
a great fancy to her, and never did dinner pass
without his giving or sending to the child something
taken from the dishes at table. When she grew up,
he made her pour out his tea in the morning and
talked to her for hours at a time. She was now
a good deal over thirty. One morning, soon after
the good news came from Ufa, Stepan Mihailovitch
said to her : ' What makes you go about looking
like a scarecrow ? Be off, you stupid creature, and
put on your best clothes that you wear on holidays.
I mean to find you a husband.' Aksyutka grinned :
she thought her master was not serious, and
answered : ' Why, who would marry an orphan
like me, except perhaps Kirsanka, the shepherd ?'
(Kirsanka, as every one knew, was deformed and
idiotic.) Stepan Mihailovitch seemed vexed ;
he went on, ' If I arrange the marriage, you can
have your pick of the young men. Go and dress
yourself, and come back at once.' Aksyutka went
out surprised and delighted ; and Stepan Mihailovitch summoned Little Ivan to his presence. We
have heard something of this man already ; he was
now twenty-four years old, with a complexion of
lilies and roses, a very fine young fellow, both tall
and stout. At the time of Pugatchoff's revolt,
when the master himself took refuge with his
family at Astrakhan, Ivan's father had been left
in charge of the serfs at Bagrovo ; and it was
generally supposed that his death was due to over-
work and anxiety at that time. He left two sons,

both called Ivan, and this one was known as Little
Ivan, to distinguish him from his elder brother,
who inherited his father's nickname of Weasel.
Little Ivan appeared before his master, ' like a leaf
before the grass.' [1] Stepan Mihailovitch looked at
him with admiration, and then said in a voice so
kind that the lad's heart leaped for joy, ' Ivan,
I mean to give you a wife.' ' Your will is law,
batyushka Stepan Mihailovitch,' answered the man,
devoted body and soul to his master. ' Well, go and
dress yourself in your best, and come back to me in
less than no time.' Ivan flew off to do his master's
bidding. Aksyutka was the first to reappear ;
she had smoothed her red hair and greased it with
oil, and put on her smartest jacket and skirt, and
her bare feet were hidden in shoes ; but alas ! she
was no more beautiful than before. She was much
excited, and her mouth was constantly expanding
into a broad grin, which she tried to hide with her
hand, because she felt ashamed of it. Stepan
Mihailovitch laughed : ' Oh, she 's willing enough
to take a husband,' he said. Back flew Ivan ; but
the sight of Aksyutka's ugly face and fine dress sent
a cold shiver down his back. ' There is your bride,'
said Stepan Mihailovitch ; ' She is a good servant
to me as your father was once. You may both
count on my protection.' His wife now came in,
and he turned to her and said : ' Arisha, the bride's
clothes are all to be made out of our stuff ; I
shall give her a cow and provide everything to eat
and drink at the wedding.' No one raised any

[1] i. e. ' instantly,' though why the phrase means this
I cannot discover. In Russian fairy-tales, a witch regularly
summons any one she wants with the words, ' Stand thou
before me, like a leaf before the grass ! '

objections, and the marriage took place. Aksyutka
was charmed with her handsome husband, but he
detested his repulsive wife, who was besides ten years
older than he was. She was jealous of him all day
long, and not without reason ; and he beat her all
day long, with some excuse on his side also ;
for nothing but the stick—and not even that for
long—could shut her mouth and keep her wicked
tongue from wagging. It was a pity, a great pity :
Stepan Mihailovitch did a wrong thing when he
made others sad because he was happy.

Of his happiness I judge partly by tradition but
more from a letter which he wrote to Sofya Nikolayevna and which I have seen myself. We have
seen that he was capable of strong and deep
affection ; yet it is hard to believe that a man with
so little refinement of manner could give verbal
expression to such tender and delicate solicitude as
breathed through the whole of this letter. He
begged her and commanded her to be careful of her
health, and sent her much advice on the subject.
Unfortunately, I can only remember a few words of
it : ' if you were living in my house '—this was one
thing the old man said—' I would not suffer the
wind to blow on you or a grain of dust to settle
on your skin.'

Sofya Nikolayevna was able to appreciate this
affection, though she understood that half of it
was intended for the expected heir ; and she
promised to carry out scrupulously his wishes and
instructions. But it was hard for her to keep this
promise. She was one of those women who pay for
the joy of motherhood by a constant discomfort
which is more painful and distressing than any real
illness : and she suffered in mind also, because her

relations with her father became daily more
humiliating and the insolence of Nikolai more
unbearable. Alexyéi Stepanitch, who saw no
danger in his wife's constant sufferings, and was
told that the symptoms were quite natural and
would soon pass away, though he was sorry for his
wife, was not excessively put out ; and this was
another cause of distress to Sofya Nikolayevna. He
worked hard at his duties in the law-court, hoping
soon to be promoted. He had become accustomed
to living with his father-in-law ; he avoided for
the present all contact with Nikolai, and looked
forward without impatience to a change in their
position. His wife did not like this either. Things
dragged on thus, as I have said already, for several
months, and it was not a happy time for any of
them.

But Nikolai was not satisfied with this state of
things : he desired a final solution. Seeing that
Sofya Nikolayevna was controlling her quick
temper and righteous indignation, he determined
to force her hand. It was necessary for his purpose
that she should lose patience and complain to her
father ; and he warned the invalid more than once
that he was constantly expecting Sofya Nikolayevna to complain of him and demand his instant
dismissal. He did not wait for any pretext or
opportunity. One day, in the presence of other
servants, when his young mistress was standing
close to him at the open door of the next room,
he began, speaking loud and looking straight at her,
to use such offensive language of herself and her
husband that Sofya Nikolayevna was struck dumb
for a moment by his insolence. But she recovered
immediately, and without a word to him rushed

to her father's room, where, choking with wrath
and excitement, she repeated the insulting words
which had been used almost to her face by his
favourite. Nikolai came in at her heels and would
not let her finish her story. Feigning tears and
crossing himself, he solemnly swore, that it was
mere slander, that he had never said anything of the
sort, and that it was wicked of Sofya Nikolayevna
to ruin an innocent man ! ' You hear what he says,
Sonitchka,' said the invalid in a peevish voice.
This was too much for Sofya Nikolayevna : stung
to the quick, she forgot her magnanimous self-
restraint and forgot also that she might kill her
father with fright. She raised her voice with such
effect that the favourite was forced to leave the
room. Then she said to her father : ' After this
insult I cannot live under the same roof with
Nikolai : you must choose which of us is to go, he
or I ! '—and then she rushed wildly from the room.
The old man had a seizure, and Nikolai hastened
to his aid. The usual remedies were applied with
success, and then master and man had a long conversation, after which Sofya Nikolayevna was
summoned to the room. ' Sonitchka,' he said,
with all the firmness and calmness he could muster,
' my weak and suffering state makes it impossible
for me to part with Nikolai ; my life depends on
him. You must buy another house ; here is the
money for the purpose.' Sofya Nikolayevna fell
fainting to the ground and was carried back to her
own room.

To this had come the tender tie of affection
between parent and child, a tie which should
surely have been made doubly strong by the
temporary coolness due to the step-mother, and

then by the father's penitence and the daughter's devotion and forgetfulness of all her wrongs. And then, when she married, she had chosen her husband with this in view, and had stipulated that she should not be parted from her father! And now they were to part at a time when the doctors declared he would not live another month! But in this forecast the doctors were mistaken, just as they often are nowadays: he lived on for more than a year.

When Sofya Nikolayevna recovered from her swoon and her eyes fell on the pale anxious face of Alexyéi Stepanitch, she realized that there was one creature on earth who loved her: she threw her arms round her husband, and floods of tears gave relief to her heart. She told him all that had passed between her and her father. The narrative revived the smart of her wounded feelings, and brought out more clearly the difficulty of her position; and she would have despaired, but for the support of her kind husband. Though weaker in character and less far-sighted than she was, he never ran into extremes and never lost presence of mind and power of judgement in the trying hours of life. It may seem strange that Alexyéi Stepanitch could give moral support to Sofya Nikolayevna; but, for all her exceptional intelligence and apparent strength of will, the effect of a sudden shock to her feelings was to make her lose courage and become utterly bewildered. As an honest chronicler of oral tradition, I am bound to add that she was too sensitive to the opinion of society and paid it too much deference, in spite of her own superiority to the people among whom she lived. What would be said by people at Ufa,

and especially by the ladies who took the lead in
society there ?   What would be thought by her
husband's family ?   What, above all, would be
said by Stepan Mihailovitch, when he heard that
she had left her father ?   As she asked herself
these questions, the injury to her pride gave her
as much pain as the wound to her feelings as
a daughter.   To her it seemed equally terrible
that her father should be blamed for ingratitude
to his daughter, and that she should be blamed
for failing in affection to a dying father.   One or
other alternative was bound to be chosen ; and
either he or she was bound to be condemned.

Alexyéi Stepanitch felt deep pity for her as he
watched these sufferings, and he felt puzzled also.
It was no easy task to administer consolation to
Sofya Nikolayevna :   her eager fancy painted
appalling pictures of disaster, and her ready
tongue gave them lively expression.   She was
prepared to brush aside every attempt to find an
issue from the situation, and to trample on every
suggestion of a settlement.   But Alexyéi Stepanitch
had love to teach him, and also that sanity and
simplicity of mind which was wanting in his wife.
He waited till the first irrepressible outburst was
over, the first outcry of the wounded heart ; and
then he began to speak.   The words were very
ordinary, but they came from a kind simple heart ;
and if they did not calm Sofya Nikolayevna, they
did at least by degrees make it possible for her to
understand what was said.   He told her that she
had always done her duty as a loving daughter,
and that she must continue to do it by falling in
with her father's wishes.   It was probably no
sudden decision : her father might have wished for

a long time that they should live apart. For a sick
and dying man it was difficult or even impossible
to part from the regular attendant who nursed
him so faithfully. Stepan Mihailovitch must be
told the whole truth ; but to acquaintances it
would be enough to say that her father had always
intended to set up the young couple in a house of
their own during his lifetime. She would be able
to visit her father twice a day and attend to him
almost as much as before. Of course people in
the town would find out in time the real reason
of the separation—they had probably some idea
already of the facts—but they would only pity her
and abuse Nikolai. ' Besides,' he added, ' though
your father talked like that, when it comes to
acting, he may shrink from the separation. Talk
it over with him, and lay all your case before him.'
Sofya Nikolayevna made no reply : during a long
silence her eyes rested with a curious puzzled gaze
on her husband. The truth of his simple words
and his plain way of looking at things—these
breathed peace and comfort into her heart. His
plan seemed to her new and ingenious, and she
wondered she had never thought of it herself.
She embraced her husband with a heart full of
love and gratitude.

So it was settled that Sofya Nikolayevna should
appeal to her father to alter his decision and let
them stay on in the house, at all events until she
had entirely recovered from her confinement ;
their household arrangements would be quite
separate, and all collisions with Nikolai would be
avoided. In favour of this suggestion, there was
one very pressing argument—that, while it was
bad for Sofya Nikolayevna in her present con-

dition to be jolted over the ill-paved streets of the town, no risk to herself would prevent her from paying a daily visit to her father. But the explanation with her father was unsuccessful. The old man told her calmly but firmly that his decision had been carefully considered and was no impulse of the moment. ' My dear Sonitchka,' he said, ' I knew beforehand that after your marriage you could not live under the same roof as Nikolai. You are not able to judge him coolly, and I don't blame you for it : he sinned deeply against you in old days, and though you forgave him, you were unable to forget his conduct. I know that he does not behave properly to you even now ; but you take an exaggerated view of it all.' At this point Sofya Nikolayevna tried to break in, but he stopped her and said : ' Wait and hear to the end what I have to say. Let us suppose that he is as guilty as you take him to be : that makes it all the more impossible for you to live in the same house with him ; but I cannot face parting from him. Have pity on my helpless and suffering condition. I am no longer a man, but a lifeless corpse ; you know that Nikolai has to move me in bed ten times a day ; no one can take his place. All I ask is peace of mind. Death is hovering over me, and every moment I must prepare for the change to eternity. I was constantly made wretched by the thought that Nikolai was giving offence to you. Our parting is inevitable ; go, my dear, and live in a house of your own. When you come to visit me, you shall not see the object of your dislike : he will be only too glad to keep out of the way. He has gained his object and got you out of the house, and now he will be able to

rob me at his leisure. I know and see it all, but
I forgive him everything for his unwearied nursing
of me day and night. What he undergoes in his
attendance on me is beyond the power of human
endurance. Do not distress me, but take the
money and buy a house for yourselves.'

I shall not describe all the phases through which
Sofya Nikolayevna passed—her doubts and hesi-
tations, her mental conflicts, her tears and sufferings, her ups and downs of feeling from day to
day. It is enough to say that the money was
accepted and the house bought, and husband and
wife were settled there before a fortnight had
passed. The little house was new and clean, and
had never been occupied before. Sofya Nikolayevna began with her usual ardour to put her
house in order and to settle the course of their
daily life; but her health, much affected by her
condition, and still more by all the agitation she
had gone through, soon broke down altogether.
She was confined to bed for a fortnight, and did
not see her father for a whole month. Their first
interview was a touching and pitiful sight. He
had grown much weaker; missing his daughter
and blaming himself for her illness, he had suffered
much by her absence. Their meeting gave happiness to both, but it cost them tears. He was
especially grieved to see her so terribly thin and
so altered in looks; but this was due, not so much
to grief and illness as to her condition. The
features of some women look different and even
ugly during pregnancy; and Sofya Nikolayevna
was a case in point. In course of time things
settled down and her relations with her father
became easy; Nikolai never ventured to appear

when she was present. There was just one person
who could not reconcile himself to the thought
that she had left a dying father to settle in a house
of her own ; and that was Stepan Mihailovitch.
She quite anticipated this, and wrote him a very
frank letter just before she was taken ill, in which
she tried to explain her father's action and defend
it as far as possible. She might have saved herself
the trouble, for Stepan Mihailovitch blamed her
and not her father, and said that it was her duty
to bear without a sign of displeasure all the
misconduct of ' that scoundrel ' Nikolai. He wrote
to his son to reprove him for allowing his wife to
abandon her father to the hands of servants.
But Stepan Mihailovitch did not realize, either
that the separation was necessary to preserve the
peace of a dying man, or that a wife could act
without the permission of her husband. In the
present case, however, husband and wife were
entirely of one mind.

To put the finishing touches to the new house
and modest household arrangements, Sofya Nikolayevna called in the assistance of a widow whom
she knew, who lived in a humble position at Ufa.
This was Mme Cheprúnoff, a very simple and
kind-hearted creature. She owned a little house
in the suburbs, and a small but productive garden,
which brought her in a trifle. She had other
means of maintaining herself and her adored only
child, a little one-eyed boy called Andrusha : she
hawked about small wares of different kinds, and
even sold cakes in the market. But her chief
source of income was the sale of Bokhara muslin,
which she went to Orenburg every year to buy.
Sofya Nikolayevna was related through her

mother to this woman ; but she had the weakness to conceal the relationship, though every one in the town knew it. Mme Cheprunoff was devoted to her brilliant and distinguished kinswoman. She used to pay secret visits to Sofya Nikolayevna during the time when she was persecuted and humiliated by her step-mother ; and Sofya Nikolayevna, when her time of triumph and influence came, became the avowed benefactress of Mme Cheprunoff. When they were alone together, Sofya Nikolayevna lavished caresses upon her unselfish and devoted kinswoman ; but when other people were present, the one was the great lady and the other the poor protégée who sold cakes in the streets. This treatment did not offend Mme Cheprunoff : on the contrary, she insisted on it. She loved and admired her beautiful cousin with all her heart, and looked on her as a superior being, and would never have forgiven herself if she had thrown a shadow on the brilliant position of Sofya Nikolayevna. The secret was revealed, as it had to be, to Alexyéi Stepanitch ; and he, in spite of the ancient lineage which his sisters were always dinning into his ears, received this humble friend as his wife's worthy kinswoman, and treated her with affection and respect all his life ; he even tried to kiss the work-worn hand of the cake-seller, but she would never allow it. He was only prevented by his wife's earnest entreaties from speaking of this relationship in his own family and in the circle of their acquaintance. This conduct earned him the love of the simple-minded woman ; and whenever there were differences in the household in later years, she was his ardent champion and defender.

She knew all the shops and was a great hand at a bargain ; and so, with her help, Sofya Nikola-yevna did her furnishing quickly and well.

When the young Bagroffs bought a house and started housekeeping by themselves, there was much talk and gossip in the town ; and at first many exaggerations and inventions were current. But Alexyéi Stepanitch had spoken the truth : the real reason came out before long. This was due chiefly to Nikolai, who boasted among his friends that he had ousted the pettish young lady, and took the opportunity to give a lively descrip-tion of her character. So the talk and gossip soon quieted down.

Husband and wife had at last a house entirely to themselves. In the morning, Alexyéi Stepanitch drove down to his work at the law-courts, dropping his wife at her father's house ; and on his return he spent more time every day with his father-in-law, before taking his wife home. A modest dinner awaited them there. To sit alone together, at a meal of their own ordering, in their own house, was a charming sensation for a time ; but nothing is a novelty for long, and this charm could not last for ever. In spite of her bad health and small means, Sofya Nikolayevna's clever hands made her little house as dainty as a toy. Taste and care are a substitute for money ; and many of their visitors thought the furnishing splendid. The hardest problem was to arrange about their servants. Sofya Nikolayevna had brought two servants as part of her portion—a man named Theodore and a black-eyed maid called Parasha ; these two were now married to one another ; and at the same time Annushka, a young laundress

belonging to Sofya Nikolayevna, was married to
Yephrem Yevséitch, a young servant who had
been brought from Bagrovo. This man was
honest and good-natured and much attached to
his young mistress, which cannot be said of the
other servants. She returned his affection, and he
well deserved it : he was one in a thousand, and
his devotion to her was proved by his whole life.

Yevséitch (as he was always called in the family)
became later the attendant of her eldest son,[1] and
watched over him like a father. I knew this
worthy man well. Fifteen years ago I saw him
for the last time : he was then blind and spending
his last days in the Government of Penza on an
estate belonging to one of the grandsons of Stepan
Mihailovitch. I spent a whole month there in the
summer ; and every morning I went to fish in
a pool where the stream of Kakarma falls into the
river Niza. The cottage where Yevséitch was
living stood right on the bank of this pool ; and
every day as I came up I saw him leaning against
the angle of the cottage and facing the rising sun.
He was bent and decrepit, and his hair had turned
perfectly white ; pressing a long staff to his
breast, he leaned upon it with the knotted fingers
of both hands, and turned his sightless eyes
towards the sun's rays. Though he could not see
the light, he could feel its warmth, so pleasant in
the fresh morning air, and his face expressed both
pleasure and sadness. His ear was so quick that
he heard my step at some distance, and he always
hailed me as an old fisherman might hail a schoolboy, though I was then myself over fifty years
old. ' Ah, it 's you, my little falcon ! '—he used

[1] i. e. the author.

to call me this when I was a child—' you're late
this morning ! God send you a full basket ! '
He died two years later in the arms of his son and
daughter and his wife, who survived him several
years.

Meantime life at Ufa took a very regular and
unvarying course. Owing to her state of health
and spirits, Sofya Nikolayevna paid few visits and
only to intimate friends, whose small number was
made smaller by the absence of the Chichagoffs.
Autumn was nearly over before those dearest of
friends returned from the country with Mme
Myortvavo. The disordered nerves and consequent
low spirits of his wife were at first a source of great
uneasiness to Alexyéi Stepanitch. He was completely puzzled : he had never in his life met
people who were ill without anything definite the
matter, or sad with no cause for sadness ; he
could make nothing of illness due to some inexplicable grief, or grief due to some imaginary or
imperceptible illness. But he saw that there was
no serious danger, and his anxiety calmed down
by degrees. He was convinced that it was all the
effect of imagination, which had always been his
way of accounting for his wife's moods of excitement and distress, whenever he found it impossible
to arrive at any reason within his comprehension.
If he ceased to be uneasy, he began to be rather
bored at times ; and this was very natural, in
spite of his love for his wife and pity for her
constant suffering. To listen for whole hours every
day to constant complaints about her condition,
which was not after all so very exceptional : to
hear gloomy presentiments, or even prophecies,
of the fatal results which were sure to follow (and

Sofya Nikolayevna, thanks to her reading of medical works, was extraordinarily ingenious in discovering ominous symptoms); to endure her reproaches and constant demands for those trifling services which a man can seldom render—all this was wearisome enough. Sofya Nikolayevna saw what he felt, and was deeply hurt. If she had found him in general incapable of deep feeling and strong passion, she would have reconciled herself sooner to her situation. She used often to say herself, ' A man cannot give you what he has not got '; and she would have recognized the truth of the saying and submitted to her fate. But the misfortune was that she remembered the depth and ardour of her husband's passion in the days of his courtship, and believed that he might have continued to love her in the same fashion, had not something occurred to cool his feelings. This unlucky notion by degrees took hold of her imagination, and her ingenuity soon discovered many reasons to account for this coolness and much evidence of its truth. As to reasons—there was the hostile influence of his family, her own ill-health, and, worst of all, her loss of beauty; for her looking-glass forced upon her the sad change in her appearance. Her proofs were these— that her husband was not disquieted by her danger, took insufficient notice of her condition, did not try to cheer and interest her, and, above all, found more pleasure in talking to other women. And then a passion, which hitherto had lurked unrecognized, the torturing passion of jealousy, as keen-sighted as it is blind, flashed up like gunpowder in her heart. Every day there were scenes—tears and reproaches, quarrels and

reconciliations. And all the time Alexyéi Stepanitch was entirely innocent. To the insinuations of
his sisters he paid no attention at all; to his
father's opinion he attached great importance,
and that was so favourable to Sofya Nikolayevna
that she had even risen in her husband's eyes
in consequence. He was sincerely, if not deeply,
distressed about her sufferings; and her loss of
beauty he regarded as temporary, and looked
forward with pleasure to the time when his young
wife would get back her good looks. Though the
sight of her suffering distressed him, he could not
sympathize with all her presentiments and prognostications, which he believed to be quite imaginary. He was incapable, as most men would be,
of paying her the sort of attention she expected.
It was really a ticklish business to administer
consolation to Sofya Nikolayevna in her present
condition; you were quite likely to put your foot
in it and make matters worse; it required much
tact and dexterity, and these were qualities which
her husband did not possess. If he found more
pleasure in talking to other women, it was probably
because he was not afraid that some casual remark
might cause annoyance and irritation.

But Sofya Nikolayevna could not look at the
matter in this light. Her view of it was dictated
by her nature, whose fine qualities were apt to
run to extremes. But what was to be done, if the
nerves of one were tough and strong and those
of the other sensitive and morbid, if hers were
jarred by what had no effect upon his? The
Chichagoffs alone understood the causes of this
uncomfortable situation; and though they received no confidences from either husband or wife,

they took a warm interest in both and did much to calm Sofya Nikolayevna's excitement by their friendship, their frequent visits, and their rational and sensible conversation. Both husband and wife owed much to them at this period.

So things went on till the time that Sofya Nikolayevna became a mother. Though she was often troubled in mind, her health improved during the last two months, and she was safely delivered of a daughter. She herself, and her husband still more, would have preferred a son; but when the mother pressed the child to her heart, she thought no more of any distinction between boy and girl. A passion of maternal love filled her heart and mind and whole being. Alexyéi Stepanitch thanked God for his wife's safety, rejoiced at her relief, and soon reconciled himself to the fact that his child was a girl.

But at Bagrovo it was quite another story! Stepan Mihailovitch was so confident that he was to have a grandson to carry on the line of the Bagroffs, that he would not believe at first in the birth of a grand-daughter. When at last he read through his son's letter with his own eyes and was convinced that there was no doubt about it, he was seriously annoyed. He put off the entertainment planned for his labourers, and refused to write himself to the parents; he would only send a message of congratulation to the young mother, with instructions that the infant was to be christened Praskovya, in compliment to his cousin and favourite, Praskovya Ivanovna Kurolyessova. His vexation over this disappointment was a touching and amusing sight. Even his womankind derived a little secret enjoyment from

it. His good sense told him that he had no
business to be angry with anyone, but for a few
days he could not control his feelings—so hard
was it for him to give up the hope, or rather the
certainty, that a grandson would be born, to
continue the famous line of Shimon.   In the
expectation of the happy news, he had kept his
family tree on his bed, ready any day to enter his
grandson's name ; but now he ordered this document to be hidden out of sight.   He would not
allow his daughter Aksinya to travel to Ufa in
order to stand godmother to the babe ; he said
impatiently, 'Take that journey for a girl's
christening ?   Nonsense !   If she brings a girl
every year, you would have travelling enough ! '
Time did its work, however, and the frown, never
a formidable frown this time, vanished from the
brow of Stepan Mihailovitch, as he consoled himself with the thought that he might have a grandson before a year was out.   Then he wrote a kind
and playful letter to his daughter-in-law, pretending to scold her for her mistake and bidding her
present him with a grandson within a twelve-
month.

Sofya Nikolayevna was so entirely absorbed by
the revelation of maternity and by devotion to
her child, that she did not even notice the signs
of the old man's displeasure, and was quite
unaffected by Aksinya's absence from the christening.   It proved difficult to keep her in bed for
nine days after her confinement.   She felt so well
and strong that she could have danced on the
fourth day.   But she had no wish to dance ; she
wanted to be on her feet day and night, attending
to her little Parasha.   The infant was feeble and

sickly : the mother's constant distress of body
and mind had probably affected the child. The
doctor would not allow her to nurse the child
herself. Andréi Avenarius was the name of this
doctor ; he was a very clever, cultivated, and
amiable man, an intimate friend of the young
people and a daily visitor at their house. As soon
as possible Sofya Nikolayevna took her baby to
her father's house, hoping that it would please the
invalid to see this mite, and that he would find
in it a resemblance to his first wife. This resemblance was probably imaginary ; for in my
opinion it is impossible for an infant to be like
a grown-up person ; but Sofya Nikolayevna never
failed to assert that her first child was the very
image of its grandmother. Old M. Zubin was
approaching the end of his earthly career ; both
body and mind were breaking fast. He looked at
the baby with little interest, and had hardly
strength to sign it with the Cross. All he said
was, 'I congratulate you, Sonitchka.' Sofya
Nikolayevna was distressed by her father's critical
condition—it was more than a month since she
had seen him—and also by his indifference to her
little angel, Parasha.

But soon the young mother forgot all the world
around her, as she hung over her daughter's cradle.
All other interests and attachments grew pale in
comparison, and she surrendered herself with a kind
of frenzy to this new sensation. No hands but hers
might touch the child. She handed it herself to
the foster-mother and held it at the breast, and it
was pain to her to watch it drawing life, not from
its mother, but from a stranger. It is hard to
believe, but it is true, and Sofya Nikolayevna

admitted it herself later, that if the child sucked
too long, she used to take it away before it was
satisfied, and rock it herself in her arms or in the
cradle, and sing it to sleep. She saw nothing of
her friends, not even of her dear Mme Chichagoff.
Naturally they all thought her eccentric or absurd,
and her chief intimates were vexed by her conduct.
She paid a hasty visit every day to her father, and
returned every day with fear in her heart that she
would find the child ill. She left her husband
perfectly free to spend his time as he liked. For
some days he stopped at home ; but his wife never
stirred from the cradle and took no notice of him
except to turn him out of the little nursery,
because she feared that twice-breathed air might
hurt the baby. After this, he began to go out
alone, till at last he went to some party every day ;
and he began to play cards to relieve his boredom.
The Ufa ladies were amused at the sight of the
deserted husband, and some of them flirted with
him, saying that it was a charity to console the
widower, and that Sofya Nikolayevna would
thank them for it when she recovered from her
maternal passion and reappeared in society.
Sofya Nikolayevna did not hear of these good
Samaritans till later ; when she did, she was vexed.
Mme Cheprunoff, who came often to the house,
watched Sofya Nikolayevna with astonishment,
pity, and displeasure. She was a tender mother
herself to her little boy with the one eye, but this
devotion to one object and disregard of everything
else seemed to her to border on insanity. With
groans and sighs she struck her fists against her
own body—this was a regular trick of hers—and
said that such love was a mortal sin which God

would punish. Sofya Nikolayevna resented this
so much that she kept Mme Cheprunoff out of the
nursery in future. No one but Dr. Avenarius was
admitted there, and he came pretty often. The
mother was constantly discovering symptoms of
different diseases in the child ; for these she began
by consulting Buchan's *Domestic Medicine*, and
then, when that did not answer, she called in
Avenarius. He found it impossible to argue her
out of her beliefs : all he could do was to prescribe
harmless medicines. Yet the child was really
feeble, and at times he was obliged to prescribe
for it in real earnest.

It is difficult to say what would have been the
upshot of all this ; but by the inscrutable designs
of Providence, a thunderbolt burst over the head
of Sofya Nikolayevna : her adored child died
suddenly. The cause of death was uncertain :
it may have been too much care, or too much
medicine, or too feeble a constitution ; at any
rate, the child succumbed, when four months old,
to a very slight attack of a common childish ail-
ment. Sofya Nikolayevna was sitting by the
cradle when she saw the infant start and a spasm
pass over the little face : she caught it up and
found that it was dead.

She must have had a marvellous constitution
to support this blow. For some days she knew
no one and the doctors feared for her reason ;
there were three of them, Avenarius, Zanden,
and Klauss ; all three were much attached to
their patient, and one of them was always with
her. But, by God's blessing and thanks to her
youth and strength, that terrible time passed by.
The unhappy mother recovered her senses ; and

her love for her husband, whose own distress was
great, asserted itself for the time and saved her.
On the fourth day she became conscious of her
surroundings : she recognized Alexyéi Stepanitch,
so changed by grief that he was hard to recognize,
and her bosom friend, Mme Chichagoff ; a terrible
cry burst from her lips, and a healing flood of tears
gushed from the eyes which had been dry till then.
Silently she embraced her husband and sobbed
for long on his breast, while he sobbed like a child
himself. The danger of insanity was past, but the
exhaustion of her bodily strength was still alarming. For four days and nights she had neither
eaten nor drunk, and now she could swallow no
food nor medicine nor even water. Her condition
was so critical that the doctors did not oppose her
wish to make her confession and receive the
sacraments. The performance of this Christian
duty was beneficial to the patient : she slept for
the first time, and, when she woke after two hours
looking bright and happy, she told her husband
that she had seen in her sleep a vision of Our Lady
of Iberia, exactly as she was represented on the
ikon of their parish church ; and she believed, that
if she could put her lips to this ikon, the Mother
of God would surely have mercy on her. The
picture was brought from the church, and the
priest read the service for the Visitation of the
Sick. When the choir sang, ' O mighty Mother of
God, look down in mercy on my sore bodily
suffering ! '—all present fell on their knees and
repeated the words of the prayer. Alexyéi
Stepanitch sobbed aloud ; and the sufferer too
shed tears throughout the service and pressed her
lips to the image. When it was over, she felt so

much relief that she was able to drink some
water ; and from that time she began to take food
and medicine. Her two dear friends, Mme
Chichagoff and Mme Cheprunoff, were with her
constantly ; she was soon pronounced out of
danger, and her husband's troubled heart had rest.
The doctors set to work with fresh zeal to restore
her strength, and their great anxiety was in a way
dangerous to their patient ; for one of them found
traces of consumption, another of *marasmus*, and
the third was apprehensive of an aneurysm. But
fortunately they were unanimous on one point :
the patient should go at once to the country, to
enjoy pure air and, preferably, forest air, and take
a course of *koumiss*. At the beginning of June
it was not too late to drink mare's milk, as the
grass on the steppes was still fresh and in full
growth.

Stepan Mihailovitch took the news of his grand-
daughter's death very coolly : he even said, ' No
reason to tear one's hair over *that* ! There will be
plenty more girls.' But when he heard later of
the dangerous illness of Sofya Nikolayevna, the
old man was much disturbed. When a third
message came, that she was out of immediate
danger but very ill, and that the doctors were
baffled and prescribed a course of *koumiss*, he was
exceedingly angry with the doctors : ' Those
bunglers who murder our bodies ', said he, ' defile
our souls also by making us swallow the drink of
heathens. If a Russian is forbidden by his Church
to eat horseflesh, then he has no business to drink
the milk of the unclean animal.' Then he added
with a heavy sigh and a gesture of disgust :
' I don't like it at all : her life may perhaps be

saved, but she will never be right again, and there
will be no children.' Stepan Mihailovitch was
deeply grieved and remained for a long time in
a state of depression.

Twenty-nine *versts* to the south-west of Ufa, on
the road to Kazan where the Ufa falls into that
noble river, the Dyoma, there lay in a rich valley
a little Tartar village called by the Russians
Alkino, surrounded by forests.   The houses
nestled in picturesque disorder at the foot of a hill
called Bairam-Tau [1] which gave them shelter
from the north ;   and another hill, Zein-Tau,[2]
rose on the west.   The Uza, fringed with bushes,
flowed to the south-west ;   the forest-glades were
fragrant with grasses and flowers ;   and all round,
oaks and limes and maples cleft the air and
imparted to it an invigorating virtue.   To this
charming spot Alexyéi Stepanitch brought his
wife, weak and pale and thin, a mere shadow of
her old self ;   Avenarius, their friend and doctor,
came with them, and they had some difficulty in
getting the patient to the end of the journey.
The owner of the village received them with
cordial hospitality ;   he had a comfortable house,
but Sofya Nikolayevna was unwilling to install
herself there, and one of the outbuildings was
cleared out for her occupation.   The family were
only too kind in their attentions to her, so that
the doctor was obliged to forbid their visits for
a time.   They spoke Russian fairly well, though
they professed the Mohammedan creed ;   and,
though their dress and habits were then partly
Russian and partly Tartar, *koumiss* was their
invariable drink from morning till night.   For

[1] Hill of Feasting.   [2] Hill of Meeting.

Sofya Nikolayevna the health-giving beverage was prepared in a cleanly civilized manner : the mare's milk was fermented in a clean new wooden bucket and not in the usual bag of raw horse-hide. The natives declared that *koumiss* made in their fashion tasted better and was more effective ; but Sofya Nikolayevna felt an unconquerable aversion to the horse-hide bag. When the doctor had laid down rules for the cure, he went back to Ufa, leaving Alexyéi Stepanitch, with Parasha and Annushka, in charge of the invalid. The air and the *koumiss*, of which small doses were taken at first ; the daily drives with Alexyéi Stepanitch through the forest which surrounded the village— Yevséitch, who was now a favourite with Sofya Nikolayevna, acted as coachman ; the woods, where the patient lay for whole hours in the cool shade on a leather mattress with pillows, breathing the fragrant air into her lungs, listening sometimes to an entertaining book, and often sinking into refreshing sleep—the whole life was so beneficial to Sofya Nikolayevna that in a fortnight she was able to get up and could walk about. When Avenarius came again, he was delighted by the effect of the *koumiss*, and increased the doses ; but as the patient could not endure it in large quantities, he thought it necessary to prescribe vigorous exercise in the form of riding on horse-back. For a Russian lady to ride was in those days a startling novelty : Alexyéi Stepanitch did not like it, and Sofya Nikolayevna herself was shocked by the notion. Their host's daughters presented an instructive example, for they constantly rode far and wide over the country on their Bashkir ponies ; but Sofya Nikolayevna

for long turned a deaf ear to all persuasions, and
even to the entreaties of her husband, whom the
doctor had speedily and completely convinced of
the necessity of the exercise. At last the Chichagoffs came on a visit to Alkino, and Sofya Nikolayevna's resistance was overcome by a joint effort.
What appealed to her most strongly was the
example of Mme Chichagoff, who, in the spirit of
true friendship, sacrificed her own prejudices and
began to ride, at first alone, and then with the
patient. This hard exercise required a change of
diet ; and fat mutton, which Sofya Nikolayevna
did not like either, was prescribed. Avenarius
probably took a hint from the habits of the
Bashkirs and Tartars, who, while moving from
place to place throughout the summer, drink
koumiss and eat hardly anything but fat mutton,
not even bread ; and they ride all day long over
the broad steppes, until the prairie grass turns
from green to grey and veils itself with a soft silvery
down. The treatment answered admirably. They
sometimes rode out in a large party with the sons
and daughters of their host. There was a potash
factory which they sometimes visited, about two
versts from Alkino, situated in the depth of the
forest and on the bank of a stream ; and Sofya
Nikolayevna looked with interest at the iron
cauldrons full of burning wood-ash, the wooden
troughs in which the dross was deposited, and the
furnaces in which the product was refined and
converted into porous white lumps of the vegetable
salt called ' potash '. She admired the dexterity
with which the work was carried on, and the
activity of the Tartars ; their skull-caps were
a novelty to her, and also the long shirts which

came down to their feet and yet left them free
command of their limbs. In general her hosts
were very kind, and tried to amuse their guest by
making the natives sing and dance before her, or
wrestle, or run races on horseback.

At first Alexyéi Stepanitch was always present
at these expeditions and entertainments; but
when he ceased to feel anxious about his wife's
health and saw her surrounded by troops of
attentive friends, he began by degrees to find some
time on his hands. Country life and country air,
with the beauty of that landscape, roused in him
a desire for his old amusements. He made fishing-
lines and began to angle for the wily trout in the
clear mountain streams round Alkino; and he
went out sometimes to catch quails with a net.
Theodore, Parasha's young husband, was a capital
hand at this sport and could make pipes to decoy
the birds. With sportsmen in general, netting
for quails does not rank high; but really I do not
know why they despise it. To lie on the fragrant
meadow grass with your net hanging in front of
you on the tall stalks; to hear the quails calling
beside you and at a distance; to imitate their low
sweet note on the pipe; to hear the excited birds
reply and watch them run, or even fly, from all
sides towards you; to watch their curious antics,
and to get excited yourself over the success or
failure of your strategy—all this gave me much
pleasure at one time, and even now I cannot recall
it with indifference. But it was impossible to
make this pleasure intelligible to Sofya Nikolayevna.

In two months she was well on the way to
recovery: her face filled out, and a bright colour

began to play again upon her cheeks. When
Avenarius paid a third visit, he was entirely
satisfied ; and he had a perfect right to triumph ;
for he had been the first to prescribe *koumiss* and
had directed the treatment himself. He had always
been attached to his patient ; and now that he
had succeeded in saving her life, he loved her like
a daughter.

Alexyéi Stepanitch sent a weekly bulletin to
his father at Bagrovo. Stepan Mihailovitch was
glad to hear that his daughter-in-law was getting
better ; but of course he disbelieved in the healing
power of the *koumiss,* and was very angry about
the riding, which they were rash enough to mention
in writing to him. His wife and daughters made
use of this opportunity, and the sneering remarks
which they let fall on purpose in the course of
conversation, worked him up to such a pitch that
he wrote his son a rather offensive letter which
gave pain to Sofya Nikolayevna. But when he
was convinced that his daughter-in-law had quite
recovered and had even grown stout, pleasing
hopes began to stir again in his breast, and he
grew reconciled in some degree to the *koumiss*
and the riding.

The young Bagroffs returned to Ufa at the
beginning of autumn. Old M. Zubin was very
far gone by that time, and his daughter's wonderful recovery produced no sort of impression on
him. All his earthly business was done, and all
ties broken : every thread that held him to life
was severed, and the soul could hardly find shelter
in the disruption of the body.

The normal course of relations between the young
couple had been, so to speak, arrested in its

development by a number of events : first, by
the birth of the child and the mother's extravagant
devotion to it ; then, by the child's death which
nearly deprived the mother of her reason and her
life ; and, finally, by the long course of treatment
and residence in the Tartar village. In the stormy
season of her distress and sickness, Sofya Nikolayevna had ever before her eyes the genuine love
and self-sacrifice of her husband. At that time
there were none of those collisions which constantly
occur at ordinary times between ill-matched
characters ; and even if there were occasions for
such misunderstandings, they passed unnoticed.
When gold is in circulation, small change is of
little importance. In exceptional circumstances
and critical moments, nothing but gold passes ;
but the daily expenditure of uneventful life is
mainly carried on with small change. Now Alexyéi
Stepanitch, though he was not poor in gold, was
often hard up for small change. When a man,
if he sees distress and danger threatening the
health and life of one whom he loves, himself
suffers in every fibre of his being ; when he forgets
sleep and food and himself altogether ; when the
nerves are strung up and the moral nature up-
lifted—at such times there is no room for small
exactions, no room for small services and attentions. But when the time of tragic events has gone
by, everything quiets down again ; the nerves are
relaxed and the spirit contracts ; the material
life of flesh and blood. asserts itself, in all its
triviality ; habits resume their lost power ; and
then comes the turn of those exactions and
demands we spoke of, the turn of small services
and polite attentions and all the other trifles which

make up the web of actual ordinary life. Time
will again apply the test and bring back the
necessity of self-sacrifice ; but meanwhile life runs
on without a stop in the ordinary groove, and its
peace and adornment and pleasure—what we call
happiness, in fact—is made up entirely of trivial
things, of small change.

For these reasons, when Sofya Nikolayevna
began to recover and Alexyéi Stepanitch ceased
to fear for her life and health, there began by
degrees to reappear, on one side, the old exacting
temper, and on the other side, the old incapacity
to satisfy its demands. Gentle reproaches and
expostulations had become tiresome to the husband, and fierce explosions frightened him. Fear
at once banished perfect frankness, and loss of
frankness between husband and wife, especially in
the less assertive and independent of the two,
leads straight to the destruction of domestic
happiness. After the return to Ufa, this evil
would probably have grown worse in the trivial
idle atmosphere of town life ; but Sofya Nikolayevna's father was now actually dying, and his
sad suffering condition banished all other anxieties
and took up all his daughter's thoughts and feelings. Obedient to the law of her moral nature, she
gave herself up without reserves to her duty as
a daughter. Thus the process which was unveiling
every corner of their domestic life, was again
brought to a standstill. Sofya Nikolayevna spent
her days and nights with her father. Nikolai, as
before, waited on his sick master, nursing him with
wonderful devotion and indefatigable care ; and,
as before, he kept out of sight of Sofya Nikolayevna, though he had now the right and the power

to appear before her with impunity. Touched by his behaviour, she had sent for him ; a reconciliation took place, and she gave him leave to be present with her in the sick-room. The dying man, in spite of his apparent insensibility to all around him, noticed this change : he pressed his daughter's hand in his feeble grasp, and said in a hardly audible whisper, ' I thank you.' Sofya Nikolayevna never left her father after this time.

I said that when Stepan Mihailovitch received the good news of his daughter-in-law's recovery, fond hopes awoke once more in his breast. They were not disappointed : before long Sofya Nikolayevna wrote to him herself, that she hoped, if God was good to her, to give birth to a son, to be the comfort of his old age. At the instant Stepan Mihailovitch was overjoyed, but he soon controlled his feelings and hid his happiness from his womankind. Perhaps it occurred to him that this second child might be a daughter, that Sofya Nikolayevna and the doctors between them might kill it also with too much love and too much medicine, and that the mother might lose her health over again ; or perhaps Stepan Mihailovitch was like many other people, who deliberately prophesy calamities with a secret hope that fortune will belie their prognostications. He pretended that he was not in the least glad, and said coolly : ' No no ! I'm too old a bird to look at *that* chaff. When the thing happens it will be time enough to believe it and rejoice over it.' His family were surprised to hear him speak so, and said nothing in reply. But, as a matter of fact, the old man for some unknown reason became convinced once more in his heart that he would have a grandson :

he gave instructions again to Father Vassili to
repeat in church the prayer for ' women labouring
of child ' ; and he fished out the family tree once
more from its hiding-place, and kept it always
beside him.

Meanwhile M. Zubin's last hour on earth came
quietly on. He had suffered much for many years ;
it seemed hardly natural that life should linger on
in a body which had lost all force and motion ;
and the ending of such a bare and pitiful existence
could distress no one. Even Sofya Nikolayevna
had only one prayer—that her father's soul might
depart in peace. And there *was* peace, and even
happiness at the moment of death. The face of
the dying man lit up suddenly, and this expression
remained long upon the features, though the eyes
were shut and the body had grown cold. The
funeral was a solemn and splendid ceremony.
M. Zubin had once been very popular ; but he
had become forgotten by degrees, and sympathy
for his suffering had grown gradually weaker. But
now, when the news of his death flew round the
town, old memories revived and evoked a fresh
feeling of love and pity for him. On the day of
his funeral every house was empty, and all the
population of Ufa lined the streets between the
Church of the Assumption and the cemetery.
May he rest in peace ! If he had the weakness of
human nature, he had also its goodness.

After M. Zubin's death, guardians were appointed for the children of his two marriages ;
and Alexyéi Stepanitch became guardian of his
wife's two brothers, who, before finishing their
education at the Moscow boarding-school, were
summoned to Petersburg to enter the Guards.

I forgot to mention that M. Zubin, shortly before his death, was sucessful in obtaining for Alexyéi Stepanitch his promotion to a higher office at the law-courts.

Sofya Nikolayevna wept and prayed for a long time, and Alexyéi Stepanitch wept and prayed at her side; but those tears and prayers were not painful or violent and had no ill effect on her recently restored health. Her husband's entreaties and the advice of her friends and doctors prevailed with her, and she began to take care of herself and to pay due attention to her condition. They convinced her that the health and even the life of the unborn child depended on the state of her own health and spirits. Their arguments were confirmed by bitter experience, and she resolutely submitted to all that was required of her. When her father-in-law wrote to her and expressed in simple words his sympathy with her loss and his fear that she might again injure her own health by excess of grief, she sent a very reassuring letter in reply; and she did in fact attend carefully to her bodily health and composure of mind. A regular but not monotonous plan of life was laid down. The two doctors, Klauss—who was becoming very intimate with the Bagroffs—and Avenarius, made her go out every day before dinner, and sometimes on foot; and each evening they had an unceremonious party of pleasant people at home, or went out themselves, generally to the Chichagoffs' house. Mme Chichagoff's brothers became great friends of the Bagroffs, especially the younger, Dmitri, who asked that when the time came he might stand godfather. Both brothers were well-bred

men and well-educated, according to the standards
of the time ; and they came often to the house
and passed the time there with pleasure. In the
Bagroffs' house, reading aloud was a favourite
occupation. But, as no one can read or listen to
reading without intervals, Sofya Nikolayevna was
taught to play cards. Klauss took the chief part
in initiating her into this science ; and whenever
the Bagroffs were alone of an evening, he never
failed to make up their table. Avenarius could not
take part in this pastime, because he never in his
life knew the difference between the five and the
ace.

Spring set in early that year, but in all its
beauty. The ice on the Byélaya broke up, and
the blocks were carried down by the stream ; the
river broke its banks and spread till it was six
versts across. The whole of this expanse could be
clearly seen from the windows of the Bagroffs'
little house ; their orchard burst into leaf and
flower, and the fragrance of bird-cherries and
apple-blossom filled the air. They used this
orchard as a drawing-room, and the warm weather
did good to Sofya Nikolayevna and made her
stronger.

At this time an event happened at Ufa which
caused a great sensation there and was especially
interesting to the young Bagroffs, because the
hero of the story was an intimate friend of theirs,
and, if I am not mistaken, distantly related to
Alexyéi Stepanitch. Sofya Nikolayevna, as one
would expect from her character, took a lively
interest in such a romantic affair. A young man,
named Timásheff, one of the most prominent and
richest nobles of the district, fell in love with a

Tartar girl, the daughter of a rich Tartar landowner. Her family, just like the Alkins, had altered their way of living to a certain extent in conformity with European customs, and they spoke Russian well; but they strictly observed the Moslem faith in all its purity. The beautiful Salmé returned the love of the handsome Russian officer, who was a captain in the regiment stationed near Ufa. As she could not be married to a Russian without changing her religion, it was perfectly certain that her parents and grown-up brothers would never give their consent to such a union. Salmé struggled long against her love, and love burns more fiercely in the hearts of women of Asia. At last, as is the rule in such cases, Mohammed was defeated, and Salmé made up her mind to elope with her lover, meaning to be baptized first and then married. The commander of Timasheff's regiment was General Mansúroff, a universal favourite and the kindest of men, who gained distinction afterwards when he crossed 'The Devil's Bridge' in the Alps with Suvóroff. He had lately married for love himself, and he knew and sympathized with Timasheff's enterprise, and promised to take the lovers under his protection. One dark rainy night Salmé sallied forth from her father's house, and found Timasheff waiting for her in a wood close by with a pair of saddle-horses; they had to gallop about 100 *versts* to reach Ufa. Salmé was a skilful rider; every ten or fifteen *versts* they found fresh horses, guarded by soldiers of Timasheff's regiment; he was very popular with his men. Thus the fugitives flew along 'on the wings of love', as a poet of that day would infallibly have said. Meanwhile Salmé's absence was quickly

noticed : her passion for Timasheff had long been
suspected, and a strict watch was kept over her
movements.   A band of armed Tartars assembled
instantly, and followed the enraged father [1] and
brothers in furious pursuit of the lovers, uttering
fierce shouts and threats of vengeance. They took
the right track and would probably have captured
the fugitives—at any rate blood would have been
spilt, because a number of soldiers, eagerly interested in the affair, were posted at different points
along the road—had not the pursuit been delayed
by a stratagem.   The bridge over a deep and
dangerous river was broken down behind the
lovers ; and the Tartars were forced to swim across,
and thus lost some two hours.   Even so, the boat
which carried Timasheff and Salmé across the
Byélaya under the walls of Ufa, had hardly reached
mid-stream, when the old Tartar galloped up to
the bank, attended by his sons and half of his
faithful company ; the other half had stopped
when their horses fell dead under them. A whole
regiment of Russian soldiers were in possession of
all the punts and ferry-boats, on the pretence of
crossing to the town. The unhappy father gnashed
his teeth in fury, cursed his daughter, and rode off
home.   Half dead with weariness and fear, Salmé
was placed in a carriage and taken to the house
of Timasheff's mother. The affair now assumed
a legal and official character : here was a Mohammedan woman asking of her own free will to be
received into the Christian Church, and the
authorities of the town took her under their
protection, informed the *mufti*, who lived at Ufa

---

[1] Another version of the story tells that the mother led
the pursuit. (*Author's note.*)

and was always called ' the Tartar bishop ', of all
that had passed, and called upon him to stop the
injured family or any other Mohammedans from all
attempts to recover by violence a person who had
deliberately preferred the Christian faith. In a
few days the clergy prepared the convert to receive
the sacraments of baptism and unction. The rite
was celebrated with great pomp in the Cathedral :
Salmé was christened Seraphima, and immediately afterwards, without leaving the church,
the young lovers were married. All Ufa was
interested in the affair. The young people and
all the men naturally stood up for the beautiful
Salmé ; but the women, some of whom, perhaps,
had personal reasons for disappointment, judged
her conduct severely. Very few stretched out the
hand of sincere friendship to the convert, whom
her husband's station admitted to the inner circle
of Ufa society. The young couple had no warmer
sympathizers than Sofya Nikolayevna and Alexyéi
Stepanitch ; and they were actively assisted by
the wife of General Mansuroff, an amiable young
woman whose maiden name was Bulgákoff. Before
long the Timasheffs had a firm footing in their new
sphere. The bride's education was taken in hand ;
she had much natural ability, and soon became
a success in society, where she aroused both
sympathy and envy, due in some degree to her
beauty and the peculiarity of her position. Sofya
Nikolayevna kept up a steady friendship with
Seraphima Timasheff till death divided them. To
the general regret, Mme Timasheff died of consumption three years after her marriage ; she
left two sons. Her husband nearly went out of
his mind with grief ; he left the army, gave up

his life to the care of his children, and never
married again. It was currently reported, though
I cannot vouch for the truth of the reports, that
her illness and death were due to secret pining
after the kinsfolk she had abandoned and remorse
for her change of religion.

These events did nothing to arrest the quick
flight of time. The day came when Sofya Nikolayevna was forbidden to go out to parties, or even
to take drives in the country. In fine weather she
walked up and down the garden for half an hour
twice a day ; if it was wet, she opened all the doors
in the house and followed the same routine under
cover. It is probable that all this seclusion and
strict regimen did more harm than good ; yet my
opinion is contradicted by the facts, for Sofya
Nikolayevna kept in perfect health. Alexyéi
Stepanitch found it necessary to let the doctors
have their way ; for he was constantly receiving
instructions from his father to watch over his
wife like the apple of his eye. Her friends also,
and especially the doctors who felt a strong personal
attachment to her, kept such a close watch on
Sofya Nikolayevna that she could neither take
a step nor swallow a morsel or drink a drop without
their permission. As Avenarius had to leave the
town on some official business, it fell to Klauss,
who was the other leading lady's doctor at Ufa,
to undertake the personal supervision of her
health. Klauss was a German, a very kind man,
clever and well-educated, but singularly grotesque
in his appearance. Though he was still of middle
age, he wore a bright yellow wig ; and people
asked where he could have got human hair of
a colour never beheld on any human head ; his

eyebrows also were yellowish, and so were the whites of his small brown eyes; but his face, which was round and rather small, was as red as burning coal. His habits in society were very odd: though he liked kissing the hands of ladies, he would never allow himself to be kissed on the cheek, maintaining that it was a gross breach of manners on the part of a man to permit such a greeting. He had a great fondness for small children, which he showed in this way: he took the child on his knees, placed its hand on the palm of his own left hand and stroked it for hours at a time with his right hand. His special favourites he constantly addressed as ' Monster ! ' or ' Turk ! ' — and Sofya Nikolayevna naturally came in for her share of these endearments.[1]

Owing to his intimacy with the young Bagroffs, Klauss knew all about Stepan Mihailovitch—his eager desire for a grandson, and the impatience with which he was awaiting the event. As Klauss wrote Russian well, he wrote out a forecast, for whose accuracy he vouched, in a distinct handwriting for the old man's benefit; he foretold that Sofya Nikolayevna would give birth to a son between the 15th and 22nd of September. When the forecast was sent to Stepan Mihailovitch, ' German liar ! ' was his only comment; but in his heart he believed it; for his excitement and joy could be seen in his face and heard in every word he spoke. About this time, our old acquain-

---

[1] Klauss became lecturer on midwifery in the Foundling Hospital at Moscow in 1791, and died in 1821 after the conscientious discharge of his duties for thirty years. He never left off the yellow wig. He was an enthusiastic and well-known numismatist. (*Author's note.*)

tance Afrosinya Andréyevna paid him a visit at
Bagrovo. He let her see more than others of his
main anxiety, lest he might have another grand-
daughter ; and she told him, that when passing
through Moscow she had gone to Trinity Church
there, to say her prayers to St. Sergius ; and
there she heard that some well-known lady, the
mother of several daughters, had taken a vow
that if her next child was a boy, it should be
christened Serghéi ; and she did give birth to
a son before the year was out. Stepan Mihailovitch
said nothing at the time ; but he wrote a letter
himself to his son and daughter-in-law by the next
post, expressing his desire that they should say
prayers in church to St. Sergius the wonder-
worker, and take a vow to call their child Serghéi
if it were a boy. In explanation of his wish he
added : ' There has never yet been a Serghéi in
the Bagroff family ' These Instructions were
carried out to the letter. Sofya Nikolayevna
spared no pains to provide everything that a careful mother could think of for her expected child ;
above all, an admirable foster-mother was found
at Kasimofka, one of the villages that had belonged
to her father. Marya Vassilyevna, a peasant
woman, had every qualification for her office that
one could wish for ; and she was perfectly willing
to undertake the duty, and moved to Ufa in good
time, bringing her own infant with her.

The crisis was now approaching. By this time
Sofya Nikolayevna was forbidden to walk.
Catherine Chichagoff was kept to her own house
by ill-health, and no other visitors were admitted.
But Mme Cheprunoff was constantly with her
cousin, never leaving her except to see her own

beloved little boy, Andrusha. Klauss came to breakfast every morning, and again for tea, which he drank with rum in it, in the evening ; then he played cards with husband and wife ; and as the stakes were too small to buy cards with, the thrifty German procured some used packs which he brought with him. Reading sometimes took the place of cards, and Klauss was present on these occasions. Alexyéi Stepanitch, who had gained some experience and skill in the art, was the regular reader ; and sometimes Klauss brought a German book and translated it aloud, which gave pleasure to his hearers, especially to Sofya Nikolayevna, who wished to get some knowledge, if only a smattering, of German literature.

Sofya Nikolayevna had experienced already the absorbing and unlimited power of maternal affection, the strongest of all human feelings, and she was filled with awe by her present condition. She accepted it as a sacred duty to preserve mental composure, and so to ensure the health of her unborn infant and secure its existence, on which depended all her hopes, all her future, and all her life. We know Sofya Nikolayevna pretty well already ; we know how apt she was to be carried away ; and therefore we shall not be surprised to hear that she gave herself up wholly to her feeling for the child she bore. Every hour of the day and night was devoted to the task of taking care of herself in all possible ways. Her mind and her thoughts were so entirely concentrated upon this one object that she noticed nothing else and was, apparently, quite satisfied with her husband, though it is probable that things happened which might have made her dissatisfied. The more

Alexyéi Stepanitch got to know his wife, the more she surprised him. He was a man singularly unable to appreciate excessive display of feeling, or to sympathize with it, from whatever cause it arose. Thus his wife's power of passionate devotion frightened him ; he dreaded it, just as he used to dread his father's furious fits of anger. Excessive feeling always produces an unpleasant impression upon quiet unemotional people : they cannot recognize such a state of mind to be natural, and regard it as a kind of morbid condition to which some persons are liable at times. They disbelieve in the permanence of a mental composure which may break down at any moment ; and they are afraid of people with such a temperament. And fear is fatal to love, even to a child's love for his parents. In general I must say, that in point of mutual understanding and sympathy, the relations between Alexyéi Stepanitch and his wife, instead of becoming closer, as might have been expected, grew less intimate. This may seem strange, but it often happens thus in life.

Just at this time Klauss was transferred to an official post at Moscow. He had already taken leave of his colleagues and all his acquaintance ; and he waited on solely with a view to Sofya Nikolayevna's confinement, hoping to be of service to her in case of necessity. He calculated that he might be able to get away on the 17th or 18th of September, and hired horses for that date. Hiring was necessary, because he intended to break his journey to visit a German friend, who lived at some distance from the post-road, so that the coach would not serve his purpose. The 15th of September passed, but the expected event did not

take place. Sofya Nikolayevna felt better and
more enterprising than usual ; and it was only the
pedantry of the doctor, she said, that kept her to
the sofa. When the 16th, 17th, and 18th had all
gone by, the German, in spite of his love for
Sofya Nikolayevna, got very angry, because he
had to pay a rouble a day to the driver he had
hired—a terribly high price, according to the
ideas of those days ; and the Bagroffs bantered
him about this in a friendly way. The reading
and card-playing went on every evening ; and if
the doctor won 60 kopecks[1] from his hosts, he was
much pleased, and said that his driver would not
cost him much *that* day. The 19th passed off
with no change. On the 20th, when Klauss came
in the morning, Sofya Nikolayevna stood at her
bedroom door and greeted him with a curtsey.
He got very angry : ' Monster ! ' he said, ' you
are treating me abominably ; ' but he kissed as
usual the hand she held out to him. ' It is too
bad, Alexyéi Stepanitch,' he went on ; ' your wife
is ruining me. Her baby ought to have been born
on the 15th, and here she is, dropping curtseys on
the 20th ! ' ' Never mind, my dear fellow,' said
Alexyéi Stepanitch, patting him on the shoulder ;
' you must rob us at cards to-night. But the packs
are nearly worn out.' Klauss promised to bring
a new pack ; he lunched there, and after sitting
on till two o'clock, took his leave. He called
again at six in the evening, punctual to the
minute. Finding no one in the hall or parlour or
drawing-room, he tried to get into the bedroom,
but the door was locked ; he knocked, and it was
opened by Mme Cheprunoff. The doctor went in

[1] 1 rouble = 100 kopecks.

and stood dumb with astonishment. The floor
of the room was covered with rugs ; green silk
curtains hung by the windows, and a fine silk
canopy over the double bed ; a candle, shaded
by a book, was burning in a corner ; and in the
bed, resting on embroidered pillows and wearing
a dainty easy morning wrapper, lay Sofya Nikolayevna. Her face looked fresh, and her eyes were
radiant with happiness. ' Congratulate me, my
dear friend ! ' she said in a strong audible voice ;
' I am the happy mother of a son ! ' The doctor,
when he looked at her face and heard her voice,
took the whole thing to be a mystification and
a hoax. ' Monster ! don't try to play tricks on
so old a bird as I am ! ' he said. ' Better get
up ; I have brought a new pack of cards. It will
be a present for the baby,' he added, coming up to
the bed and shoving the cards under a pillow.
' My dear friend,' said Sofya Nikolayevna, ' I
swear to you I have got a son ! Look at him ;
there he is ! ' And there, resting on a large down-
pillow trimmed with lace, and wrapped in a pink
velvet coverlet, he really saw a newborn infant,
a strong boy ; and Alyona Maksimovna, the midwife, was standing near the bed.

The doctor flew into a furious rage. He sprang
back from the bed as if he had burnt himself, and
roared out, ' What ! in my absence ! after my
staying on here for a week and losing money every
day, you did not send for me ! ' His face turned
from red to purple, his wig came half off, and his
whole stumpy figure looked so ridiculous that the
lady in the bed burst out laughing. Then the
midwife tried to soothe him : ' *Batyushka*,' she
said, ' when God's gift came, we had no time to

think of anything; when we had got things straight, we meant to send for your Honour, but Sofya Nikolayevna said you would be here at once.' The worthy man soon recovered from his vexation; tears of joy started to his eyes; he caught hold of the infant in his practised hands and began to examine it by the candle-light, turning it round and feeling it till it squalled loudly. Then he thrust a finger into its mouth, and when the infant began to suck lustily, the doctor was pleased and called out, ' How fine and healthy he is, the little Turk ! ' Sofya Nikolayevna was frightened when she saw her priceless treasure so freely handled; and the midwife tried to take it from him, fearing it would be ' overlooked '. But Klauss was inexorable : he ran about the room, holding the child, and called for a tub of warm water with a sponge and some soap, and a binder. Then he turned back his sleeves, tied on an apron, threw down his wig, and began to wash the babe, talking to it like this : ' Ah, my little Turk, that stops your crying; you like the feel of the warm water ! '

Then Alexyéi Stepanitch hurried into the room, almost beside himself with joy. He had been dispatching a special messenger to carry the good news to Stepan Mihailovitch, and writing letters to his parents; and there was a separate letter for his sister Aksinya, begging her to come as soon as possible and stand godmother to his son. Before the doctor had time to dry his hands, the happy father embraced him till he nearly choked him; he had already exchanged greetings with every one in the house, and many tears of joy had been shed. And Sofya Nikolayevna—but

what *she* felt, I dare not try to express in words :
her bliss was such as few on earth ever feel and
no one can feel for long.

The event produced extraordinary rejoicings
within the house, and even the neighbours shared
in it. The intoxication of joy was prolonged by
liquor ; and soon all the servants were singing and
dancing in the court. Some who never drank at
other times now took a drop too much ; and one
of these was Yevséitch. They found it impossible
to control him : he was always begging to go to
his mistress's bedroom to see the little son. At
last his wife, with Parasha's help, tied him tightly
to a heavy bench ; and even then he went on
kicking out his legs, cracking his fingers, and
attempting to articulate the chorus of a song.

Tired out by his exertions and by joyful excitement, Klauss at last sat down in an armchair and
much enjoyed a cup of tea. He was somewhat too
liberal with the rum that evening, and felt a buzzing
in his head after the third cup. So, after giving
instructions that the baby was to have no milk
but only syrup of rhubarb till the morning, he
took leave of his happy host and hostess. He
kissed the baby's hand, promised to call early
the next morning, and went off to spend the night
at his own house. As he passed through the court
he saw the dancing, and the sound of singing came
from every window of the kitchen and servants'
quarter. He stood still ; and though he was
sorry to interfere with the good people's merriment, yet he advised them to stop their singing
and dancing, because their mistress needed rest.
To his surprise, they all took his hint and lay
down at once, intending to sleep. As he passed out

of the gate he muttered to himself : ' Well, he's a lucky child ! How glad they all are to have him ! '

And it is really true that this child was born under a happy star. His mother, who had suffered constantly before her former confinement, had perfect health before his birth ; his parents lived in peace together during those halcyon days ; a foster-mother was found for him who proved to be more devoted than most real mothers ; he was the answer to prayers and the object of fond desires, and the joy over his coming into the world spread far beyond his parents. The very day of his birth, though the season was autumn, was warm as summer.

But what happened at Bagrovo, when the good news came that God had given a son and heir to Alexyéi Stepanitch ? This is what happened at Bagrovo. From the 15th of September, Stepan Mihailovitch counted the days and hours, and waited for the special messenger from Ufa. The man had been told to gallop day and night with relays of horses. This method of travelling was new, and Stepan Mihailovitch disapproved of it as a foolish waste of money and an unnecessary tax on the country people. He preferred to use his own horses ; but the importance and solemnity of this occasion made him depart from his regular practice. Fortune did not keep him in suspense too long : on the 22nd of September, when he was sleeping after dinner, the messenger arrived, bearing letters and the good news. The old man woke from a sound ·sleep, and had hardly had time to stretch himself and clear his throat when Mazan rushed into the room and, stammering with joyful excitement, got out the words, ' A

grandson, *batyushka* Stepan Mihailovitch ! Hearty
congratulations ! '

The first movement of Stepan Mihailovitch was
to cross himself. Then he sprang out of bed, went
barefoot to his desk, snatched from it the family
tree, took the pen from the ink-bottle, drew a line
from the circle containing the name Alexyéi,
traced a fresh circle at the end of the line, and
wrote in the centre of the circle, ' SERGHÉI.'

Farewell, my figures, bright or dark, my
people, good or bad—I should rather say, figures
that have their bright and dark sides, and people
who have both virtues and vices. You were not
great heroes, not imposing personalities ; you
trod your path on earth in silence and obscurity,
and it is long, very long, since you left it. But
you were men and women, and your inward and
outward life was not mere dull prose, but as
interesting and instructive to us as we and our
life in turn will be interesting and instructive to
our descendants. You were actors in that mighty
drama which mankind has played on this earth
since time immemorial ; you played your parts
as conscientiously as others, and you deserve as
well to be remembered. By the mighty power
of the pen and of print, your descendants have
now been made acquainted with you.[1] They have
greeted you with sympathy and recognized you
as brothers, whenever and however you lived, and
whatever clothes you wore. May no harsh judgement and no flippant tongue ever wrong your
memory !

[1] This work first appeared in parts in a Moscow magazine.
When they were collected in a book, this epilogue was added.

Printed in the United States
40731LVS00001B/16-36

9 781589 639515